CORPSE IN THE CASE

She was baking bread — until an unknown party choked her with a wad of raw dough. Now the heat is on, and only Trewley and Stone can find out who cooked up this fiendish murder . . . Detective Superintendent Trewley has years of experience probing the dark secrets of cozy English village life, but even he can use a bit of help sometimes. That's where Stone comes in: with the mind of a scientist and a black belt in judo, she's the perfect partner for tough old Trewley.

SARAH J. MASON

CORPSE IN THE CASE

Complete and Unabridged

LINFORD
Leicester

First published in 1993
in the United States of America
under the title 'Corpse in the Kitchen'

First Linford Edition
published 1999

British Library CIP Data

Mason, Sarah J., *1949*–
    Corpse in the case.—Large print ed.—
Linford mystery library
    1. Detective and mystery stories
    2. Large type books
    I. Title
    823.9'14 [F]

ISBN 0–7089–5590–8

Published by
F. A. Thorpe (Publishing) Ltd.
Anstey, Leicestershire

Set by Words & Graphics Ltd.
Anstey, Leicestershire
Printed and bound in Great Britain by
T. J. International Ltd., Padstow, Cornwall

This book is printed on acid-free paper

1

As the universe is governed by immutable laws, so are its various component parts, no matter what their size or whereabouts in that universe.

Newton's Law of Gravitation, for example, states that the force of attraction between any two masses is directly proportional to the product of those masses, and is inversely proportional to the square of the distance between their centres of mass.

Allshire's Law of Speculation states — perhaps more importantly — that there is always more gossip on Fridays. The buildup begins modestly, at around seven o'clock in the morning. It thereafter increasingly gathers speed and momentum until it peaks approximately four hours later, at eleven, when those inhabitants of the country too parsimonious to have the local paper delivered with their daily post pop out to their newsagents and buy one, in order to find out what everyone else already knows their fellow citizens are rumoured to be doing.

The police, of course, must not be seen to disobey the Law. In Allingham, county town of Allshire, they traditionally regard Friday as Funnies' Day: particularly so towards the end of September, after the equinox, when days grow ever shorter and nights spent indoors, slaying absent characters cheerfully before the fire, grow longer . . .

It was on a morning just before the equinox that Detective Superintendent Trewley and Detective Sergeant Stone sat over elevenses in their office, each with a mug of tea and half a packet of biscuits to hand, each with assorted pages of the latest *Allingham Argos* spread on the blotter between the in tray and the out on their respective desks.

Detective Superintendent Trewley buried his nose in his share of the *Argos*, firmly closing his eyes against all evidence of paperwork unaccomplished in the overflowing files on either side of his blotter. As he contemplated page

2

after page of local doings, he munched chocolate-coated digestives and drank well-sugared tea with a defiant air. He was no more fond of documentation than any other serving policeman: his job (he would grumble) was to catch crooks, not to write books about the beggars — an epithet which, before the advent of Stone (a small, slight brunette whose looks did not suggest the judo black belt which she held) would, with different vowels, have been as forceful as himself. A stolid, heavily built man in late middle age, the superintendent had mournful brown eyes and a face so wrinkled that nobody could ever decide for certain whether he resembled a bloodhound more than a bulldog. Constabulary colleagues, when safely out of earshot, had been known to refer to him as the Plainclothes Prune.

'Just listen to this, sir,' said Stone. 'In the Personal Column. *Thank you very much to the person who stamped and posted a letter to Kelling Ferry. If you would like to telephone, please do* — and it gives a number. I wonder what on earth it means. Do you think I'd find out if I rang and said it was me?'

Trewley glowered across at her as she nibbled her third biscuit. 'Trying to make young What's-his-name jealous, are you?' His sergeant had a long-standing relationship with an officer from Traffic, of whose identity the superintendent, for some whimsical reason of his own, professed to be ignorant. 'No particular mystery about it, if you ask me. It'll just be some silly kid been trying to get in touch with her boyfriend when her parents hate the sight of him.'

'My goodness, sir — surely that's not the voice of experience I hear? You amaze me. I'd never have dreamed any of yours could ever stoop to such subterfuge . . . Sorry, sir. Not very funny, I suppose.'

'No.' Trewley glowered again. As the father of a trio of personable teenage daughters, he had more than his fair share of worries. He even claimed that his face had been unlined until his oldest child reached her thirteenth birthday, though photographs gave him the lie. 'Not funny at all. The young idiot,

4

whoever she is — if she's not careful, she'll have our friendly Peeping Tom paying her a visit — or worse.' Brooding, he slapped a hand on the *Argos*, and sighed. 'Let's hope her parents spot the ad before anyone else does, because . . . '

'Hear, hear.' Stone knew the topic of Peeping Tom was best ignored, if remotely possible, even though he and his exploits had been in the news a great deal over past weeks. She returned to her share of the paper in search of less controversial inspiration. 'Oh — and hear this, sir. *Found in Ayrde, four laminated chipboard-covered shelves, teak effect*. I expect they fell off a roof rack when someone was driving back from that new do-it-yourself place.'

Trewley grunted, stretched, and shuffled his portion of the *Argos* into a tidy pile, rattling his empty biscuit wrapper as he did so. 'Probably never have bothered putting in the ad in the first place if the brackets and screws'd fallen off too — or if he'd had to pay more than a few bob to advertise for the bloke. Once this rag ups its charges, it won't take nearly

5

so long to read . . . '

Stone observed the elaborate contortions her superior's face had suddenly begun to undergo, especially about the eyes. 'Finished with your half, sir?' She was, after all, a detective. 'Er . . . would you care to swap?'

'Thanks.' He stopped squinting, and chuckled as he held out his folded sheets for exchange. 'There's one letter in here you'll enjoy, I daresay. Usual moan about the bypass and why won't County Hall make up its mind? Silly clot. I could've saved him the stamp. Because it'd mean another bob on the rates, that's why, though I imagine young What's-his-name'd think it money well spent.'

The intimate friend of the Traffic Officer nodded as she hopped up from her desk to effect the swap. She'd lost count of the number of mealtime harangues to which her loved one had subjected her over recent weeks as the controversy raged between councillors, ratepayers' representatives, and the Department of the Environment. Breakfasts would be

6

far more easily digested, she always felt, if he'd only calm down long enough to realise he was preaching to the converted.

'You know as well as I do, sir, that if we don't have a bypass, what we *will* have is more and more juggernauts leaving the motorway at the wrong junction and thundering along the side roads demolishing walls and hedges all over the place until they finally end up where they were heading hours late, because they wasted so much time being lost — '

'Lost?' snarled the superintendent. 'Don't breathe that word within a mile of me, my girl, if you value your life!' He let the *Argos* fall from trembling fingers, shuddered, and reached weakly for his steaming mug. 'And whatever you do, Stone, don't you dare say anything about the *Property* pages, or I swear I won't be responsible for my actions!'

As he took a great gulp of tea, Stone — who'd been blinking in some surprise — laughed. The conundrum had suddenly solved itself: there were certain words which, when uttered by her superior in that tormented manner, could only mean one thing: that Desk Sergeant Pleate, in charge of lost property, was on the warpath again. With a rueful grin, she settled herself on Trewley's visitors' chair, cheerfully pushing what remained of her share of the biscuits across his blotter. 'I came in the back way this morning, sir, but I . . . er . . . deduce that you didn't. Is he — is he very . . . ?'

'Ha!' Trewley slammed down his half-empty mug, reaching absently for the biscuits as they rolled towards him. 'What do you think?' He unwrapped the packet, gazed inside, then recollected himself with a start, shaking his head as he put the packet down again, 'Isn't he always, blast him! Which you know as well as I do, my girl, so you can just stop grinning like that, or I'll have you back in uniform before . . . Oh, what's the use?'

A man of weaker will would have buried his face in his hands at this point: Detective Superintendent Trewley merely raised despairing eyes to the ceiling and sighed, his bloodhound jowls aquiver. 'Don't mind me, Stone. It's not your fault, I suppose — or his, come to that. He's just getting to me more than usual today because — oh, damnation, because all of 'em at home are going on at me again. My Susan had that blasted gleam in her eye while she was clearing away the breakfast — enough to make a man's blood run cold . . . ' He snatched up the biscuits, removed the topmost, and crunched it defiantly.

Stone's eyes danced, though she managed to extinguish the grin, and her tone was sympathetic as she replied. 'So Mrs. Trewley thinks you should go on another diet, does she, sir? Well, taking your likely blood pressure into consideration, I must say — '

'Don't!' This time it wasn't so much a snarl as a howl of anguish. 'For pity's sake, Stone, let me enjoy my last few days of freedom without having you rabbit on at me at work the way I'm getting it under my own roof!' A bloodhound can look pitiful and accusing at the same time: Trewley was at his most bloodhoundish now as he surveyed his mischievous sidekick. 'And there's no need to drop all the hints about your blasted expert knowledge, either. That was hitting below the belt, that was.'

'Sorry, sir.' Stone, who had been a medical student before the sight of real — as opposed to textbook — blood made her abandon the course, made a silent bet with herself that Susan Trewley's latest nutritional regime would be imposed upon her husband within a matter of days, probably over the coming weekend, which he and his sergeant had booked as free time. It did not sound as if Allingham's top detective was going to enjoy his little break.

A dutiful sidekick would at least try to take her superior's mind off his troubles for a little while. 'Do you think the man with the laminated shelves didn't bring them in to us because he knew the Lost Property cupboard was full, sir? Sergeant Pleate — '

'Damn and blast Pleate to perdition! If I've heard him once about his blasted cupboard, I've heard him a hundred times — and I'll tell him a thousand times I think one month is enough.

Three months takes up space we could do with for real live coppers, never mind some of the dead-and-alive rubbish the blasted public brings in . . . '

The Lost Property War had raged for years between Detective Superintendent Trewley, nominal head of the Allingham police, and Desk Sergeant Pleate, who had been there a lifetime and ruled the station with a rod, or rather a truncheon, of iron. The general position was not so much an uneasy truce as an ongoing series of ambuscades. From time to time a new lock would appear on a little-used office door, to be countered with a pointed delivery of dustbin liners, or a visit from the proprietor of the local junk-shop, touting for wares. Hints were dropped about crowbars, and the risk of fire or infestation. The lock would, in the end, vanish as suddenly as it had come — temporarily, until Desk Sergeant Pleate could work out his next ploy. It seemed unlikely that either he or the superintendent would ever achieve complete victory, but frequent skirmishing kept both men on the tips

11

of their mental toes.

'Lost Property be damned!' Trewley reached broodingly for the biscuits, which Stone had continued to nibble as they talked. He scowled. 'Good grief, I thought you women liked to keep an eye on your weight. There's only one left — and I didn't get my last bit of toast this morning . . . '

'Your need is greater than mine, sir.' Stone grinned at her suffering as she relinquished all claims to the remaining treat. 'Tell you what — I'll buy you lunch. We could pop down to the pub as . . . as compensation, if that's what I mean.' She frowned. 'Reparation?'

'I know very well what you mean.' The responses sounded through embittered crumbs. 'And I think I might just take you up on the offer, thanks very much. May as well make the most of it while I still can. I'll get the drinks, though. All Right?'

'Fine, sir. Tell you what — if we go early, we can bag a seat outside. As you say,' said Stone, wilfully misunderstanding, 'we may as well make the most of it while we still can. It's such a glorious day . . . '

* * *

It was, indeed, a glorious day. Even as Trewley and Stone chatted over their newspaper, a powder-blue coupe was racing along the Allshire lanes. It was driven by one Andrew Ryan, a youthful Adonis whose blond hair waved just a little too close to his collar, whose eyes exactly matched the open-necked silk shirt which toned so beautifully with the three pieces of luggage strapped to the back of a car painted in an identical shade, and gleaming with customised chrome.

Other indulgences were a souped-up engine, mag wheels, real leather seats in a delicate shade of cream, and quadraphonic speakers. The car was Andrew's present to himself for having at last won through his earlier problems to start a new life in a new job with — as his friend and senior partner had made clear — every opportunity of climbing to the

13

top of the tree. The tree in question had various names; Management Consultancy and Organisational Psychology were only two of them. A third, cynics would say, might be Money for Old Rope . . .

Andrew and his colleague used yet another.

Today heralded the apotheosis of Andrew Ryan. Today he was to handle the very first Consultancy Course at the newly opened Campions Crest Conference Centre, midway between the Allshire village of Campion Morse and Campion Dexter. Andrew's training had been thorough, his preparations precise. He felt, for once, utterly confident that the past was behind him, that he could cope with whatever Fate might bring. His luck had turned at last.

'This is my lucky day!' he exulted, looking back on his motorway journey from London. It had been one long, high-spirited orgy of speed and self-congratulation: yet not a single police car had spotted him as he hurtled up the outside lane, and he had passed scot-and-ticket-free through several counties. He sang rousing old songs learned in his school days, and crooned ballads, once the quieter country byways were reached, in a light tenor. As he followed the final signposts, he warbled love-songs, or chanted snatches of martial verse in keeping with his mood.

'Four great gates has the city of Damascus,' he intoned, as he neared his goal, the appointed stage for his coming triumph. The Centre had until recently been the manor house for the Campions. Its gates certainly numbered four, as Andrew had discovered on reading the brochure his friend, colleague and boss had brought back from the brief visit he had contrived after the sale had gone through, when the syndicate had suggested that its new Management Consultant should stop theorising and planning for a few hours to explore the area of future operations.

Mr. Ryan continued to quote Flecker as he drew up outside the imposing archway. Even the stones seemed newly scrubbed to Andrew's hopeful gaze, and he gloated over the neatly lettered notice which told him he had arrived, savoured the sight of fresh paint, and admired the glass in the lodge windows and the gold-tipped spears of the wrought-iron gates as they glittered in the September sun.

An impatient hooting startled him as an unexpected tractor, too wide to pass, came up behind him shedding wisps of straw from the bales on its trailer. With a blush and an apologetic wave, Andrew let in the clutch, slipped into first gear, and turned the car off the road to disappear up the drive in a blissful blur, blue as the sky . . .

The sky which a cloud, as yet no bigger than a man's hand, was about to darken.

16

2

Allshire had in recent months heard a good deal, one way and another, about Campions Crest. For generations it had been the manorial seat of the Jervaulx family, who took pride in their heritage and allowed only intimates to misspell the name, for a joke, as Jarvis. But, like several other manors of the county, Campions Crest had fallen on hard times; running costs rose, faithful retainers retired without being replaced, and return on investments was much reduced.

Family pride was still further humbled with the death of Joscelin Jervaulx, son and sole heir to Sir Joyce, a widower. Young Joscelin, whose birth had cost his mother her life, had been indulged by his father until he believed that even the forging of the older man's signature on various cheques would be forgiven him . . .

17

He was wrong. Once the forgery was discovered, there was a monumental quarrel. Joscelin found himself banished from hearth and home, making his way to London, where he fell in with a doubtful crowd, turned to drink, and eventually became a junkie, dying at last a squalid, sordid, premature, lonely death. Sir Joyce, his heart as broken as his exchequer — thanks to Joscelin's pillaging — was empty, sold up in despair and left the district.

He also left his cousin, Miss Melicent Jervaulx, in the home his father had long ago granted her. In the West Lodge of Campions Crest, Miss Melicent did her dauntless best to restore the tarnished honour of the squire's family. Her spine was straight, her shoulders unbowed, her look heroic. Not even to Squadron Leader Kempshott would she betray her shame at the manner of Joscelin's demise.

Squadron Leader Robbie Kempshott lived in the South Lodge. A wartime fighter pilot and — disillusioned early by death — an apparently confirmed bachelor, he was keen on history, bird-watching, and similar solitary pursuits. He had even written one or two books on such subjects which had been published without his having to pay for the privilege. Opinion in the Campions had him as a quiet sort, but one with brains. The villages were secretly rather proud of Robbie's scholarship, though they doubted whether Miss Melicent would ever condescend to accept him should he venture to make her an offer — or whether, indeed, medals or not, he was good enough for her. Miss Melicent was, after all, the old squire's cousin, never mind that she only lived in the West Lodge . . .

The aristocracy traditionally have at least one faithful old retainer who lives on their charity. The Jervaulx were never a family to flout tradition, and a retainer — certainly faithful, though perhaps not so old — duly occupied the East Lodge.

The North Lodge had squatters.

They were, by hippie standards, a small commune, and, as such, hardly noticed at first. Nobody in the Campions could say for certain how long they had been there. Their peaceful and unobtrusive arrival, whenever that was, had heralded an equally peaceful and (almost) equally unobtrusive way of life, seen (by some) as a blessing in disguise.

The North Lodge had for several weeks stood empty after the death of the nonagenarian widow who had been its previous (legal) tenant, her death being followed by the astonishingly swift decampment of her son, Young Walter (a mere sixty-five) to the fleshpots of Allingham, where he made an honest woman of the peroxide barmaid at the Seven Bells.

The resulting scandal rocked the Campions to their very foundations. What with Old Thomasine so against the evils of Strong Drink, and Young Wally been and gone and wedded with a wench from an inn, wasn't his mother sure to be spinning in her grave? No surprise if she Walked as well, to make her displeasure known . . . And so, while Walter revelled in the embraces of Allingham-born Ruby, he relinquished any claim he might have had to the continuation of the lease in his own right: and nobody from either of the Campions could bring themselves to apply in Walter's stead.

And there quietly came another family to replace that lost to Campion Morse and Campion Dexter: the Family of the Phoenix — whose members, having been (so they said) reborn into a new life, had adopted forenames symbolising the freedom of spirit and freshness of opportunity for those who had abandoned their unhappy pasts, liberated prisoners of a malignant Fate. The Phoenixes wore strange, handmade clothes; never seemed to cut their hair, though it seemed, the Campion admitted, clean enough, so far as anyone could tell; and appeared, again so far as anyone could tell, to cohabit happily in a mutual and amoral harmony.

'Although their *morals*, Mr. Kempshott, cause me no particular concern,' said Melicent Jervaulx, who, it being Friday, was driving Squadron Leader Robbie into Allingham for their biweekly shopping excursion. 'Heaven knows, the villagers need no encouragement from outsiders in *that* direction. We are no strangers to

21

the seven-months' child in the Campions, are we?'

'Uh . . . ahem . . . no. That is . . . no,' replied the squadron leader, twirling his moustache and feeling a hot flush creep under his collar. 'No, indeed, Miss Jervaulx.'

'At one time,' said Melicent, with a sigh, 'I had hopes that some of the energies with which our young folk are so — so remarkably *endowed*, as it were, might be channelled into the Girl Guide movement, but . . .'

She sighed again. No blue-uniformed, trefoil-badged patrol frolics could long past puberty compete with the attractions of muscular and virile village youth — of which (the Campion birthrate being a by word in the county) there was always an ample supply.

'Although why,' she now mused, '*haystacks* should be so popular, I cannot imagine. So very *prickly*, I would have supposed . . . and then what about when it rains?'

'Ah — ahem!' Robbie Kempshott, scarlet of face, cleared his throat twice,

22

and stared at the road ahead. 'Ah . . . well, Miss Jervaulx,' as Melicent seemed to be waiting for his reply, 'I cannot . . . that is . . . ahem!' He cleared his throat again, twirled his moustache, and fell silent.

'It can hardly,' continued Miss Melicent, 'come as any great surprise to *you* — ' Robbie jumped, turning from scarlet to purple — 'who have made such a close a study of the historical records of this parish, that *almost half* the children in the Campions are apparently conceived out of wedlock. While the other half,' she went on, as the historian gurgled helplessly in the passenger seat beside her, 'appear to be *born* out of it.'

He had to say something — she seemed to expect it. 'Ah, quite so, Miss Jervaulx. Er, yes.' He glanced sideways at Melicent, bolt upright in the driver's seat of her little grey Morris, her knuckles white as she gripped the steering wheel. 'Quite so — yes, indeed.' His eyes glazed over, and he spoke as if he hardly knew what he was saying. 'Most — most unfortunate . . . '

'Unfortunate in *moral* terms, no doubt,'

returned Melicent promptly, 'but at least one may say that such behaviour is perfectly *natural*. One might almost add that it does at least suggest our young people are less likely than we feared to mingle with these — these ridiculous Phoenixes for the purposes of *sexual experiment*. There can be little, if anything, I imagine, that this so-called commune could show our village youth about such matters, I should say.'

The hint of regional pride in her tone roused poor Robbie from his trance. 'Ah . . . yes, Miss Jervaulx. Couldn't agree with you more. Young Campion seems to have very, ah, broadminded and, uh, *catholic* tastes. That is — '

'And of course we must remember' — Melicent seized upon the latter adjective, and turned it to her own purpose — 'to mention the dear vicar's visit to the lodge, must we not? In my opinion, it is that remarkable incident which provides the *ultimate proof* for our suspicions.'

'Suspicions?' Boiling with a myriad different emotions, the squadron leader's mind had lost its grasp of the matter immediately under discussion. 'Of their indulgence in' — he gritted his teeth — 'in nameless debaucheries? But — but surely, my dear Miss Jervaulx — '

'If they please, they may debauch themselves into *utter physical exhaustion*,' Melicent retorted, to his astonishment. 'In fact, I would go so far as to say that it might be a very good thing if they did!' Squadron Leader Kempshott blinked, and could find nothing to say. 'In such a state,' enlarged the squire's cousin crisply, 'they would then have neither the time nor the inclination to attempt the seduction of our Campion youngsters — *attempt* being the operative word. The, ah, less robust attractions of this commune could hardly present any great challenge to the — the *native-born competition* . . .

'Nevertheless, Mr. Kempshott,' continued Melicent, as poor Robbie gurgled again at her side, 'we do *not* want these Phoenixes in our village, do we? For reasons which I need hardly state.' She coughed. 'Do we?'

The squadron leader could feel the perspiration on his forehead, and prickling hotly on his upper lip. 'Ah — oh, certainly not, Miss Jervaulx.' He stroked his moustache with shaking fingers. 'Certainly not. Er — couldn't agree with you more, in fact. Ought not to be allowed.'

'You are, as ever, right, Mr. Kempshott.' Melicent, having bullied him into backing her every inch of the way, was now inclined to look kindly on the hapless Robbie. 'Your summing-up of the case has been no less than *masterly*, if I may say so. And I am delighted to have your views so firmly expressed: that these Phoenixes have *got to go*!'

★ ★ ★

Most of the Course attendees had been instructed to arrive at the Conference Centre between five and six in the evening. Most, but not all. Andrew Ryan, breathing deeply, combed his hair for the seventh time, re-adjusted yet again the flowered cravat he had tied around his neck, twitched the crease in his trousers with geometric precision, and, pale of face, hurried from his room to pose on the front steps of Campions Crest. He remembered just at the last minute to turn his best profile towards the black Rolls-Royce now describing a slow circle on the gravel drive.

The Royce came to a halt, and four curious eyes stared from behind its tinted glass at the slim figure hovering on the steps. There was a thoughtful pause.

'*Not* what I was expecting,' murmured Sir Lionel Tobias at last, as Andrew looked across, bowed, and smiled a too-wide toothpaste smile. 'Although . . . '

Chauffeur Simpson emitted a discreet cough. 'It would appear that the young . . . gentleman is of a somewhat nervous disposition, sir. If I may venture to say so, that is.'

Tobias grunted. 'Venture away. At a guess, he's been suddenly left in the lurch, and he's starting to realise it'll be a long time before reinforcements arrive — too long for comfort, knowing how these places work. Still, now I'm here . . . ' Not even to Simpson would he voice his unspoken thought that the coming weekend could be even more rewarding than he had hoped.

He was out of the car and heading for the steps as Simpson unloaded the luggage. Andrew, continuing to radiate an uncertain welcome, advanced to meet him.

'Sir Lionel Tobias? How do you do.' His handshake was almost too firm, his eyes, beneath their long lashes, restless. 'My name's Ryan — Andrew Ryan — and I'm . . . lucky enough to be running the first-ever Attitudes Analysis Course at the Campions Crest Conference Centre.' He took another deep breath. 'Do come in, and I'll show you where — '

'*Running* the course? You?' Tobias, a tall man, seemed even taller as indignation and surprise brought the ejaculation from his lips. 'I was expecting to meet — '

'Oh, yes, I know.' Andrew licked his lips. 'I'm sorry, but — he's been delayed, you see. An emergency — some last-minute panic — he rang about half

28

an hour ago and told me to carry on regardless until he managed to get here, only he couldn't be sure when . . . He, er, said to tell you he was very sorry . . . '

Sir Lionel looked him up and down without speaking. If Andrew Ryan thought he could rely on nothing but his fragile good looks to make his way in the world, he was mistaken. And yet . . .

The clothing magnate managed to return Andrew's shaky smile with some show of enthusiasm, and began to mount the steps at the young man's side as Simpson brought the cases. Relieved at being over the first hurdle, Andrew began emitting a flood of informative chatter.

'Banter will show your driver where everything is, your room and so on — there's a buffet lunch ready laid in one of the side rooms — we hope you'll be comfortable . . . '

'Banter?' Sir Lionel's eyebrows arched. Andrew stifled a giggle, and lowered his voice as he replied.

'The, er, butler — an amazing man, a real character. He knows this place inside out, you know. He used to work for the Jervaulx family before they, er, left, and he was persuaded to stay on — or rather to come back. Without him, I doubt if Campions Crest would be half so successful.'

Tobias was tempted to make some remark on the wisdom of claiming success for a venture still in its opening throes, but decided against it. Light conversation should be the order of the day, at least for the moment.

'I thought he might be another Attitude Analyst, that's all.' He favoured Andrew with a genial nod. 'And if you say there's a meal waiting — well, lead me to it. It may be only a short drive from Allingham, but long enough to work up an appetite if you've skipped your elevenses as I did.'

'Oh, yes.' Andrew nodded back, his blond forelock falling over his eyes. He shook it back with an instinctive gesture, and pointed along the hall.

'Down here, Sir Lionel — do let me show you. It's the old morning room. We've kept most of the original furniture and fittings . . . ' He opened the door to reveal a spacious, high-ceilinged chamber with leaded windows around which long velvet curtains fell in festoons. 'We wondered,' said Andrew with another giggle, 'whether we could use some of your pyjama cords — dyed, you know — to tie these back, but I'm afraid they aren't, er, in the correct proportions.'

Sir Lionel forced a chuckle at the pleasantry. Feeble as it was, the intention had obviously been to compliment. The Allshire and Farther Clothing Company, of which he was both chairman and managing director, was second only to Marks and Spencer in its number of stores and range of quality goods. Like Marks and Sparks, Allshire had started in a small way: originally the Allingham Clothing Company, it had enlarged first to cover the rest of the county, then had spread still farther afield across the entire country.

The Tobias who effected this expansion had been a man of plain speech, setting forth his intentions in the company's altered title; his great-grandson shared many of the same characteristics. He now dropped the enormous tasselled cord which looped the lush velvet folds, stared out of the window, and said: 'Good God, I must be dreaming! I could have sworn I recognised that car — yes! It is!' He leaned forward with narrowed eyes as the driver opened his door and stepped out. 'I thought so — I'd know that man anywhere.' He turned a furious face to Andrew, who took two steps hurriedly back.

'Ryan — what the devil is this all about?'

3

Trepidation and dismay wrought together in the heart of Squadron Leader Kempshott as Miss Melicent Jervaulx, every inch of her thin, tweeded form betokening Resolution and Duty, strode along Allingham's main street, her eyes fastened on the hanging blue lamp she confidently believed was not only her target, but his. Robbie had done his best to dissuade his companion from her self-appointed task, but the willpower of a Girl Guide captain is stronger even than that of one numbered once among Churchill's Few.

Desk Sergeant Pleate, inevitably brooding over the Lost Property, looked up with a frown from his personal copy of the *Allingham Argos* as the ill-assorted pair made their entrance. It took no more than a second for him to recognise the lady as the one in command: it was the way she beckoned her all-too-reluctant escort inside with the stern insistence of

33

a competitor at a sheepdog trial . . .

'Come along, come along. Do please *hurry*, Mr. Kempshott. The sooner this matter has been cleared up, the better.'

Wishing himself a million miles away, Robbie hurried, as far to the rear and as slowly as he could, his hands thrust deep in his pockets as he caught Pleate's curious eye. He huffed unhappily through his handlebar moustache, flushed, and lowered his gaze as the sergeant's frown grew more acute with the effort of trying to put a name to the voice and face he was beginning to think he'd encountered before.

'Good morning — madam.' The name had proved too elusive. 'Sir . . . ' Pleate did his best to sound like Dixon of Dock Green, but in his present mood his best was not good enough. 'What seems to be the trouble?'

Melicent's sallow cheeks turned a discreet pink as she hastened to correct the misapprehension. '*Miss*, Sergeant. I am Melicent Jervaulx — Miss Jervaulx, from the Campions — and this is Squadron Leader Kempshott. My neighbour.'

'Ah, yes, of course.' He thought he'd recognised that voice and he'd been right. He nodded in what he believed was an avuncular way. This time, he was wrong. Robbie flinched at the sergeant's expression, and shuffled his feet as he moved behind Melicent again, glumly fingering his moustache, then thrusting his hands in his pockets as Pleate looked across at him with some interest.

'Well, Miss Jarvis, Mr. Kempshott — how can we help you?' Something made him wonder whether he was to be called on to explain to this emphatically spinster lady that prosecutions for breach of promise had long since gone out of fashion.

'Squadron Leader Kempshott and I, Sergeant, come from Campions Crest.' Pleate nodded again. Melicent, turning a sallow shade of pink, coughed, and quickly continued: 'The squadron leader lives in the South Lodge, while I live in the West — quite half a mile or more apart, you understand,' she added, as a light gleamed in the sergeant's eye.

Pleate was not, in fact, thinking the

worst. That gleam betokened nothing but the effort involved as he dredged up what else he knew of the Campions beyond the scandal, muted in the press but rampant on the streets, of young Joscelin's death. There had been a wedding, he recalled, where his wife's cousin had worn a preposterous hat, and he had whiled away the tedium of the vicar's sermon by counting the number of cherries and flounces fastened about the brim. If either of these two intended to confess to having killed the reverend gentleman, Sergeant Pleate not only didn't blame them, but he might even volunteer to speak in their defence.

'I — we — have a *serious complaint* to make.' Melicent paused, and stared pointedly at the sergeant's stripes. 'To whom should we make it? Is there anyone of higher rank that we might see?'

The gleam brightened to a gleeful, unholy glow as Pleate saw his chance, and sighed happily. 'Higher rank? Well, it had best be the very highest, if it's a *serious* complaint you want to make. Our Superintendent Trewley's the man you should be talking to . . . '

Squadron Leader Kempshott retreated yet further behind Melicent's back as the sergeant glared in his direction and slammed down the telephone. Superintendent Trewley was not in his office; nobody knew where he had gone. Detective Sergeant Stone also seemed to have vanished without trace. Thwarted of the Lost Property revenge for which he had been thirsting, Sergeant Pleate was in an angry mood as he snatched the Occurrence Book from its place under the counter and pulled his fountain pen out of his breast pocket.

'A serious complaint,' he repeated grimly, pen poised; then caution prevailed. 'Suppose you tell me all about it first, Miss Jarvis?'

Melicent cleared her throat. 'We have, perhaps, been just a little remiss in not registering our complaint earlier, but there are so few convenient buses these days. And we drive into town, you see, only twice a week — that is, on Tuesdays and Fridays, to do our shopping and change our library books. And today, of course, is Friday.'

Pleate, who knew very well what day it was, scowled at the squadron leader's moustache, which was jerking up and down in nervous support of Melicent's self-evident remark. Robbie huffed, pushed his hands back in his pockets, and tried to look as if he wasn't there.

Melicent lowered her clarion tones to a thrilling murmur. 'The problem may be expressed in one word, Sergeant. *Drugs*!'

Pleate put down his pen — he hadn't written anything yet — and stared. 'Drugs? In the Campions?'

'So we have good reason to believe. A group of loose-living young persons has recently chosen to set up a . . . a commune — ' the aristocratic nose twitched with distaste — 'in the North Lodge of the Campions Crest estate.' The old squire's cousin tried to sound an impartial note, difficult though this might be. 'The lodge, admittedly, has been empty for some months now,

38

and as to whether or not they broke in, I have been unable to ascertain, although, naturally, I suspect the worst, given the type of persons they seem to be. They call themselves the Family of the Phoenix — heathen nonsense!' Miss Jervaulx drew herself to her full height. 'Doubtless you now fully appreciate our — my — particular concern. In the circumstances.'

'Quite so, Miss Jarvis. Only natural you'd be concerned about drugs — in the circumstances. Most regrettable.' The sergeant contrived to look sympathetic without committing himself to belief in her accusations until she could provide him with hard facts. 'You say this commune is in the North Lodge, eh? What exactly are they doing?'

'Squatting,' said Melicent, her nose wrinkling again. 'Or so I understand the term to be. Pah!'

Pleate raised an eyebrow at Robbie Kempshott, who found himself jerking his head in confirmation of Melicent's tale. 'Trespassers,' agreed the squadron leader, his moustache bobbing up and down. 'Lawbreakers — shocking.'

'Unlicensed hordes,' said Miss Jervaulx. 'Disgraceful!'

'You think they're running a brothel, Miss Jarvis? Now, that sounds more like it,' said Pleate, 'always assuming you can prove it, with not being so sure about the breaking and entering. Can you?' Once more he turned a questioning eyebrow in Squadron Leader Kempshott's direction. Robbie gasped, and went purple. Miss Jervaulx flushed, but rose nobly to the occasion, and contrived to click an irritable tongue as she began to spell.

'H–o–r–d–e–s, Sergeant, not w–h–o–r–e–s. Barbarians. The rabble. The unruly mob.'

'The Mob?' A Mafia connection with Allshire seemed unlikely, but nowadays you could never tell. Maybe he hadn't been making such a joke of it when he told the old girl she'd best speak to Trewley about all this. 'The big boys, eh? Some London syndicate, I daresay, running a bawdy-house to launder the money. Sounds serious, Miss Jarvis — can you give me some details?'

Melicent clicked her tongue again. This was what came of failing to insist on one's right, as a taxpayer as well as a member of the manorial family, to speak with someone of sufficient rank to understand fully the gravity of the situation. 'Sergeant, Mr. Kempshott and I are doing no more than trying to make clear to you the natural distress and disapproval which must be felt by any right-minded person over these — these *lawless individuals*. They may well come from London: we neither know, nor care. Nor can their — their sexual habits be of the slightest interest to us, save insofar as they would seem to indicate the appalling lack of *decent inhibitions* which these — these self-styled Phoenixes evidently enjoy.' She frowned at the final word, but did not correct it.

'Nor,' she went on, 'are we necessarily concerned should they indulge in *strong liquor* — always provided that they make no public exhibition of themselves, which as yet, it is generally agreed, they seem not to have done.' Melicent did not sound as if this temperance entirely met

41

with her approval. 'One might reasonably expect them to have by now displayed some signs of such indulgence if it was a regular habit . . . ' She sighed, and shook her head. 'What, however, must surely be considered as an almost proven habit is their taking of drugs, Sergeant. For what else but the taking of drugs could explain,' as Pleate looked another question and Robbie Kempshott squirmed, 'their *very strange behaviour*?'

It seemed to Sergeant Pleate, trying to make sense of Miss Melicent's rigmarole, that her companion was behaving pretty strangely, too. He scowled at the blank page of his Occurrence Book, and said: 'Now look, Miss Jarvis, I'm afraid we're going to need a bit more than what you've told me so far. If you'd got real proof, now, you'd have done just the right thing coming to tell us about it, but *almost* isn't good enough, not by a long way it isn't. The police can't act without evidence. We can't go bursting into anyone's house on somebody else's say-so — that's the law of the land, and even squatters're covered — and

I'm not too sure,' as she opened her mouth to protest, 'as trespass is covered, neither, if it was trespass in the first place — which is no more than you said yourself, remember. There's been no complaint from the owners of Campions Crest — the new owners, I mean, this conference syndicate there's been such a to-do about in the papers of late.'

As Melicent gasped weakly, Robbie Kempshott was moved to speak without being spoken to. 'But Miss Jervaulx is a member of the family,' he began. 'Surely that counts for something?'

Melicent tilted her chin and glared down her nose as Pleate began shaking his head; before he could speak, she spoke first. 'Really, Sergeant, I should have thought you could find some pretext for a — a routine visit to check up on them — to drop a hint or two and frighten them away. We do not welcome such people in our neighbourhood, corrupting our young folk with their *evil opiates* — of which, I might point out, I have indeed almost definite proof.'

'Have you now? Good.' Once more,

Pleate picked up his pen, and waited for her to continue.

'I have. Yesterday morning,' said Melicent, 'our vicar went to call upon these — these *depraved young people*. At my request,' she added. 'As a member of the family . . . However,' she continued as Pleate sighed, 'that is no great matter, except that he told me later what occurred, and one would have supposed the word of a Church of England clergyman to be sufficient for anyone.' Pleate said nothing. Melicent frowned.

'The vicar, so he said, remonstrated with them — at some length, I imagine. He is, you must understand, a most eloquent speaker' — Pleate remembered that long-ago wedding, and sighed — 'who is neither given to mincing his words, nor to shirking his duty.' Did Melicent also sigh? Pleate couldn't be sure. 'He told them that their presence might be considered undesirable in our village . . . and their response to his accusations is proof enough for me!'

'Beat him up, did they? Now, if it's

a charge of common assault, I should think — '

'They *listened* to him, Sergeant — listened to him without once interrupting! Our vicar is a sterling character, Sergeant, but one has to admit that it is not easy to endure his sermons without some — some degree of ennui, I fear. These — these Phoenixes, however, simply smiled at him, and heard all he had to say without interruption — and then invited him to join them in a singsong afterwards as a — a gesture of friendship!'

'Oh,' said Pleate. 'Oh . . . Well, I grant you it's a good argument, Miss Jarvis, but I'm still not sure it's good enough. You can't put someone on a charge just for wanting to sing a few songs, not unless they're kicking up a row in the middle of the road, or someth — '

'Singing songs is neither here nor there, Sergeant! My point is that for anyone to listen willingly to the vicar — a worthy man, a true Christian, but tedious in the extreme — they must either be *mad* . . . or *on drugs.* Alcohol alone would hardly produce the required effect — moreover, he mentioned that he saw no sign of liquor, which is not the sort of indication even he could miss. And, since one finds it hard to credit an entire household of lunatics, the inference — '

'You may be right, Miss Jarvis.' Pleate, brooding on that wedding sermon, nodded. 'Yes, you may be right — but then again, maybe not. I'll talk it over with my superiors as soon as I can, believe me, and we'll make sure something gets done — though I can't say what,' he added quickly, before she could hold him to some promise hindsight might make him wish he'd never given.

Melicent looked at him sharply. 'I hope, Sergeant, that you do *something* as soon as possible — if not sooner. Feeling in the Campions is very strong, let me assure you. These hippie Phoenixes simply have to go!'

★ ★ ★

The advantage of a buffet is that you may start when you choose, and may draw it out for as long as you please. You may also sit at whichever table takes your fancy: and it was plain that Sir Lionel Tobias had no fancy to sit at the same table as the man whose unexpected arrival at Campions Crest had so disturbed him. It was well-known in business circles that the Allshire and Farther Clothing Company had done no business, and had no dealings, with Brazier's Boots for over seventy years. Which explained why Archie Brazier pointedly dined at one end of the morning room, and Sir Lionel Tobias, with equal point, at the other . . .

The Family of the Phoenix, those graceless hippies from the North Lodge, also enjoyed the benefits of flexible mealtimes, governed as their lifestyle was by the natural functions of sunrise, sunset, and their stomachs. The Phoenix rises with the sun, breaks a hearty fast, and feeds by snacking and grazing throughout the day, returning to the roost only if the weather turns against it, or if (it being mainly a juvenile fowl) boredom sets in. Otherwise, this early bird spends the day in gleaning, scrounging, and foraging from fields and hedgerows; but it tries not to trespass, and does no damage to fences, gates, or even buildings — whether squatted in or not.

Such was the Philosophy of the Phoenix, which met with the strong and continued disapproval of Miss Melicent Jervaulx (and, by inference, of Squadron Leader Kempshott) as they drove home from Allingham towards their own sedate, and separate, midday meals.

'I confess,' said Melicent, 'that I am more than a little disappointed at the reception given by the police to our complaint. The sergeant appeared to be — to be *humouring* me as if I were no more than a — a foolish old woman. I cannot say,' she went on, above Robbie's embarrassed mumblings of denial, 'that I am particularly pleased by such an attitude. Nor do I find it entirely credible that the man's superior officer should be absent from the building in the middle of the working day, with no indication as to his whereabouts. I fear, Mr. Kempshott, that I — we — have been *fobbed off,* which is a distasteful notion.'

Robbie tried to say something, but she ignored him. Her eyes glittered as she gazed at the road ahead, and her hands gripped the steering wheel with ferocious intensity. 'One has, Mr. Kempshott, *obligations* which a mere policeman may not hope to understand — and I have no intention of shirking those obligations, never mind what the opinion of others might be. I shall go,' she announced, 'to the North Lodge this instant — we are, after all, almost there — and I shall speak to these Phoenixes myself.' The Morris swooped across the road as she glanced at her wristwatch. 'There is ample time, I would think, before luncheon, since what I have to say will not take long. Plain speaking seldom does.'

'Here — I say, Miss Jervaulx, should you really . . . ?'

Melicent sniffed, and slowed the car, favouring her passenger with a scathing sideways glance. 'You may await my return, Mr. Kempshott — or,' she added witheringly, 'since it is a fine day, why not walk on through the park and straight home to the South Lodge? I can always bring along such of your shopping as you feel unable to carry yourself . . . '

And Squadron Leader Kempshott, mopping his brow, accepted Melicent's offer, and escaped thankfully from the car as she pulled in outside the North Lodge, leaving her — spinster of the parish, member of The Family, staunch churchgoer, Girl Guide captain — to lock both doors; to walk, her spine straight as a tent pole, up the path to the front of the North Lodge; and to rap fearlessly upon the closed door.

4

As the sun sank slowly at the end of the day, and streetlamps flickered one by one into life, people began to think of suppertime, and home.

Trewley slammed shut the Peeping Tom files he'd been studying, tossed them on top of his in tray, and told Stone he didn't suppose he'd see her again until Monday, and he hoped she enjoyed her time off. For himself, he was looking forward to a good fry-up at least once between now and the start of next week . . .

The Phoenixes came in from the fields to a warm welcome from those of their number who had remained at home during the day, busy with indoor tasks to the comfort and advantage of their fellows. Newly baked bread and freshly gathered nuts — hazel, beech, sweet chestnut — were eaten with hedgerow fruits and a tasty casserole of edible roots and fungi. Water drawn from the lodge well was the only drink on the table as candles and paraffin lanterns were lit, and everyone settled comfortably round the huge, white-tiled kitchen table. It was one of the few items of furniture Young Walter hadn't bothered to take with him on his decampment to the arms of Allingham's Ruby.

While Walter's illegal successors ate, more water was heating on the range; the washing-up afterwards was a shared endeavour. Once everything was tidied away, the Phoenixes retired to their cushion-filled Parley Room until, lured by the rising moonlight, they wandered severally — in silence or singing, according to their mood — out into the fresh coolness of an autumn night.

Squadron Leader Kempshott stoked his inner fires with a serving of macaroni cheese, put the dish to soak, collected his binoculars, and headed for the great outdoors.

Miss Melicent Jervaulx heated tomato soup, grilled a chop, locked and bolted her front and back doors. Then she loosened her whalebone stays and plumped herself down in the deep fireside armchair with a thriller or two to hand — the manorial family had scorned television — and a bottle of tonic wine, with a tumbler, on a convenient table.

The Campions Crest Conference Centre's first seminar dined uneasily, but with considerable style. There were damask cloths, shining cutlery, gleaming glassware, and food and drink of the highest quality — which was more, the seminarians felt, than could be said of their companions . . .

It had been an awkward three-quarters of an hour in the morning room at Campions Crest. Andrew Ryan tried to set a few conversational balls rolling, but gave up after his seventh struggling gambit was greeted with monosyllabic replies from Archie Brazier ('Braziers make the Best Boots') and Sir Lionel Tobias, neither of whom seemed willing to converse with anyone except Banter. Andrew's 'amazing man' did sterling work behind the serving dishes, and helped his guests to the food of their choice with all the lofty disdain of the well-bred butler. He refused to be drawn into more than 'Indeed, sir?' or 'Certainly, sir,' or 'I would particularly recommend the kedgeree,' but compared to Andrew's nervous chatter, this counted as repartee of the highest order.

Sir Lionel had finished his meal first, muttered something, and left the room without pudding. Archie Brazier requested a second helping of apricot fool, lavished cream and sugar into his coffee, and rubbed his stomach with satisfaction before announcing that he could do with some fresh — a meaningful look at Mr. Ryan, a scowl in the direction of Sir Lionel's vacant seat — air.

The Boot Baron and the Clothing King managed to vanish successfully from the scene until five o'clock, the appointed hour for the other members of the Course to start arriving. Arrive they duly did — in their own cars, sharing taxis, singly or in groups — and each arrival was as startled as the two magnates had been on realising who their companions for the weekend were to be.

'For heaven's sake!' The sentiment was expressed in a variety of ways around the entrance hall as people collected room keys and Course folders before their luggage went upstairs. 'Haven't the idiots running this place ever heard of the Wardrobe War? If they're not careful, they can expect blood on the carpets long before Sunday night . . . '

The Wardrobe War was the title popularly given to the disagreement, some seventy years earlier, which had occurred between the Tobias of that time, in charge of what was still the Allshire Clothing Company, and the Brazier then running Brazier's Boots. There had been talk of a partnership, of expansion with intent to supply the entire head-to-foot outfitting requirements of young Empire-builders at competitive prices in convenient locations. Hands had been shaken on the deal, words given as the directors' bonds . . . and then the lawyers somehow — details had never been made clear — managed to destroy not only the prospective partnership, but also the decades of mutual goodwill which had grown up between the two companies. From the day when twin copies of the contract had been angrily consigned to flames kindled from the tips of two cigars in separate offices, no Brazier would have anything to do with a Tobias, and vice versa. When an obscure Tobias niece married a distant Brazier nephew, both parties were promptly disowned by their respective families, and thereafter pursued highly rewarding careers with neutral Marks and Spencer. People once taking employment with Allshire and Farther knew they could never hope to work for Brazier's Boots; those whose non-company husbands or wives moved jobs to towns where there were no branches of Brazier's knew it would be worse than useless to apply to the omnipresent Allshire establishment . . .

In the light of so stirring a history, it should perhaps come as no surprise that the Course attendees dined uneasily together. There were around a dozen members of each company present, including Sir Lionel Tobias and Archie Brazier, who was known to the popular press as 'Brash Archie' from the playboy lifestyle he had enjoyed until the unexpected death of an uncle and two cousins left him head of the family firm. Archie was tall, dark, dashing, and rakishly handsome; he enjoyed gambling, and the company of beautiful women; he had a gourmand's relish for good food, and good wine.

Good food and good wine he had in abundance that night at Campions Crest, as did everyone else. Andrew Ryan, whose presence had hardly been conducive to merriment, sighed with relief as the unobtrusive presence of butler Banter oversaw the giggling village girls who served the meal and cleared away afterwards. Andrew himself poured wine, and more wine, though he drank little himself. All was done to perfection. Mr. Ryan was seen to smile at last as the mellowed Course members heard the butler clear his throat, and announce in his most imposing tones: 'Coffee will be served, with liqueurs, in the drawing room. If you would care to follow me, ladies and gentlemen?'

Everyone dropped napkins beside plates and pushed back chairs to follow Banter's lead. Those who smoked pulled out sleek metal cases or cellophane-wrapped packets, and offered them loudly to colleagues, ignoring the opposition, hoping their behavior would score points with the big bosses.

Banter, in his turn, ignored both sides, walking with measured tread, soft-footed as a panther, across the marble-tiled hall to the half-open door of an airy, pleasant room where a fire burned and trays were set ready.

'Your coffee, sir — madam,' he murmured, bowing, ushering the ill-assorted group inside. He closed the door firmly behind the last to enter, and allowed the broad grin he had been holding in check to cross his face in the first natural movement it had shown all day. He rubbed his hands, suppressed a chuckle, and reached cautiously for the knob, turning it to ease the door barely three inches open, enough and no more for him to hear everything that went on.

58

At first, he heard nothing but the shuffle of feet, the clearing of uneasy throats as people looked at one another, the repeated click of cigarette lighters and the striking of an occasional match. For a time, it seemed as if nobody was prepared to speak.

'Ah — coffee,' someone said at last, in a voice that was far too hearty: this was, after all, the first time the Allshires and Braziers had been alone without witnesses since they had arrived at the Conference Centre. 'And liqueurs. Very — very hospitable.' There was a nervous laugh. 'I bet that butler's gone sneaking off to his pantry for a glass or two of port . . .'

A few, hurriedly stifled chortles arose from Allshire and Brazier alike, followed by embarrassed shufflings as they drifted in the direction of the side table where crisp white linen enhanced the rich glow of filled decanters, the diamond sparkle of hand-cut glass, the silver-swan elegance of coffeepots.

'I take mine black,' said another voice, firmly. Bruno Morland, Allshire

Advertising Manager, had made up his mind. 'Anyone else? How about you, Sir Lionel? Good grief!'

Bruno stood with a coffeepot in his right hand, his left frozen in midair, stretched towards the row of waiting cups. His surprise was so evident that, without realising they did so, everyone moved to see what had disturbed him, crowding together to stare: at neat glass dishes of sugared almonds, at saucers of thin mints; at a box of ready-trimmed cigars, at an ornate silver casket of cigarettes; at bottles — chunky, slim, frosted glass; at steaming coffeepots and milk jugs; at shining dishes of crystals — white, brown, rainbow-hued; and at the row of squat, stark, white plastic beakers in front of this epicurean display.

A statuesque redhead picked up one of the beakers, and turned it over to read the letters embossed on the base, crinkling her eyes to focus them. '*FetherFome Containers for Hot or Cold*,' announced Geraldine Burghley, second-in-command of Brazier's Marketing Department. She shrugged. 'Oh, well, then they won't melt — pity they don't have handles, though I'm sure we'll manage.' She thrust the FetherFome Container with a bridge-burning gesture towards Bruno Morland. 'I take mine black, too.'

Bruno shut his mouth, which was still open in surprise, and after a quick glance at Archie Brazier, poured Geraldine's coffee: she was a very good-looking young woman. Geraldine nodded her thanks, spooned sugar, stirred, and moved away with the faintest of smiles.

Bruno's eyes were not the only ones to watch as she settled herself in a comfortable armchair and raised the beaker of black coffee to her lips. She drank, and smiled again.

Sir Lionel smiled too. 'White for me. Thanks, Morland, but I'll add the milk myself.'

Archie Brazier's saturnine face appeared by Lionel's side. 'Same here — please,' he said, through perfect white teeth no girlfriend had yet found soaking in the bathroom. Archie's smile seemed forced on this occasion, but a smile it was, though it did not seem to reach his eyes. Once Tobias had been served he moved rapidly away to a chair near Geraldine without once looking at his Brazier counterpart.

An Allshire employee may have poured the first cup, but no Brazier was going to be beaten by this. Other people began to follow Bruno's example, and several cups of coffee were poured for members of the rival company. It was hardly, however, what anyone would call a party atmosphere . . .

A motherly little typist from the Allshire Purchasing Department plunged into nervous speech. 'Isn't it funny — this beautiful house, and this lovely room, and the silver and glass and everything — and these funny plastic cups!'

'FetherFome,' Geraldine corrected her, with some feeling. 'As a marketing person myself, I can readily imagine how annoyed the FetherFome marketing department would be to hear the product referred to as plain plastic!'

'Whatever it is,' smoothly interposed a fellow Brazier from Public Relations, 'it's hardly the best bone china, is it? I'm sure there must have been some mistake — perhaps those giggling girls who served our meal broke all the good stuff washing up.' And Jason Hockworthy permitted himself a smile as he glanced round at the band of coffee drinkers.

'I'm not so sure,' ventured a thoughtful Allshire man, tapping his spoon on the rim of his beaker. 'I thought that butler had a — a knowing sort of expression as he showed us in here — and there was the way he slammed the door . . . '

'We could always ring the bell and ask him,' someone suggested. 'Assuming he's still sober, that is.'

'Perhaps,' put in Sir Lionel, 'Mr. Ryan has the solution to the mystery. Can you tell us, Mr. Ryan — ? Dear me!'

Andrew's silence had passed unnoticed until now, so quiet had he generally been during dinner; but, as everyone began to search amongst themselves for their nominal leader, they realised that the young man was indubitably absent.

'You know, I don't believe he can have come in with us,' said Geraldine.

63

'We'd have noticed him going out again, wouldn't we?'

Bruno's voice rose above the general murmur of assent. 'Maybe he never meant to. Maybe it's all part of the Course — no cups, no Ray, no idea what's going on. We didn't expect any of it to start until tomorrow morning, did we? But if you ask me, the Attitudes Analysis has already begun!'

5

Saturday morning dawned cloudy, with a hint that worse might come. A bright grey blanket hung low over the earth, which smelled damp, though no rain had yet fallen; and the gloomy atmosphere accorded only too well with the mood of Detective Superintendent Trewley, who felt that Nature and his wife were joined in conspiracy against him.

Susan Trewley had made it woefully clear to her spouse that she was too busy to cook his usual eggs and bacon for breakfast. His daughters set the table with racks of wholemeal toast instead of white, sunflower margarine instead of butter, and only scrapings of marmalade in the dish. After this scanty repast, hints were dropped about the pleasures of digging the garden in the healthy fresh air . . .

Trewley tried to read the morning paper, and willed the telephone to ring before his wife could remind him of her idea that they should walk, rather than drive, to the corner shop (which he supposed he didn't really mind) to carry the bags back for her (which he did). The girls babbled in the background about pollution, and atmospheric lead, and the greenhouse effect . . .

With a muffled oath, he threw the paper down. They'd hear the car starting up, he knew — they'd guess he was making a run for it — but, good grief, they wanted him to take a spot of exercise, didn't they? So they could hardly complain if he *walked* to freedom . . . And Detective Superintendent Trewley, terror of Allshire's criminal classes, twice commended by the Chief Constable for bravery, sidled from the dining room, crept into the hall, shrugged on his raincoat, and sneaked out of the house.

Automatically, his footsteps headed in the direction of the police station. Better a life of crime than a day digging the garden . . .

He remembered to go in by the back door, keeping his fingers crossed he wouldn't run across Sergeant Pleate taking time off from Front Desk duty. He tiptoed the last few steps to his office door, opened it — and stood transfixed on the threshold.

'You! What the hell d'you think you're playing at?'

Stone looked up, swallowed, put down the rest of her sandwich, and grinned. 'I do work here, sir,' she reminded him gently. 'And I might well ask the same of you — as it's Saturday, I mean.'

'Don't bandy words with me, girl.' Trewley stamped across to her desk, dragged out the visitor's chair, and sat down with a weary thump, his bulldog face scowling. 'I'm in no mood for women's nonsense just now. Give me a straight answer. I thought you were going somewhere exotic with young What's-his-name this weekend. Where is he? And what are you doing here?'

Stone stifled a sigh. 'Extra duty, sir — they're two men short, and you know how everything's building up to that equinox nonsense next week. Apparently, there are vanloads of hippies wandering all over the place and, well . . . ' She

67

shrugged. 'So I decided I might as well try catching up on the paperwork instead. I brought in a picnic, and — '

'Don't!' As his sergeant reached again for her sandwich, the superintendent groaned, and closed his eyes.

After two seconds, light dawned. Stone chuckled. 'Er — family troubles, sir?' She paused, delicately. 'Again?'

He grunted, but said nothing. Stone munched cheerfully for a few moments, and at last he opened his eyes to stare at her with deep loathing.

'I was right,' he snarled. 'They've got it into their blasted heads I need to lose weight, all four of 'em. What else d'you expect me to do except get out of the house, with everyone nagging me about blood pressure and calories and cholesterol and Lord knows what? And don't you' — as she opened her mouth — 'start on at me too, girl, or you'll be back in uniform before you can blink!'

Stone sighed. She recalled too many previous occasions when Mrs. Trewley and her daughters had decided there was rather more of the nominal head

68

of their household than they would like. Mrs. Trewley and her daughters hadn't had to work with the aftereffects of their calorific ban . . .

She made up her mind quickly, pushing the grease-proof-wrapped packet across the desk towards her stricken superior. 'Wholemeal bread, sir, though I have to confess it's butter, not low-fat spread. Go on — I won't tell a soul, I promise. Take two, if you like,' as he hesitated. 'I made the bread myself.'

Trewley hesitated no longer. With a sigh, and a nod of thanks, he took three.

'What's in 'em?' he enquired, starting to munch. 'Not bad at all. Haven't taken too many, have I?'

'I'd almost finished, sir, thanks. I was going to save the rest for lunch, but now — well, we can always pop out to the pub, can't we? Just as long as we make sure we're back in good time . . . '

'In time for what?' Trewley chewed on a crusty corner, and frowned. 'This equinox rubbish won't bother us, I'd've thought. My days of standing in the

69

middle of the road in white gloves waving my arms about are long gone, and so are — well, yours're gone too, anyway.'

'Yes, sir. And with so many people called back from their days off, I don't suppose anyone else will be needed — but just because Traffic is unlikely to need us doesn't mean someone else won't, remember. In good time for whatever's going to happen, and for whoever eventually needs us — that's what I meant, sir. Because it's almost like Fate — here you are, and here am I. Something's bound to happen, if you ask me — and before I'm very much older, too . . .'

★ ★ ★

Breakfast had been the best part of the day so far at Campions Crest. Butler Banter's virtuoso performance on the gong had reverberated around the building to summon Course delegates from bed and bathrooms, and by five past eight — having collided furtively with one another in corridors and on the stairs — Allshires and Braziers were together, in the dining room, investigating the display of silver covers on the sideboard. Kippers, kidneys, cutlets, mushrooms, tomatoes, sausages, eggs, ham, fried bread, pancakes, porridge, fruit juice, cereal, toast: everything wafted tempting odours to hungry noses.

But the tables, damask cloths notwithstanding, were laid with paper plates, and the cutlery was plastic.

It seemed that Banter intended to rest on his percussive laurels, for he was nowhere to be seen as the delegates entered the dining room; and again it seemed that Andrew Ryan's presence was to be denied his charges. There were no bells to push to summon assistance; no giggling girls appeared to pour from the tea and coffeepots which were set out, with milk jugs, on every table.

Bruno Morland surveyed the scene before him, and nodded as if some secret suspicion had been confirmed. 'I said it was deliberate,' he remarked, carving bacon with a bendy knife. 'It's all done to fool us — we're probably

71

halfway through the Course without even realising it.'

'Hardly halfway — a quarter, perhaps.' Geraldine Burghley looked at her watch, and consulted a mental timetable. 'No, say a fifth . . . '

Somebody sniggered, but nobody spoke. Breakfast was a silent, dragged-out meal, as everyone pondered what might happen next. The Course notes, while extolling the undoubted benefits of attending, had been particularly vague as to how those benefits might be achieved. Deliberately vague? People started to wonder . . .

And to wander, as nobody came to attend to them. Some drifted into the hall, where they found a selection of newspapers on a table beside the coffee-lounge door; they took the papers into the lounge to read. Jason Hockworthy made sure Archie Brazier saw him with *The Financial Times*; Archie himself selected one of the racier tabloids.

Others went outside, making the most of the day before the threatened rain arrived; but nobody could have wandered too far, for by nine o'clock everyone had joined the newsreaders in the lounge, waiting . . .

By twenty past nine, they were becoming restive. They were all — with the continued exception of Andrew Ryan, the original Invisible Man — present, and as correct as so ill-assorted a group of people can be when one half is in a permanent state of feuding with the other, and when within the halves no two persons have equal rank or similar interests.

The grandfather clock in the hall chimed once, for the half hour.

There was a rustle of movement, and Andrew Ryan stood in the doorway — to a chorus of gasps. Gone was the suave Adonis of the previous night. This young man, white-faced and drawn, was as unshaven as a blond can be. His hair was tousled. Instead of trim trousers, silk shirt, and cravat, he wore paint-stained corduroy jeans, and a pullover with baggy sleeves and several ill-made darns.

'Good morning.' He forced a smile, as if nothing could be less unexpected than his appearance. 'Is everyone here?' He checked his watch, then looked round the room. 'Good.'

Without another word, he turned on his heel and, hands thrust deep in his pockets, walked across the hall to the foot of the stairs, where he leaned against the newel post with his arms folded, watching the lounge door from blue, blank-gazing eyes.

The eyes of Sir Lionel Tobias and Archie Brazier flashed unfathomable messages across the startled room. Archie, a strange expression on his face, rose to his feet.

'We don't want to miss any of the fun, do we?' Without waiting for a reply, not bothering to check whether any of his staff had heard him, he headed after Andrew Ryan.

There was an immediate surge of Brazier employees behind him. The Allshire crowd, determined not to be outdone, soon caught them up. Sir Lionel, on his dignity, came last.

Andrew nodded as they all drew near, but said nothing. Again he turned away, and began to climb the stairs. This time, people were quicker to take his lead. Puffing a little, but game, everyone hurried in his wake to the top of the first flight, along the landing, and up the druggeted second in the direction of what must surely be the third — leading, they deduced, to the attic.

When Andrew opened the creaking door and went in, everyone saw that this attic, from its shape and size, must run the whole length of the house. Boards had been fixed across the rafters for storage, and still bore witness to generations of bygone Jervaulx. There were footprints in the dust, and cobwebs lay thickly on crates, trunks, and boxes; sturdy suitcases, corded and strapped, were ranged beside them. A giant water tank, lidded against pigeons, gurgled grey and cold in the corner opposite the wide dormer window.

Andrew, his eyes half-closed, leaned against the slope of the raftered ceiling with his arms once more folded, and listened.

'Quite a climb,' said Archie Brazier,

puffing less than might have been expected from a playboy but recently reformed. He went over to the window. 'Not a bad view. Looks as if it may clear up later.'

'Clearing up?' The Allshire typist giggled as she gazed about her. 'There's so much dust — and they've left so much luggage — at least, I suppose they left it when they went. He, I mean — Sir Joyce, poor man.'

'He had more on his mind than shifting a few old suitcases,' said Brazier's Warehouse Manager grimly. There was an uneasy pause.

'Let's all sit down, if we're going to be here for a while,' suggested Geraldine Burghley, just before the hush grew deafening. 'If we pull a few of those trunks and cases out into the middle, and dust them off — '

'We're hardly dressed for shifting furniture,' retorted Bruno Morland, who was wearing a fawn cashmere pullover.

All eyes drifted to Andrew Ryan in his cords and scruffy sweater. His eyes were now completely closed and there was a faint twist to his lips that might have been a smile.

'Perhaps,' said Sir Lionel, 'we should have come better prepared, Bruno.' He gazed ruefully at his own neat suiting. 'The dry cleaners will have a fine time of it on Monday — and Allshire and Farther as well, I hope. Dear me — it's an ill wind.'

'Sir Lionel! You can't — '

'Why not?' Tobias twinkled in Geraldine's direction. 'An excellent suggestion, young lady; but, if I may venture a slight amendment — near the window, I think, rather than here in the centre. On so grey a day — even if it *may* clear up later . . . '

'Throw a little more light on the subject,' agreed Archie Brazier. Then he scowled. Everyone looked at everyone else, unwilling to take a lead.

'Maybe there's electric light,' said an Allshire Buyer.

'There isn't,' said a Brazier Export clerk.

'Then near the window it is,' said Geraldine, dusting her hands in anticipation. She studied the assortment of cases and trunks with a thoughtful smile. 'Teamwork,' she said, as the males of the group automatically flexed their muscles. 'We'll never move anything by ourselves.'

'Suppose the sun *does* come out?' A Brazier Accountant not overfond of physical effort had been calculating the likely weight of so much left luggage. 'Best leave things as they are. We won't be able to see what's happening if we're dazzled half to death . . . '

Geraldine looked at her watch, then shook her head and smiled. 'I forgot — it's new. Digital,' she explained.

Bruno Morland was unable to resist the opportunity. 'Very impressive — a new digital watch. Tells the time in three separate continents, I suppose?'

His remark had drowned out Geraldine's request for the loan of a timepiece with hands; but there was no need for her to repeat it. Sir Lionel Tobias had been watching her with interest, and, even as Bruno spoke, was unfastening from about his wrist an old-fashioned leather strap. 'Be prepared,' he said with a bow, and handed his watch to Miss Burghley: who smiled back, as if at some shared joke, then took the watch over to the window with a murmur that she would certainly do her best.

'A simple trick,' said Tobias, 'but invaluable — always provided that you remember to convert to Greenwich Mean Time during the summer, of course.'

Geraldine's knowing smile suggested only too well that she had remembered to allow for this conversion. Others of the group might feel annoyed by her smugness, but Sir Lionel smiled back, and went on:

'If Miss — Burghley, thank you — if Miss Burghley, as I'm sure she's going to, points the hour hand of my watch directly to the sun, and bisects the angle it makes with the figure twelve on the dial, then the bisecting line will run due north and south — and it should be perfectly possible to work out which way the sun is travelling, and where anyone should sit to avoid being dazzled by sun in the eyes. Isn't that right, Miss Burghley?'

'Good grief!' burst from Bruno Morland, as Geraldine nodded, and smiled again. 'Where on earth would anyone pick up a trick like that?'

'In the Girl Guides,' replied Geraldine smoothly, returning Sir Lionel's watch to its owner. 'That hearty outdoor life palled after a couple of years, but while I belonged I did pick up a few really useful tips — like how to tie a parcel using a packer's knot with the minimum of string, or how to tell the time at night from the handle of the Plough.'

Sir Lionel was listening and nodding. 'My boy Michael,' he said with pride, 'is a Cub, you know.' There was little that newspaper-reading Allshire did *not* know about the Tobias son and heir, though it never stopped the doting father enlarging on his favourite topic whenever possible. 'Passed his First Class youngest of his pack, and is going up to the Scouts in three weeks' time, the clever little chap. You should see him on a hike, building a fire from stones and turf and twigs — splendid! Even before he came to us, you know, I was interested in youngsters of his sort — the Boys' Brigade, the local Cadets. That trick,' and he tapped his watch with an approving finger, 'was taught me on my first outing, many years before Michael was born. I'm surprised anyone remembers it now, with so many' — twinkling again — 'digital watches around. So what, may I ask, was your conclusion, my dear?'

Geraldine shrugged. 'That we'll have to wait for the sun to come out properly before we can work out where the rays are going to fall at any particular time.' She smiled. 'Sorry, but there you are. Nature — the weather — Fate . . . you can't fight any of them, can you?'

She was not the only person at Campions Crest that day to be of the same opinion.

6

Desk Sergeant Pleate's Occurrence Book
was always written up in a neat,
unflurried hand, no matter what the
contents. So far that morning he had
noted a lost dog, a stolen handbag,
and three minor traffic offences, all
apparently unconnected with the convoy
of equinoctial hippies Traffic Division
seemed to have been successful in
deflecting from Allingham town centre.

The emergency message, when it came,
was logged in his normal copperplate
hand. *One-seventeen, three nines call
from Campions Crest. Body of a young
woman, believed victim of violent attack,
found in the kitchen of the main lodge
by Mr. Simeon Gotobed.*

Two discreet cars — no need for
blaring horns or flashing beacons in
Allingham, even on a Saturday afternoon
— made their swift exit from the rear
of the police station. The first was

driven by Detective Sergeant Stone, with Detective Superintendent Trewley at her side. Trewley knew this was an emergency, but he couldn't help brooding on the pub lunch he'd been forced to leave half-finished when, sent in pursuit by Desk Sergeant Pleate once telephone messages to his house had failed, PC Benson had run him almost immediately to earth. Benson and his colleague PC Hedges followed in the other car with others of the forensic team.

'I haven't been this way for years, sir,' said Stone, as she steered the car round a high-hedged corner and decided it might now be wise to switch on the siren. 'Really the sticks, isn't it?'

Trewley grunted. 'Expensive sticks. There's more millionaires to the square inch in the Campions than in the rest of Allshire put together, some say.'

'I suppose that's why poor old Jervaulx took it so badly when he realised the games his son had been playing with the family fortune.' Stone shook her head. There were obvious advantages in the middle-class mortgage ethic she

83

and her Traffic colleague had embraced: not that she disapproved of inherited wealth, but she could see that it had its inconveniences.

And its privileges. The car had been running for some time beside a high stone wall, in which a gap now appeared — if *gap* was not too ridiculous a word for the wrought-iron splendour which now met her gaze, for the spacious parklands and glorious vista which stretched beyond the gold-tipped gates as far as the eye could see.

'Very nice,' said Stone, flicking the indicator as she slowed to complete the turn through the high carved archway. 'Pity we have to go barging in on all that . . .'

'Umph. Too good to waste on a load of blasted trick cyclists, if you ask me.' Thwarted hunger made Trewley irritable, and the sight of the new notice board did not inspire him as it had inspired Andrew Ryan the previous day. 'These business syndicates have money to burn — all gimmicks and rubbish and government tax allowances, just because they can call it training. Wouldn't surprise me if one of the ordinary mortals around the place'd taken it into his head enough was enough, and bumped off one of 'em just to chivvy the rest into selling up and leaving. They might have better luck with the next buyer . . . '

Stone was pulling the car around in a neat half-circle. 'Or perhaps it's a publicity stunt that went wrong — they haven't been open long, remember.'

'If they've been monkeying about wasting police time — ' Trewley broke off. 'Good grief!'

Stone, applying the brakes, stared as hard as her superior at the figure which now met their eyes. A gnarled and weather-beaten old personage, his shirtsleeves rolled up and his midriff leather-waistcoated, stood calmly in green gum boots before a low hedge, clipping it with a large pair of shears. So methodical and soothing was the rhythm into which he had apparently worked himself that he did not seem to notice the arrival of the police car. On he clipped regardless, even when Benson, braking on loose gravel, sent a crunching spray of small stones and earth rattling against Stone's paintwork as she opened her door.

'I know they say folk in the country live at a slower pace,' muttered Trewley, 'but this is ridiculous. Doesn't this character realise what's been going on?'

'Perhaps it's a — a displacement activity, sir.' Stone often found that her lapsed medical training had its uses. 'Shock can do funny things to people . . .'

While his superiors were discussing in low voices the remarkably phlegmatic demeanour of Leather Waistcoat, PC Benson took matters into his own hands. He strode forward across the gravel, his buttons agleam with efficiency. He cleared his throat.

'Er — Mr. Simeon Gotobed?' The leather waistcoat slowly turned its front buttons to face him. Benson pressed on. 'Mr. Gotobed, we understand — '

'No,' returned the leather waistcoat, polite but firm. Its wearer stared thoughtfully at the two intrusive police cars, and shook his shears with some impatience.

Benson blinked, then rallied as Trewley and Stone came up beside him. 'Er — no? You — you mean you're *not* Simeon Gotobed?'

'Yes,' returned the leather waistcoat at once, and the shears clashed emphatically together.

Benson was thoroughly bewildered. 'Yes? You mean you *are* him — Gotobed — after all? Then why — ?'

'No,' returned Leather Waistcoat. The shears clashed again. 'I mean nothing of the sort. My previous affirmative, which you appear to have woefully misunderstood, was no more than a positive response to your question as to the bearing of my original negative. Yes, I meant that I was not Simeon Gotobed. I still mean it. I am not he.'

As Benson turned pink about the ears, Trewley came to the rescue. 'Then may we ask who — ?' he began; but his words were drowned out by the irritated tones of Leather Waistcoat.

'It is a lamentably common failing in

townspeople,' he complained, brandishing his shears accusingly beneath poor Benson's startled nose, 'to assume that all country-dwellers sport only such picturesque appellatives as Diggory Venn, or Kester Woodseaves. They — we — do not.'

'Or Gabriel Oak,' supplied Stone, hearing Trewley snort at her side. 'Or' — her eyes twinkled — 'Adam Lambsbreath.'

'Ah.' Leather Waistcoat turned to her with the faint beginnings of a smile on his nut-brown face. He favoured her with a bow. 'Good — very good. And how might I be of service to you, my well-read young friend?'

Trewley muttered something Stone chose not to hear. She addressed Leather Waistcoat firmly. 'So you're not Simeon Gotobed,' she said. 'And you didn't telephone an emergency call to Allingham police station to say there was the dead body of a young woman on these premises?'

Not-Simeon-Gotobed bowed again. 'You are entirely correct in your assumption — or should I say in your deduction?' His gaze flicked from Stone, in her sensible split skirt and discreet blouse, to uniformed Benson and his colleagues. 'The Criminal Investigation Department, I in my turn deduce. Detectives.' At her nod, he permitted himself a smile, and waved the shears in the direction of the little house behind the half-clipped hedge. 'There are no dead bodies here, male or female — although you are at liberty to search the premises, if you feel you must.'

Stone glanced at Trewley, raising an eyebrow. The superintendent frowned, scowled, then shook his head. Stone said: 'I don't think that will be necessary, thank you, sir. Not yet, that is. Not as far as we know.'

'Ah.' The leather shoulders shook. 'Yes, indeed. This temporising will be in the nature of insurance, of course, in case I am lying. I might genuinely be this murderous Gotobed — or an accomplice, perhaps — intent on delaying you with vacant and specious chatter while the body is disposed of, and my friend makes good his escape.' Trewley snorted again, and Leather Waistcoat's eyes gleamed. 'The theory, I venture to suggest, is as good as any other you may have, is it not?'

'No,' retorted the superintendent, as Stone smothered a choking sound. 'No, it isn't, because if you say you didn't make that call — '

'I have no telephone,' interposed Leather Waistcoat.

' — Then somebody else made it,' Trewley said, 'and from some*where* else — and with three other lodges to choose from, I'd say it was one of them we need instead of yours. Wouldn't you, Mr . . . ?'

'Smith.' Another bow, the shearless hand placed across the leather waist. 'Pensioner of the Jervaulx estate, former tutor to young Joscelin, for my sins — although to lay the blame for Joscelin's recent sins at the door of my tutelage would be more than a little unjust. And John, if you please — no middle name . . . ' From his tone, it sounded as if the explanation was one he was accustomed to giving at some length, but on this particular occasion he seemed to cut it short.

'A body in one of the other lodges — a young woman? And the police in full cry . . . Dear me.' Mr. Smith sighed. 'Far be it from your humble servant to cast aspersions upon the moral character of Squadron Leader Kempshott — and one would hesitate to describe Melicent Jervaulx as in any way of tender years — which leaves, alas, the Phoenixes. And what a matter for regret should this be the case, with their whole lives ahead of them . . . '

'You mean the commune?' Trewley's voice was eager as Mr. Smith chopped sadly in the air, a horticultural Grim Reaper with shears instead of a scythe. 'You've had dealings with them — you know them, do you? Any particular reason for thinking it's one of them that's been killed?'

Mr. Smith stared at his boots, evidently considering his reply. Trewley, irritated, was about to press the question when: 'I would hardly call any of them particular friends,' said Mr. Smith at last, 'but I

certainly feel that I may claim some
. . . acquaintance with the Phoenixes.
Some,' he said again, firmly. 'We meet,
you understand, on occasion in the fields
and hedgerows hereabouts, and in the
course of such meetings we naturally pass
the time of day.' Mr. Smith drew himself
up, and spoke in dignified accents, all
frivolity forgotten. 'Although retired some
years now from my pedagogic pursuits,
I maintain a professional curiosity in
. . . certain aspects of youthful behaviour.
The, ah, Phoenixes, I cannot help but
feel, regard me as a rusticated — in the
literal sense of the term — old hermit.
It . . . amuses them to narrate stories
of their past and present lives in an
attempt — or such is the impression I
have gathered — to shock my simple rural
mind with tales of urban degradation and
city squalor.'

Mr. Smith permitted himself a sardonic
smile. 'I have a strong suspicion that most
of their tales are less than true — if not,
indeed, downright falsehoods. I am not
a man easily shocked, you see. These
young people no doubt feel it necessary

to go to extremes of invention in their efforts to *épater* such *bourgeois* instincts as they deem me still to possess . . . but enough of this idle chatter. You and your companions have a death to investigate. I will bid you all good day, and wish you Godspeed.'

Trewley had been trying for some minutes to break into Mr. Smith's conversational flow to ask for directions to the Phoenix lodge, but now felt irrationally annoyed that the old gentleman had as good as given the forces of the law their marching orders. He held up a hand as Mr. Smith seemed about to turn back to his hedge.

'Just a minute, if you don't mind, sir. From what we've been given to understand, there's not many people in these parts have more than a nodding acquaintance with these — these Phoenixes, so your opinion could be worth something if it turns out it's them we're dealing with. Hippies — an odd bunch, by all accounts. Could be we'll need a — an interpreter when we're interviewing 'em, for a start, seeing as you say they talk to you. And another thing that's a bit odd, if you don't mind me saying so, is that they tell you lies to . . . ' Trewley hesitated. He had never been much of a scholar, and his knowledge of French was limited. ' . . . to tease you,' he brought out at last, daring anyone to argue. 'They tell you lies, yet you don't seem bothered about the way they might be trying to make a fool of you? Like I said — a bit odd.'

Mr. Smith shrugged. 'They might well be trying, but they do not succeed. It is harder than one would expect to make a fool of someone who has, despite his advancing years, kept his wits about him — and then, for all I know (as opposed to suspect) to the contrary, they may be telling me the truth.' He shrugged again, spreading his hands in a world-weary gesture. 'The longer one's experience of life, the more one comes to realise that there is indeed very little which can, in the end, be ruled out as unlikely. Did not one of your — forgive me — infinitely superior, albeit fictional, colleagues have some thoughts on the advisability of eliminating the impossible to be left with the merely improbable? Had he lived in this century rather than the last — '

Trewley might not have been much of a scholar, but it was a rare policeman who didn't know his Doyle. He emitted a monumental snort. 'Never mind Sherlock Holmes, Mr. Smith, I've got a real-life murder on my hands — well, a sudden death, anyhow, and I want to get on and solve it. The message said the main lodge. We thought that was you, and now you say it isn't.' Mr. Smith seemed prepared to argue with this, but Trewley hurried on: 'So, if it's not you — where is it?'

'Ah.' There was an inexplicable gleam in John Smith's eye. 'The main lodge — yes, indeed, an understandable error on the part of your informant, whoever he or she might have been. Certainly not a local, unless — improbably — one with sufficient wit to devise so cunning a double-bluff as to take advantage of this snippet of Allshire history of which none of you' — his glance swept over Trewley, Stone, Benson, Hedges and the rest — 'is apparently possessed . . . '

He saw something in the superintendent's face which made him turn serious again. 'I apologise. Shock, you know, can do . . . ' Briefly, his eyes met those of Stone. ' . . . Funny things to people — and there can be no denying that the news you bring has been something of a shock to me. To the Phoenixes, also, it will be unwelcome; but then, as they believe themselves to be guided by the higher hand of Fate, if Fate has so ruled that one of their number should perish, they will accept the ruling with a better grace, perhaps, than you or I less . . . philosophic mortals may achieve . . . '

As the cars at last pulled away in the direction of the North Lodge, Trewley was frowning. 'Smith's a queer sort of tutor for the Jervaulx lad to've had. No wonder he — Joscelin — went off the rails like he did. That bloke's at least halfway round the bend, to my mind — spouting such nonsense, trying to bamboozle us with his fine talk — and who,' he demanded, his tone accusing, 'were those characters you and he were having such a nice chat about? Diggory and Adam and I-don't-know-who . . . '

Stone, with a smile, confirmed that they had indeed been characters, briefly explaining the references to Thomas Hardy, *Precious Bane* and *Cold Comfort Farm*. Trewley grunted, rubbed his chin, and muttered that it was no doubt fine for some, but *he* hadn't been to university, and had to muddle along speaking ordinary English like the rest of the world. Stone would oblige him if she didn't get too chatty with the suspects, just in case.

The sergeant was slowing the car for the turn into the North Lodge, and did not reply. At first sight, this gateway was even more impressive than the one at the East Lodge: the stone arch was higher, and ornately carved; the gates themselves were wider, their wrought-iron curlicues more elaborate. Yet a second glance showed that all this splendour seemed just a little faded, by comparison.

Stone had too much sense to ask Trewley whether he had earmarked John

Smith as a potential suspect: she knew that at this stage of an investigation, comments like that would be worse than useless. 'Smith certainly seems a — an interesting man, sir,' was all she was prepared to say; and Trewley, with another grunt, agreed with her.

'There's a car,' said Stone, bringing theirs to a halt. 'Not a local one, from the number.'

'AA SG 1,' Trewley read aloud. 'Oh, no, of course, it can't be. AAS 61 — he's had one of those blasted gimmicky plates made up. SG — Simeon Gotobed, maybe? Let's go and find out . . .'

'And what's the betting, sir,' murmured Stone, as they left the police car and made for the sleek little sports model in the shelter of the wrought-iron gates, 'that AA stands for Alcoholics Anonymous? He's probably got the D.T.s and only *thinks* he saw a body . . .'

'Wasting police time!' growled Trewley, then stopped in his tracks. Stone whistled softly under her breath.

'No doubt of it, sir — he's seen

something nasty in the woodshed, all right . . . '

A man — a stranger, trendily clad in a stonewashed denim suit — was slumped in the driver's seat of the little sports car, half in and half out of the open door, his feet flat apart on the ground, his elbows on his knees, his head buried in his hands. At the sound of approaching feet, he lifted his head.

'Oh,' he said, in a wavering voice. 'Oh — thank God!' And he buried his face in his hands again.

'Mr. Simeon Gotobed?' enquired Trewley. The buried head nodded without looking up. A muffled murmur informed anyone who might be interested that Simeon Gotobed felt terrible.

'Mr. Gotobed!' This was no time for witnesses to mollycoddle themselves. 'You made an emergency call to Allingham police headquarters at one-fifteen, didn't you?'

Gotobed groaned, and raised an ashen face to meet the superintendent's gaze. He gulped. 'In — in there — in the kitchen. The door . . . was open, and . . . I can't — I can't! It — she — was . . . horrible — you just won't believe . . . '

He tailed off, and gulped again. Stone surveyed him with an expert eye, and decided that, once he had given full vent to his emotions, he would undoubtedly live. Trewley ordered the forensic team inside, then turned back to Simeon Gotobed, determined to find out something, no matter how the man might moan and groan.

'The body of a young woman, you said, sir? Now — '

'Oh! Oooohhh . . . ' Simeon turned from white to green, gulped, gasped, and flung himself out of the car and into a convenient clump of shrubbery, beneath which shelter he was shudderingly sick. Stone, about to hurry across, felt Trewley's hand grab her arm.

'He'll live,' he muttered, echoing her earlier thought. 'Mr. Gotobed — we're going to want to talk to you, ask you a few questions. And if you're not well . . . would you like our medical people to take a look at you? If you'd care to wait for the doctor to arrive . . . '

There was a shaky pause, while Simeon adjusted his loosened cravat and dusted down the knees of his trousers after scrambling to his feet. His face was still pale, though no longer green, and he even managed a feeble smile. 'There's no need,' he brought out at last, 'to drop hints that I'm not to go anywhere — I don't think I could, just now.' He closed his eyes, and shivered. 'I think — I think I'd be only too happy to hang around out here until you're ready to talk to me — and you can ask me anything you want, except — except to go back into that — awful . . . kitchen . . . '

7

Simeon half opened his eyes, groaned, and began groping his way towards the open door of the car. Trewley favoured him with a long, thoughtful look.

'My sergeant here,' he said, as the young man staggered the final few steps and collapsed, shuddering, on the front seat, 'she's medically trained, Mr. Gotobed. I'm sure she'd say you oughtn't to be left by yourself, after the shock you seem to have had.' He turned to Stone, rolling his bloodhound eyes in a meaningful way as he spoke through the side of his mouth. 'Just watch our green-faced friend, will you, while I fetch someone along to keep an eye on him? They can make out they're listening for radio messages, if he starts agitating.'

The superintendent strode to the open front door of the lodge, and bellowed an order which, within seconds, produced PC Hedges. The young constable's face was unusually pale, and he threw his superior a glance of mingled relief and sympathy as he listened in his habitual silence to Trewley's swift instructions before hurrying to take his place in the second police car, leaving his colleagues to face whatever horror he himself had just left.

'Umph.' Trewley rubbed his chin, and frowned. 'Maybe Gotobed's not playacting, after all — all that moaning and groaning,' he enlarged, as with Stone beside him he hastened to trace in reverse the steps of PC Hedges. 'I thought he might be trying to pull the wool over our eyes. First on the scene's always suspect, remember, and I had the idea he perked up just a bit too quickly once we'd put in an appearance — but Hedges doesn't look too bright, either, and the lad's used to corpses by now, I'd've said.'

'He could,' Stone pointed out, 'be the world's best actor, sir — Gotobed, I mean. It's not impossible, though' — with memories of John Smith's little lecture — 'very improbable, I suppose. And even if he'd deliberately taken an

103

emetic, I don't quite see how he could have timed it to work so well when — '

She broke off, sniffing. She pulled a face. Trewley looked at her, sniffed in turn, and nodded grimly.

'Hippies,' he growled. 'Sticks of incense burning left, right and centre to cover up something they'd rather nobody else knew about, I'll be bound. Ten to one that character out there's a dealer, togged up like that. Why else would a bloke in a poncy suit be hanging round a crowd of long-haired layabouts? Did in the girl when she double-crossed him, most likely — aaachoo!'

The sneeze brought a forensic figure, signalling wildly, out of a doorway at the end of the flagstoned hall. 'In here, sir. And — and — oh, sir, it — she — she looks . . . ' He shook his head, and swallowed. 'You'd best see for yourself, sir . . . ' His eyes drifted to Stone, who was unable to fathom their expression. 'Sarge, she — she — '

'Don't you worry about the sergeant, Constable,' Trewley told him, before Stone could deliver a blistering speech on woman's equality with man. 'She'll cope with whatever's in there as well as the rest of us, I don't doubt.'

A faint smile crossed the drawn face. 'Better, sir, if you ask me. It's what I was trying to tell you, she — she's not alone in there . . . '

The kitchen was tiled in quarry red, sun-warmed through wide, low windows, with a black-leaded Aga crackling gaily against one wall. Beside the Aga, in a wicker basket, lay a swaddled baby, plump and pink. Beside the baby, on the floor, lay a female body, plump and pink.

Horribly plump. And hideous, black-faced pink . . .

Her head was a purple puffball, her features distorted beyond recognition by a pale, seething, sick-brown ooze which overflowed from her mouth, from her nose — which bulged her cheeks, and swelled shut her eyes — an ooze that had choked and smothered and suffocated her to death.

Trewley found his voice at last. 'What — what the hell has happened to her?'

Stone cleared her throat with unnecessary force. 'I — I think . . . '

A large earthenware crock, half full of that same sick-brown, spongy mass, stood on the kitchen table. Stone moved slowly across the room, and sniffed. Without touching anything, she indicated that side of the table closest to the kitchen range. There, caught in the rays of the sun, were two or three baking trays on which had been set out in rows smaller, neatly formed lumps of the mysterious oozy substance.

'I think,' said Stone, more firmly, 'she must have been making bread, sir. Smell the yeast?' She sniffed again. 'It's still working. He — he probably shoved a lump in her mouth to keep her quiet, sir, and — and the fire, and the sun, not to mention her own body heat, will have . . . will have done the rest . . . '

'Good God!' And Trewley forgave, on the spot, every affection of weakness on the part of those who had already seen the body. He found himself gulping and drawing in deep breaths . . .

'Aaaachooo!'

Everyone turned automatically to shush him, pointing.

'The baby, sir!'

But the baby did not wake, slumbering on peacefully, safe in its crib. Trewley tiptoed across to stand, staring down at it, beside Stone. He put his hand on her sleeve, and drew her away.

'Is it all right to leave the kiddie here?' he muttered, with a nod in the direction of the swollen figure on the floor, the flowing simplicity of her homespun robes horribly incongruous in such a setting. Stone whispered back: 'If it can sleep through . . . what's happened, I should imagine it can sleep through anything — but I'm no expert, sir. You're the one with three children, remember.'

'Umph.' He rubbed his chin, brooded for a moment, then nodded. 'Fair enough. I only hope the poor little brat *was* asleep when it happened.' He roused himself from the unpleasant daydream into which he was in danger of drifting, and turned to the others. 'Right! Sergeant Stone's agreed we can all carry on, so once the doctor's done his stuff — any sign of

Doc Watson, by the way?'

'Talk of the devil, and see his horns.' The voice came from the doorway as Dr. Watson — a tall, bushy-bearded, bespectacled man who had long ago given up reacting to the inevitable jokes about his name — marched briskly into the kitchen, then stopped in his tracks as he saw the grim tableau by the Aga.

'Oh,' he said. 'Yes, indeed. Very nasty. I only hope the poor creature was unconscious when it happened.'

'If it's managed to sleep this long — ' began Trewley, then stopped, as Dr. Watson shook his head.

'No, no, I didn't mean the baby, I meant the mother, if that's who she is. The victim. Let's hope he knocked her out before he shoved that stuff inside — though I suppose he must have done, otherwise surely she'd have done her best to get rid of it — spit it out, pull it with her hands or whatever. She's not tied up, is she?'

Trewley replied in an almost steady voice that, while the doctor examined the woman on the floor in order to

108

pronounce her dead, he could keep a lookout for signs of ropes around her wrists. The sooner he did so, the happier the police would be.

Dr. Watson settled himself to his grisly task as everyone else turned their backs and began the inevitable examination of the rest of the room. Photographs were taken, measurements noted. At last, the doctor rose from his knees, packing his instruments away.

'Dead,' came the legally required confirmation, with a nod. 'I'll be able to tell you more about her once I've got her on the slab, of course, but there's some fairly conclusive bruising on the skull which would have felled an ox, let alone a young woman. Late twenties,' he added, as Trewley was about to put the obvious question. 'Young by our standards, at any rate. That bump on the head occurred before death rather than after, although whether she was bashed deliberately, or whether she fell and knocked herself out, I can't say — unfortunately, the position of the bruise can be read either way. But, for what it may be worth — and not simply

109

because I didn't find any signs that she'd been tied up, because I didn't, though that's neither here nor there — I'd say the poor girl *was* unconscious when she was gagged with that muck.'

A general sigh of relief floated round the kitchen. Dr. Watson ignored it, and went on talking to Trewley.

'Let me have her as soon as you can, and you should know pretty well all there is to know — physically speaking, that is — within a couple of hours. For now, I can tell you that's not her child you've got there. She neither gave birth recently, nor was she expecting a happy event in a few months' time.'

'Time of death?' Trewley suspected he was asking the impossible, but nevertheless he had to ask it.

Dr. Watson confirmed his suspicion. 'Have a heart, man. At a guess, she's been dead a couple of hours, but a guess isn't much use to you, is it? You want to know the likely time she was first — first gagged, and I wouldn't care to venture an opinion on that. Too many variables.'

Unconsciously, he echoed Stone's earlier

words. 'The strength of the yeast, warmth of the room, heat of the body . . . but we can say between ten and twelve, if you insist, though don't take it as gospel, by any means.'

They stared more closely at the flowing and dishevelled robes of the dead girl. 'Sexual assault?' Trewley asked.

'No. Not straightforward sex, anyway, though there's always the possibility of something a bit kinky gone wrong. There are tales I could tell you of hot water bottles and wet suits and half-pound pats of butter — ' Dr. Watson broke off, with an apologetic nod for Stone. 'Sorry, Sergeant. Hardly germane to the present case — which I'd call ordinary murder, if there is such a thing. It's for you, of course, to put a definite label to it, though if we take the bump on her head into account I'd guess the kinky side of things can be pretty well ruled out — but that *is* only a guess, and I could be wrong. Do let me know if I am, and I'll write to Havelock Ellis about it.'

'The Peeping Tom, perhaps,' suggested Stone, as Trewley frowned in thought.

The superintendent grunted.

'What d'you reckon, Doc? Could it be a peeper caught in the act and for some reason gone clean over the top?'

Dr. Watson's eyes glittered behind his spectacles. 'I'm no expert in these matters, of course, but from the few rusty memories of my medical training which remain I'm willing to risk saying that almost any form of sexual deviancy can either remain at a constant level, or escalate, entirely according to circumstances — which, I admit, doesn't really help you much. For example, take your ordinary foot fetishist. Goes merrily along year in, year out just cuddling shoes, then one day he happens to stroke some girl's ankle. She kicks out at him, naturally enough — but, by kicking, she could just tip the balance and trigger the desire for violence to be incorporated from then on as a regular part of the perverted activity.' Did those bespectacled eyes glitter even more? It wasn't easy to tell.

'Mind you,' Dr. Watson went on, 'I don't think it often happens without some sort of trigger — and I wouldn't suppose it happens in enormous leaps, either. From peeping to killing in one fell swoop . . . somehow I think I'd expect a more gradual progression. You'll have to check your records to see what other types of complaint you've had concerning the unknown Thomas, or his confrères. Is, ah, a culinary perversion part of his anonymous charm?'

'Not that we've a — ah — ay-heard-choo!' Everyone except the still-sleeping baby jumped at Trewley's sneeze. He scowled. 'Damned filthy joss sticks — *hippies*,' he added with a snarl, groping for his handkerchief. 'Never mind covering up for drugs, they probably think it saves 'em having to wash like honest citizens, as well. Back to nature, and all that nonsense — bells and beads and free love — the poor kid ought to be in a decent home, not being brought up by a load of draggle-tailed layabouts high on dope half the time — no?' For Dr. Watson was shaking his head.

'No. No immediate signs, that I could see. No blisters on the skin, no injection marks — not recent, anyway. But once

I've had the chance for a proper check, I'll be able to let you know for certain. Make it snappy, will you?' And Dr. Watson was gone, leaving Trewley and his team to plan the next move.

With the privilege of rank, it was the superintendent who quickly made it. 'This is no place for a kiddie,' he announced, with a wary look at Stone. 'We ought to get him, her — whatever it is — out of here while . . . everything's going on. The rest of the house'll have to be given the once-over — suppose you and I, Stone, take him with us on the guided tour? Or at least move her cradle into another room,' he amended, as the sergeant's doubts about this proposal became apparent. 'It just doesn't seem . . . decent, to leave him. Her.'

'In theory, sir,' Stone said at once, 'I agree with you, but practice is a rather different matter. I mean, we've been lucky so far, haven't we? And with luck, our luck will hold. Despite your doubts, it does seem she — er, he, is well cared for and contented. He hasn't woken up and started yelling for food, or because

114

he needs changing — '

'If these hippies condescend to use nappies like honest folk,' Trewley muttered. 'Or soap — or even hot water . . . ' Stone couldn't help grinning.

'They'll use something, sir, I'm sure of it — but please don't ask me to find out what it is.' She became serious again. 'If we disturb him now, even if all anyone does is lift up the blanket for a peep, what's the betting that's the time he starts to yell blue murd — ' She broke off, and looked uncomfortable. 'Oh. Sorry, sir, that just slipped out. I wasn't thinking — babies are a bit out of my line, I'm afraid, and . . . '

'And *I've* got three daughters,' he supplied, feeling as awkward as she. 'Umph. Well, I suppose one thing you learn with three daughters is to let sleeping babies lie. You're right as usual, Sergeant, we must leave this little chap to the tender mercies of Benson and his friends while we scout round the other rooms — and heaven help you,' he added to the startled Benson and company, 'if you wake the poor kid up. I'm the

115

wrong generation, thank the Lord, to know anything about bottles, and though I've no doubt the sergeant learned how to mix one in her student days, I need her with me. So just watch your step, all of you. Keep those clodhopping feet of yours under control — don't shout, or tap dance on the table — don't drop things, or knock the cradle over. And if him or her that's in the cradle wakes up . . . '

He was pushing Stone hurriedly out of the kitchen as he spoke, and turned to throw the final words over his shoulder. 'Take him outside to Hedges for a bedtime story!'

On which cheerful note, Trewley left his team chuckling as, with Stone, he prepared to explore the rest of the North Lodge of the Campions Crest Conference Center.

8

Out in the hall: 'Would you like me
to check the bedrooms, sir?' Stone, her
hands thrust deep in her pockets with
the automatic gesture of the trained
investigator, stood contemplating the
broad white ribbon of unstained wood
running in regular creases up the stairs
between two far darker, mock mahogany
bands. 'I wonder what happened to all
the carpets around here?'

Trewley surveyed the bare floorboards
with a grimace. 'And most of the furniture
— but don't ask. Most likely this precious
crowd sold the lot to the highest bidder,
or put the stuff on a bonfire to save
buying honest coal — Downstairs for
you, I think. I'd better do the bedrooms
myself — and that's not to spare your
innocent eyes the awful sight of what else
might have been going on up there, it's
to give me a spot of exercise to keep my
wife happy. Just make sure you tell her

117

I've been following her good advice next time you see her, all right?'

'Right,' said Stone, sketching a cheerful salute as she set off on her solitary prowl around the lower floor of the North Lodge.

It was second nature for the two detectives, when they were on a case, to walk with careful feet and watchful eyes, their hands kept safely out of the way where they could not by accident disturb some vital piece of evidence. Stone heard the slow, steady tread of Trewley up the stairs, and jumped as he suddenly emitted an ear-splitting sneeze; she hesitated, listening for signs that, unable to grab the banisters, he'd lost his balance and fallen — but all was well. There came the muffled blast of a be-handkerchiefed nose, and then a further slow, steady tread . . .

Six minutes later, Trewley was back in the hall, where Stone joined him within thirty seconds.

'It's *cleaner* than I'd've thought,' observed the superintendent, sounding at once surprised and aggrieved.

Stone smiled faintly. 'You've already pointed out that they don't have much in the way of furniture, sir, so there aren't too many fiddly bits to keep dusting round. Just cushions and rugs on the floor — no carpets to hoover, no curtains to wash — clean as the proverbial whistle,in fact. No drugs,' she enlarged, as he shot her a sharp look.

'That's as maybe. There's enough incense upstairs to keep the Brompton Oratory going for a year, I might tell you — filthy stuff.' And Trewley trumpeted once more into his pocket handkerchief.

'Quite so, sir. I could hear you sneezing through the floorboards every now and then. Punctuation marks to your progress, as it were.' Stone ventured a chuckle. 'It rather startled me, the first once or twice. But at least it wasn't sudden screams for help — so may I assume everything is all right up there?'

'Depends what you mean by all right. For a start, you can say they've got no curtains downstairs — but they don't even have them in the bedrooms! What did I tell you about the blighters having

119

no sense of decency?' Then moral outrage gave way to further factual account. 'Granted I didn't find anything — any more than you did, but this ghastly horrible smell from the joss sticks has got to be covering up something worse than, well, nothing . . . '

'I looked,' said Stone, 'for hypodermics, or aluminum foil and spoons, or even packets of mysterious white powder — but I didn't find a sausage, sir, though I admit I drew the line at tapping for secret panels or taking up the floorboards. And if you didn't find anything either, then perhaps they really are clean — '

'Clean?' The word came out in a horrified bellow. 'Let me tell you, Stone, that the only furniture this so-called clean crowd've got upstairs is more cushions — and they're *all in the same room!*'

'Er — oh,' said Stone, not entirely sure how to respond to this shattering revelation. 'Yes, well, that's more or less how it is down here, too. There's one particular room — from the layout I'd guess it was originally the sitting room — where they seem to hang out. There's a guitar, and a flute, and a penny whistle on the hearth . . . ' Remembering his cynical reference to coal, she added: 'The fire's wood, sir, and ready laid. The place is crammed with cushions and rugs, and there are posters all over the walls . . . '

The superintendent was nodding as he listened, looking more and more depressed. 'Snap,' he said, 'even down to the posters. They've got one with some damned great ugly golden bird nesting on a fire — meant to be a phoenix, I suppose, bearing in mind what Pleate told us about Miss Jarvis and the Kempshott bloke — but it didn't look at all how I'd imagined the phoenix from school.' His depression gave way to suspicion. 'A vision from the drugs, most likely.'

Stone shook her head. 'I'm not so sure about that, sir. I'd have said they thought of it as a — a totem, or a good luck charm — they've painted one on the wall in what I think must have been the dining room — '

'On the wall?' Trewley was scandalised.

'You mean it's right on the paper? The young vandals!'

The superintendent's face was growing red, and Stone, mindful of his blood pressure, tried to lighten the mood by remarking that some people might consider the mural in the dining room a distinct improvement on the original paper, which in her opinion was very ugly. The argument failed to impress her superior.

'Vandals,' he said again, though with rather less vehemence. 'First they commit trespass to break in — you'll say you didn't find the marks, I suppose, but they've had time enough to repair a broken lock or a smashed window — then they draw graffiti all over the walls . . .'

'Perhaps,' suggested Stone, bracingly, 'the new owners of the lodge will be able to sue for criminal damage and evict them — '

This was not the consolation she'd intended. 'Nobody,' threatened Trewley, 'is evicting anyone before we find out which of 'em did for her! Because ten to one it's another of the blighters, drugged to the eyeballs and forgotten he's done it by the time we catch him — so much for peace and love and those damned silly bells they used to wear! Hardly a loving way to treat your friends, is it?'

Stone was busy thinking. 'Of course, it could always be an outsider, sir. A hippie squat's bound to have made quite a few people unhappy — though it's a pretty drastic way of removing them from the neighbourhood — but just think how worked up Sergeant Pleate said Miss Jervaulx seemed to be, not to mention the squadron leader, all strong and silent and hopping from one foot to another. And they're just the first complainers we've heard about, sir . . . '

'So far,' he agreed. 'Queer customers, the pair of 'em — talking of which — '

They had been so engrossed in their preliminary theorising that they had failed to hear the feet approaching from the kitchen along the hall. PC Benson cleared his throat, and made Stone jump.

'Just bringing her out now, sir. D'you want to take one last look? Sarge?'

Stone's features moved in an involuntary gesture of refusal, and even Trewley shuddered. 'No, thanks — but hold on a minute, lad. We'll go ahead and warn friend Gotobed to keep looking the other way — it'll be a good excuse to have a talk with him. Like finding out,' he went on, as he and Stone made their way to the front door, 'just what he was doing prowling round the house in the first place.'

'He's hardly the hippie type,' Stone said thoughtfully. 'I'd find it hard to credit he came looking for drugs — even if these people have them, which we don't know for certain one way or the other, sir, do we? Perhaps,' she hurried on, as Trewley emitted an irritated grunt, 'he lost his way, and was looking for directions to . . . to the main conference centre, perhaps. I know Mr. Smith had a notice outside, but there's nothing at this entrance, is there?'

As they emerged from the North Lodge, it seemed at first that there was no Simeon Gotobed there, either, although a second glance showed that he had merely moved his car farther along the drive. Under the watchful eye of PC Hedges, Mr. Gotobed had been encouraged to clear a space for the ambulance, and took advantage of this removal to turn himself firmly away from any sight of the lodge and those whose business had brought them there. He now sat in the driver's seat, with the door closed, the window down, and his head resting weakly on the steering wheel.

As the feet of Trewley and Stone approached across the gravel, Simeon's shoulders stiffened. Slowly, he sat up, and risked a cautious peep from the corner of one eye. His cheese-faced expression became slightly more cheerful as, recognising reinforcements, he opened the car door.

'I expect you'd like to ask me a few questions,' he said, forcing a smile which, the two detectives supposed, was intended to express the willing cooperation of an honest citizen. To Stone, at least, it looked more like the grimace of someone who has had his arm wrenched up and round behind his back and yet tries to remain stoic about the experience.

'Just a few questions, yes, sir — if you feel more up to it now, that is.' Trewley glanced quickly at Stone, who nodded: Simeon seemed over the worst of his initial shock, and questioning wouldn't kill him. 'Mind if we hop in the car with you?' The superintendent lowered his voice. 'It's my sergeant, see. There's a bit of a nip in the air, and she's a great one for her creature comforts, is Detective Sergeant Stone.'

It was with considerable difficulty that Stone contrived to look frail, but her histrionic efforts were good enough to deceive a still shocked Mr. Gotobed. He reached as would any gentleman, with another smile, and the polite response that the sergeant — and her colleague — were of course more than welcome to join him. Although he looked welcoming, he sounded less than sincere in his invitation: but that (reasoned Trewley and Stone) was, in the circumstances, only to be expected.

With a silent jerk of the head, Trewley

directed Stone to the passenger seat, while he climbed in the back. Simeon forced another smile as the young woman settled herself at his side, and prepared himself to be grilled from the rear. Stone took out her notebook and pencil; Trewley cleared his throat.

'Now then, Mr. Gotobed, perhaps we'll start with what you were doing here in the first place. This isn't exactly the middle of civilisation, is it?'

Simeon sighed. 'If the middle of civilisation's anything like that county town of yours I spent all morning trying to get out of, give me the backwoods every time — except when . . . when . . . '

The bustle of stretcher-bearers going about their business in the near distance made him draw a sudden deep breath. Trewley said quickly: 'Come from London, do you, sir? Not that I could tell for sure, from the number plate, but . . . '

The superintendent's mention of the personalised number plate brought a feeble light to Simeon's eyes, although he had to draw several more breaths before he could confirm that he had, indeed, come from Town.

'Not the usual route, through the centre of Allingham,' remarked Trewley, in questioning tone.

Simeon achieved what in lighter moments might have been a laugh. 'It — it sounds ridiculous, I know — incredible, even, when I'm meant to be working here, but I'm afraid I — I lost my way, Superintendent.' His voice throbbed with the utter sincerity of one who has made a mistake for which a little sympathy would be in order. 'I've only been in these parts once before, you see, and that was with someone else driving. This time, I overshot the motorway exit — '

Something in the way Trewley cleared his throat made him add: 'It's — it's not terribly well signposted, for someone who doesn't know the area. There are trees all along that stretch, and I think they must have had overhanging branches — anyway,' as Trewley cleared his throat again, 'I went on to the next junction, and turned off. I knew if I followed the Allingham signposts I'd end up within striking distance of Campions Crest — only my map showed there was a bypass, and before I'd realised there wasn't I was — was stuck in your one-way system and couldn't get out.' He paused as Stone, beside him, uttered a choking little cough which she hastily smothered. Trewley, glaring at the back of his sergeant's head, instructed Mr. Gotobed, in a voice even he found hard to keep steady, to continue.

'It took what felt like hours before I was out of the town at last and on what I thought was the right road . . . ' Simeon's tone, as he warmed to his narration, was accusing. 'And when I managed to find a lay-by to check my map, I realised the bypass was only a — a projected route, and I'd have done better to go back down the motorway and — well, anyway, I got as far as this, and from what I'd remembered it looked just like the lodge I'd seen before, but I couldn't see the notice — which made me wonder if it was the right place after all. The syndicate never intended to hide our light under any sort of bushel when it set up the Conference Centre, believe me! So I was, well, a bit confused. I wondered if they'd known I'd be expecting . . . '

Simeon recollected himself with a start. 'I didn't want to turn up what looked like a private driveway, so I thought I'd check exactly where I was, and — and I knocked on the door.' He paused. 'And nobody answered. So I thought I'd try round the back — and the door was open — and . . . '

'Wide open?'

'What? Oh, sorry.' Mr. Gotobed gulped. 'Not locked, I mean. The door was closed — but the window was open, and I thought I could hear someone moving about inside. I called, and knocked again, and I could still hear someone, so I . . . tried the door. It — there was a baby, in a cradle . . . '

'You'll have touched the handle, of course, to open the door,' said Trewley, in a bracing tone. 'Touch anything else, that you can think of?'

'I — I'm not sure. Oh, I don't know! I can't remember — I don't want to remember. I just want to forget I ever saw . . . saw . . .'

'Yes, sir.' Trewley, having seen what Simeon had seen, was slightly more sympathetic to this self-imposed amnesia than he was inclined to be with other witnesses on similar occasions. 'You checked the young woman was dead, naturally. And then what did you do?'

Simeon shuddered. 'Legged it out of the house as fast as I could, and called for help.'

Trewley said at once: 'We've had a good look round the lodge, Mr. Gotobed. The people living there don't seem to hold much with what you'd call modern conveniences — no furniture to speak of, no television, no washing machine — *and no telephone*. Now, when we arrived you had all the appearance of a man in shock, and you gave us the distinct impression you hadn't felt up to leaving the grounds. So how come you managed to raise the alarm?'

Stone, taking notes in the front seat, shifted her position towards the side window, giving Trewley a clear line of sight to the open compartment under the dashboard. 'Ah, a mobile phone,' said the superintendent, before Simeon had time to reply. 'Hope you don't use it while you're driving, sir — easy to lose control when one hand's off the wheel, though I'm not saying they aren't handy little gadgets to have around. Business, or pleasure?'

'Er — business,' said Simeon, after a startled moment or two. 'Business,' he repeated, more firmly. 'This isn't your common or garden off-the-shelf mobile phone, Mr. Trewley — this is something rather special. In fact I'd be amazed if even you have ever seen one before, because this is the very latest technology . . .'

The chance to show off his new toy so heartened Simeon Gotobed that he completely missed Luddite Trewley's exclamation of disgust for all those worshipping at the altar of the goddess Mechanica. 'This, Superintendent, is a videophone!' He unclipped it from its under-dashboard niche, pointing to the miniature screen with a proud finger.

'You have absolutely no idea how seeing this impresses the chairman of the board, or the managing director, or whoever is responsible for taking the final decision to make use of our services — it encourages them to treat us on at least equal terms right from the start, because of course they all have mobile phones themselves, but very few indeed,' with irritating smugness, 'one of these. If anyone should have any doubts about us, they take us seriously when they see this — especially in such a small car . . . '

Simeon had begun to relax as he gave this explanation, and now switched into what sounded a well-rehearsed sales patter.

'You wouldn't *expect* to find a mobile telephone with a video facility in a car like mine, would you? I wouldn't expect you to! Because that element of surprise forms the basis for the theory of Attitudes Analysis — which is the consultancy theory the syndicate running this Centre intends to promote.'

'Attitudes Analysis,' repeated Trewley. 'Oh, yes, the local paper gave your lot

133

quite a good write-up recently — my sergeant, she found it most interesting. She's been to university, you see, and they've got lively minds, these educated types — but me, I'm just an ordinary copper. Suppose you give me a run-through on what it's all about? Go easy with the fancy words, mind,' as Simeon drew in his breath and prepared to perorate.

While Mr. Gotobed paused to rearrange his teeming thought processes, Trewley tried to recall what he had read of the Attitudes Analysis feature in the *Argos*. Despite his mock-mystified pose, the superintendent had taken a lively interest in what little had been reported about the newcomers to Campions Crest, reasoning that if a crowd of trick-cyclist lunatics was about to invade his patch he needed some idea of what to expect. The paper had printed columns about the physical refurbishment of the manor, and about the many miracles the new Centre hoped to achieve, but had given very few details as to how it hoped to achieve them. Simeon was the first Attitudes Analyst

Trewley had encountered, and thus an unknown quantity — as well as being the person who had discovered the body . . .

'The theory of Attitudes Analysis,' announced Simeon, with an almost audible smirk, 'is the result of an original research programme undertaken by myself at university into . . . ' His hesitation hinted at some doubt as to policeman Trewley's ability to appreciate his brilliance. He frowned. ' . . . Into certain promising aspects of Behavioural Science, although at this stage there is no real need to go into details, I think. It should be enough to explain that I was able to develop considerably from my findings once I had obtained the greater freedom and more dedicated input of a commercial, rather than a purely academic, background — '

'You mean sponsorship,' interposed Stone; not that she didn't believe Trewley incapable of translation, but she didn't want Simeon to think he'd succeeded in blinding the flatfoots of the force with science.

'Sponsorship,' agreed Mr. Gotobed,

after a pause, though he soon rallied. 'Given such encouragement — and with virtually unlimited funding — I have succeeded in improving the psychological understanding of behaviour and attitudes pertaining to society today in a way which I — which we all — feel is far more meaningful, and has far greater contextual relevance, to every aspect of twentieth-century life — and, especially to life in a business context.'

Trewley's cough sounded a warning behind him, and Stone condensed the rigmarole into a cynical shorthand squiggle. *College dropout who conned his way into a proper job? Check this!* Mr. Gotobed, too engrossed with his own words to notice hers, continued: 'My theory takes an in-depth look at existing attitudes to life, work, our role in society, the way we react and respond to other people, different situations and so on — and it Analyses these Attitudes, in the literal sense of breaking them down into their various component parts — having first, of course, ascertained the nature of such parts — '

136

'Oh? How?' demanded Trewley, more convinced than ever that what he was hearing was a load of — his eyes flicked across to Stone, and he modified the thought — rubbish.

Simeon was by now so carried away with his sales pitch that he hardly heard the question. 'We explore the very fundamentals of an individual's personal characteristics, ideals, and beliefs — or those of a company, which is no more than the individual writ large — and we demonstrate to him exactly what these fundamentals are. Then, we deliberately introduce an element of doubt. We make him question everything, to ensure that he understands *why* he thinks what he thinks. Only then can he begin to wonder whether there might not be a better way of looking at, and responding to, life. In other words,' as Trewley uttered an exasperated snort, 'having Analysed his Attitudes, we aim to alter them beyond recognition — to his greater benefit, of course . . .'

'In other words,' said the superintendent sourly, 'you brainwash the poor devil!'

9

Brainwashing! he'd had his suspicions right from the start that this new conference centre might make life a bit awkward, and what he'd just heard proved that *awkward* was probably the understatement of the year. It was all he needed: to find a gaggle of certifiable, jargon-spouting lunatics right on the doorstep of a murder as offbeat as this seemed to be . . .

Simeon was so put out by Trewley's suggestion that he swivelled round in his seat to explain. The bones in his neck cracked loudly. 'Brainwashing? Certainly not, Superintendent! We merely prevent the indulgence of traditional, regressive modes of thought and behaviour during our seminar sessions through a system of continual surprise — a system which renders the subject receptive to the required modifications in his behaviour. Or hers,' he added, more conscious of

Stone's presence now that he was twisted sideways and could see the glint in her disapproving eye.

'People with — with fossilised and oppressively formulised ideas,' he went on, as she rearranged her features to mask the irritation she felt, 'have certain *expectations* of life, and it is these expectations we do our utmost to overset, so that nobody can ever be certain of undergoing normal, everyday experiences while in the care of an Attitudes Analyst. This overbalancing process enables them to decide for themselves if they really want — or even need — to continue thinking as they do. Or whether, with our help, they can work out for themselves a modified system of thought which will be an improvement on the thinking processes they followed prior to undergoing Analysis.'

There was a grim, puzzled silence while his audience digested the full horror of what they understood him to have said. Stone found her voice first, though it was toneless and unnaturally controlled as she replied: 'Expect the unexpected . . . I see.'

'I don't,' said Trewley, in a bulldog rumble. 'Except that you seem to be saying your idea's to end up with a crowd of folk who're half out of their minds, if that's what you meant by unbalancing them — which doesn't sound particularly healthy to me — '

'*Over* balance, Superintendent!' Simeon was far too anxious to correct the misapprehension to bother with manners. 'A — a slight loss of psychological equilibrium, no more than that, believe me, and any stable, fully rounded personality should be able to cope with the aftereffects without suffering any emotional trauma whatsoever — the system was, remember, designed with that very purpose in mind.' One hand clutching the back of his seat to hold himself steady, with the other he stabbed an expressive forefinger in the air.

'Let me explain how it works in practice, Mr. Trewley, and then you'll realise you need have no cause for alarm.'

Trewley longed to take issue with such

glib assurances, although at this stage he knew better than to voice any doubts. He grunted, scowled, and rubbed his chin as he nodded for Simeon to continue: he had more than a suspicion he was going to need as much information as he could get about the victims (as he was coming to think of them) of Attitudes Analysis presently in the neighbourhood, but that didn't mean he had to make approving noises while the sales pitch went on.

'When attending a business seminar,' began Mr. Gotobed, 'what does one normally expect?' He remembered that he was addressing a constabulary, rather than a commercial, audience, and hurried on: 'Briefcases, polished shoes, smart suits, an air of general authority . . . ' He waved an expressive hand, and smirked self-consciously.

It was Stone who wearily obliged. 'In some ways, rather as you appear now?'

'Er — just so.' Simeon chose in the end to accept her remark as the compliment he'd expected. 'And can you guess why?' He left no time for a reply. 'It's because Andrew Ryan, my assistant,

141

who is hosting our current course in a — a tutorial capacity — is casually dressed in sweatshirt and jeans! Moreover,' as this information failed to evoke a response in either detective, 'Andrew — a sterling character, a most talented chap — he isn't *me*. He's not the person they'd been led to *expect* would be there to welcome them. In reality I had no intention of arriving before today — and he behaves in a vague, unsatisfactory manner, quite unable to assist or to control the group, so that they all end up arguing with him and with each other.'

'And that's . . . good?' This time it was Trewley who managed to bring out the words; Stone was speechless.

'It's according to plan,' said Simeon. 'Eventually, Andrew admits that he's out of his depth, but adds that I will soon be . . . coming to the rescue, as it were.'

'And you arrive' — Stone spoke at last, her voice sounding strained — 'looking as you do — not scruffy, I mean,' hastily, in case he misinterpreted her observation as showing more than professional interest.

'Not scruffy — and with an air, I trust,

of considerable command. The course attendees await my arrival with uneasy expectations. Will I be as nervous and uncertain as Andrew? Will I takc charge — or will I ignore them as he appears to have been doing? They have no idea what to expect of me . . . and such unexpectedness is deliberately maintained, in various ways, throughout the entire course.'

'Poor beggars,' muttered Trewley, thankful that it had been a life of crime, not commerce, which he had elected in his youth to pursue. He risked a look at Stone: no steam, as yet, coming out of her ears. Surely she didn't believe in this maniac and his crazy notions? And, for heaven's sake, how much crazier were they going to get?

'What happens,' he demanded, 'once you've got 'em all nicely — overbalanced — in their ideas, Mr. Gotobed? How do you reckon to put things right again?'

'Ah,' said Simeon, 'I'm so glad you asked that question, Superintendent. Because now comes the tailor-made application of Attitudes Analysis! Once we have shaken the seminarians to the very foundations of their personalities — once they're automatically questioning, asking *why*? about everything — then, and only then, do we assist them to rebuild. But — and this is the beauty of the system — the rebuilding will be entirely according to the requirements of the company for which they work! Hence,' with a would-be airy gesture limited by his physical position, 'the considerable interest shown in my work by the consortium which put up the money to buy the manor and turn it into a conference centre — one we hope will, in due course, draw clients from a country-wide catchment area — '

'To brainwash them,' said Trewley again, more grim than ever. 'You mean to tell me any reputable firm's gone along with your fancy games? The whole setup sounds downright dangerous to me! Never mind what you might be doing to the poor devils on your perishing course — have you ever stopped to think why you're asked to do it in the first place, or to wonder just who's doing the asking?

Could be a nasty can of worms, I reckon. Very nasty indeed.'

'There are, naturally,' Simeon informed him with as much hauteur as a man twisted round in the seat of a small sports car can achieve, 'safeguards imposed, Superintendent, before we agree to undertake the Analysis programme. All clients are subjected to the most careful scrutiny, and I assure you that if there were indeed any . . . sinister motives behind the apparently genuine desire to obtain the best possible results from a hitherto demoralised workforce, the assignment would be refused almost the instant the application was received, and certainly once the initiators had been — investigated.' He hesitated over the final word, evidently troubled for the euphony of the entire sentence.

His hesitation allowed Stone to pose the question which now most concerned her. 'Who exactly carries out this . . . 'careful scrutiny,' Mr. Gotobed?'

The grip on the back of his seat relaxed, and Simeon turned to face her, smiling. 'Why, I do, Miss Stone!

I am the possessor of an honours degree in psychology, and two postgraduate qualifications in sociology. And, since it is on my research that the whole theory is based, who better to vet applicants to our courses than myself?'

Stone did not — could not — answer. Her hazel eyes met those of Trewley, and a silent message flashed between them. Simeon Gotobed sounded — must surely be — completely and utterly crazy. At the very least, he had a power complex — compensation, perhaps (it occurred to the medically trained Stone) for the lifelong handicap of his unusual name . . .

But did that make him a murderer?

Trewley could take no more. 'You'll be wanting to get on up to the house now, I *expect*, Mr. Gotobed.' Simeon nodded, though he did not smile at the superintendent's little jibe: he seemed to be deep in a happy daydream of the remarkable Theory he had just propounded. 'We'll be along presently,' continued Trewley, 'to take your written statement — about finding the body,' he

146

added, as Simeon looked startled. 'And we'll need to talk to everybody else up at the house as well, of course, so we'd appreciate it if you'd let them all know, once you get there, that they aren't to leave Campion's Crest until we've seen them. And I should think,' he added, as Simeon, brought thus abruptly back to the harsh realities of life, began to gulp again, turning pale, 'that being suspects in a murder enquiry ought to be quite . . . unexpected enough for anyone who's following your theory, Mr. Gotobed. Wouldn't you?'

But for once Mr. Gotobed seemed reluctant to venture an opinion, and drove off, after Trewley and Stone had climbed out of the car, in a flurry of nervous gravel. Trewley stood staring after him, rubbing his chin.

'He *was* real, wasn't he?' he said at last, turning to his sergeant with a worried look in his eyes. 'I'm not off my head — I didn't dream him? He sounded stark, staring bonkers to me, and if I've started imagining people like our Mr. Gotobed I'm in worse shape than ever my Susan thought!'

'You can tell her to keep the strait-jacket in the cupboard just a little longer, sir — he was real, all right.' Stone shuddered. 'Only too real! If you'd told me before I met him, I'd have said he must be drunk, but I couldn't smell anything, could you? Perhaps he's on drugs. It would explain his connection with the hippies — although why he should kill one of them . . . '

'Search me, girl. Peeping Toms are one thing, but your well-dressed weirdos with a good line in patter are a sight more worrying . . . ' He brightened slightly. 'Kept us out of the house for a while though, didn't it? Gave 'em time to take her away, and leave us — ah.' He frowned, and rubbed his chin. 'Yes, that baby. I was forgetting. Wonder whether they — no, surely they won't have done, they'll have left the poor little beggar to sleep it off until somebody comes along to take care of . . . '

He turned a speculative eye upon his sergeant, who firmly shook her head. 'I don't mind mixing a bottle for him if there's such a thing in the house — not that I remember seeing one, sir, though maybe you do — but if you're dropping hints about anything more, um, individual, then you can pick them right up again, please. Besides, you're the one with three daughters, not me.'

Trewley chuckled, kicking cheerfully at the gravel as they began to walk back to the lodge. 'There's always Benson. He's probably holding the kiddie upside down to wind it, or singing it rugby songs — which is probably,' he added in a bleaker tone, 'the sort of *unexpected* thing that Gotobed lunatic would think was a good idea . . . '

They did indeed find PC Benson in the kitchen, dancing uncertain attendance upon the still-sleeping infant, and extremely thankful for his superiors' return. Trewley's bulldog features re-arranged themselves in a grin.

'Having fun?' he rumbled, treading softly towards the kitchen range. 'Coped all right, have you?'

'He sort of — snorted at me once, sir,' hissed Benson, as he crept away from the cradle and prepared to hand over this most unusual of charges. 'But he went back to sleep again straight after. Don't they make, well, funny noises? Do you think he's all right?'

Trewley's glance into the crib was cursory, but expert. 'You'll know soon enough if he isn't, lad. Born survivors, babies are. With any luck, his mother'll be along before long, and then — '

'His mother? Thank goodness,' broke in Benson, so relieved by Trewley's remark that he forgot police protocol. 'I mean, it's good that wasn't his mother who — who was here, sir.' Inspiration struck. 'Want me to have a look for her, sir? She probably isn't far away, and — '

'Desertion in the face of the enemy,' Trewley informed him, 'used to be a hanging matter, lad. If a six-footer like you's scared of one small baby, I despair, I really do, of what the modern copper's coming to — though you could be right,' as he caught Benson returning Stone's wink. 'About her likely enough not being too far away, that is. According to the chap at the other lodge, these Phoenixes spend half their time rummaging about for nuts and what-have-you in the great outdoors. If you're seriously minded to desert, I daresay I could stretch a point and let you try one or two of the nearest fields . . . Go out the front way, and tell Hedges to stay on watch. Sergeant Stone and I'll get on with the detecting in here while you're gone.'

Hurriedly, Benson went; but he was not gone long. Trewley and Stone had barely begun their examination of the sinister chalk outline on the kitchen floor before they heard footsteps returning down the hall. They looked at each other, dusted off their knees, and rose quickly from the quarry tiles to find out if it was indeed Benson, or somebody else, who disturbed them at their work.

It was Benson — with somebody else. Pattering in his wake came a young, female somebody, so slightly built and lightly stepping that even the keen ears of Stone had missed her approach beneath the barrage of Benson's size twelve boots. She was dressed, as the dead girl had been, in a garment of homemade appearance, its weave uneven, its colours drab, its folds ample and flowing about a bosom which seemed of generous proportions for so small a frame. Her hair, like her clothes, was long, though clean, and worn shaken forwards so that these strangers should not easily see her face . . .

But she could see them. As the two detectives first emerged from the kitchen she had stopped, glowered at Benson through her fringe, and then thrust her way past him to face the intruders.

'More of you! I don't understand. The one outside tried to stop me coming home — then him,' with a contemptuous backward toss of her head. 'And now you — police, the whole lot of you!' Her voice grew shrill. 'Why have you come interfering with us? What are you doing here? Why don't you leave us alone? Why can't you just *go away!*'

And as Trewley opened his mouth to reply, a pitiful wail arose from the kitchen behind him.

10

Everyone jumped, not least the girl. 'Baldur!' she cried, as the wails grew louder. 'My baby! If you've hurt him . . .'

Hitching up her gown, her sandalled feet slapping, she darted down the hall, pushed past a startled Trewley, and rushed into the kitchen to seize the baby from its — his — cradle. The wails momentarily ceased as the baby gasped, so surprised at being snatched from his cosy nest that he could only stare as his mother clutched him to her bosom, rocking him to and fro, crooning his name over and over again, while she glared at the police as they followed her into the room, daring them to disturb her. 'Baldur — oh, my Baldur — have they hurt you? Baldur . . .'

Baldur began wailing again, on a different note, as she rested him on one arm and fumbled at his wrappings with her other hand. Trewley, watching her, coughed. 'We're police officers,' he announced, rather more loudly than he'd intended. 'As you seem to know already, miss — er, as you seem to know already. And we're here because . . . '

The girl had been so preoccupied with the welfare of her child that she completely failed to notice the evidence of police activity all around her. Even though she quickly satisfied herself that Baldur had come to no apparent harm, her attention was still focussed more on him — as his wails turned to chuckles, then to blowing bubbles and gurgling in a manner quite out of keeping with the circumstances — than on the superintendent. Trewley found himself having to repeat his explanation before she even began to take it all in. When he started over for the third time, the girl's mouth dropped, and her grasp on the baby tightened. He let out a startled squeak.

For once, she was oblivious of Baldur's welfare. 'Alpha — she's dead? Are you sure — quite sure? Alpha . . . dead?'

'I'm afraid,' Trewley told her, 'that if

she was a young woman with long, dark hair, wearing sandals and a dress not unlike yours, there's no mistake about it, miss — er . . . umph. No mistake at all.' He rubbed his chin, and frowned.

She followed his gaze to the chalk marks on the floor. Her eyes widened. She swallowed, and licked her lips before whispering, in a choked voice: 'Alpha was — was the only one of us who stayed home today . . . It must be so . . . '

Holding Baldur's head so that he should see nothing of what she saw, she moved across to the table, her long skirts whispering against the tiles as she pulled out a chair and sat down, settling the baby on her lap with one hand, while making the sign of the cross with the other.

'Poor, poor Alpha.' She closed her eyes, and shivered, holding the baby close. 'But at least he didn't hurt darling Baldur . . . ' She blinked her eyes open, shaking her head as if banishing tears she scorned to shed in front of strangers. 'I think — I think I would have died if anything had happened to my own, precious baby. It would have been so — so very cruel a fate — when I *know* life can be cruel, but not to one so young, someone untarnished by the pollution of the world, as Baldur is. Nobody could ever believe such a — a terrible thing could possibly be Meant To Happen . . .'

Her final words were so clearly capitalised that Trewley at once recalled the remarks of the East Lodge's John Smith with reference to the guiding hand of a higher fate. 'Meant to happen? So if it did, that would upset all your beliefs, would it? Because you think what's happened to your friend was unavoidable? Destined, as you might say.'

'Oh!' She sat up, looking surprised, and not a little wary. 'Well, yes, I believe in destiny — we all do.' Gently rocking Baldur, whose eyes were drifting shut in slumber, she enlarged: 'Destiny . . . Fate . . . Life itself, you can never — *should* never — fight them. Not unless you withdraw completely from the world, once you have seen the error of its ways. I tried, once before, to withdraw, but the way I chose was a mistake, it was ill-fated, it didn't work for me — and then I met Apollo, and Alpha, and the rest. And they explained that it's up to *you* and nobody else to change your fate, your future — by withdrawing to contemplate it at *your* pace, in *your* time, not the world's, not that of anyone else. Only then can anyone be honestly, essentially themselves.'

She shook back her hair, and her eyes shone with a distant light as she swayed to and fro. 'I am the master of my fate,' she quoted, her voice husky with emotion. 'I am the captain of my soul — as everyone should be, as we of the Family of the Phoenix *try* to be. We have chosen to be free spirits, unfettered by the conventions of the world, in charge of our own lives, not ruled by the petty actions of other people — '

This repetitious adolescent claptrap was too much for Trewley's self-control. 'For heaven's sake,' he exploded, 'I'd hardly call it being in charge of your own life when somebody can just come along and smother it out of you, the way they did for your friend — Alpha, was it? I'd say *that* was being ruled by the actions of other people, all right — and not in such a *petty* way, either, ending up murdered!'

The girl shook her head, and her voice was grave. 'The death of Alpha was Fated, from long ago in the past, when her own actions — her freedom to act — must have forged the steel which made the knife which cut the thread at the destined hour today.' The rocking motion seemed to send her into a trance, and her next words were in a singsong chant. 'There is no one who can escape their Fate once it has been decreed by Wyrd, and Verdandi, and Skuld . . . '

Trewley's face began to turn purple, and before he could explode Stone slipped in a comment derived from schoolday memories. 'The three fates of Norse mythology, right? The Norns, you mean?'

'Yes . . . of course.' Once more, it was clear the girl was surprised, speaking in a more normal voice, and, from the look of her, increasingly wary. 'The Norns — the Fatal Three who rule our lives . . . '

'And is that,' persisted Stone, not quite quickly enough to mask Trewley's exasperated snort, 'why you called your baby Baldur? He was more or less the only person to survive the, er, Last Battle, wasn't he?'

'The Ragnarok,' agreed the girl, with a sigh. 'The Last Day, when evil will contend with good, and all shall perish save those few whose survival leads to rebirth — rebirth into a new world order. As we in the Family of the Phoenix,' she said, for the first time looking directly at the two detectives, 'have already chosen to be reborn — to forget our pasts — as Alpha has been reborn with a double blessing, once by her own choice, as a Phoenix, and once today, by the hand of Fate. Even now, she rides among the stars with the Valkyries — '

She broke off, brought back to reality by the stupendous snort emitted by Detective Superintendent Trewley of the Allingham police. He caught Stone's eye, spluttered, and managed at last to say, with a straight face:

'Interesting ideas, I've no doubt,' hoping he'd be forgiven. 'Still, we've no time to bother with 'em now. You

159

called her Alpha, didn't you? Not her real name, of course. You'd better tell me what that was — we need to know for our records.'

The girl's face crumpled in a scowl, and again she retreated behind her hair. 'It *was* her real name — her true, only name! She chose it for herself, it wasn't forced on her by anyone else — she chose it the way we've all chosen new names for our new lives . . . '

Trewley's bulldog wrinkles quivered as he struggled to suppress his emotions and force his blood pressure down. The girl was obviously in shock. If she wouldn't — perhaps couldn't — tell him what he wanted to know, there'd be someone else later who could. He hoped. 'Well, never mind that for now. How about telling me what your name is? Real or otherwise,' he couldn't help adding, and silently cursed the day that had brought him not one, but two lunatics so far — with, no doubt, more to come.

The girl glanced up, and tossed her hair back from her face. She hesitated, then smiled. 'You can call me Breeze.

I've had enough of being confined — I go where I want, without harshness, freely and quietly like a summer wind — and this,' dropping a kiss on the baby's head, 'is my Baldur.' She raised her head again. 'I'm not married,' she said.

Trewley restrained himself with difficulty, and merely remarked that he was sorry if his questions upset her, but that she must understand they really did need to be asked, no matter how irrelevant they might seem, in order to help in finding out who killed — he made the effort — Alpha.

'What for?' Breeze was not rude, but careless, in the most literal sense. 'What does it matter? Why should you need to know who spared Alpha the weary horrors of this world, and brought her in early triumph to the next? What good will it do you? She's gone — you won't be able to bring her back. We shall miss her, of course we shall, but we hate cruelty to other people, and if you ever find out who — who did this to her, you'll put them in prison, and lock them away — away from the free air — you'll kill them! I know it would kill me — and Alpha is gone, for good. It would be no more than . . . than vengeance on your part to hunt down the man who killed her — and Alpha, I'm sure, would be like the rest of us. She would wish nobody to suffer vengeance on her behalf.'

'But what,' snapped Trewley, 'about justice? What about the law of the land? For goodness' sake, girl, do use your common sense for once! There's some maniac wandering around killing young women — aren't you the least bit bothered it could be you next? Oh, in an ideal world, I won't deny your way of life sounds lovely, all hearts and flowers and everyone friends — but this isn't an ideal world. Believe me, it can turn pretty nasty from time to time. And everyone in it's got at least one person who isn't particularly friendly towards them — and with some it goes further, the way your friend *Alpha*' — the control with which he said her name was evident — 'found out. Want to end up like her, do you? Shall we let some lunatic come along and get rid of the lot of you, one by one?'

'Lunatic?' She stared. 'I — I don't understand. She's dead — that's all we need to know, surely?'

Trewley had suspected she hadn't taken in his earlier attempts to explain; and now that he'd tried talking to the girl, he wasn't even sure if it would be safe to give her the facts of her friend's death — and, if it was, he had no idea how to do it. He threw a helpless glance at Stone . . .

Who responded at once. 'Your friend was smothered,' she said, matter-of-factly. 'In a rather — peculiar — way . . . '

'Oh.' A blush coloured Breeze's pale cheeks. 'There's a — a Peeping Tom, we've heard, going round the villages at the moment . . . Do you think he might have, well, come upon poor Alpha at the wrong time? They — they can take advantage, so I believe, even if there are some people who think he wouldn't need to take advantage of Alpha because she . . . because they . . . because the village believe the Peeping Tom is one of us! And they believe far worse of us, too. We're blamed for everything awful that happens — when all we want to do is be free!'

Her passionate gesture woke the baby, whose eyes opened in a startled blink. He uttered a little yelp, and Breeze, glaring again at the detectives, jumped to her feet.

'I ought to be feeding the poor darling, not poisoning his ears with these — these horrible things, wasting my time talking to you of vengeance, and enemies, and evil gossip we've done nothing to deserve. Nothing! Why should we? We try to love everyone! We try to be friends — we believe in freedom — in life — in a happy life to come.' She nuzzled Baldur close against her breast, and fumbled with the folds of her woven dress. 'Happiness, and hope, and faith, and charity — not cruelty, and prisons, and dark days of punishment in narrow cells! Life is for — for living!'

And, with a sob rising in her throat, she jumped up from the chair. Before either Trewley or Stone could stop her, she dodged past them out of the kitchen, along the hall, and swiftly up the stairs,

164

her sandalled feet pattering on the bare wooden boards . . .

Leaving the two detectives to stare at each other in silent surprise.

But their silence was soon broken, as Trewley tapped a forefinger to his temple and rolled his eyes. 'I knew it,' he groaned. 'Stark, staring bonkers — and I hate to say this, but if the other girl talked half as much half-baked balderdash as this — this Breeze does, whoever did her in probably did it out of sheer desperation, to shut her up.'

Stone hid a smile. The superintendent's three daughters were on the verge of the dangerous years: it came as no surprise that he should feel some apprehension about the types of youthful idealism he would have to suffer around the house until the girls grew up.

She tried to find a non-controversial reply. It wasn't easy. 'The trouble is, sir, that if the rest of them think the way she seems to, and talk the same way, we're going to find it rather difficult to make much sense of anything they tell us — '

'If they tell us anything at all,' growled the superintendent. 'Probably take one look at young Benson's buttons and leg it to the other side of the country . . . '

He clumped across to the kitchen window, and stood staring out into the garden. It was, even he was forced to admit, neat and well-tended, with rows of cabbages, tripods of pea-sticks, and well-turned earth now beaded with moisture. 'Umph. Rain seems to have started while young Breeze was on her soapbox. With luck, the rest of the gang'll get sick of blackberrying, or whatever they do, and come on home before much longer. Still, there's enough for us to be getting on with while we wait.' He moved away from the window, rubbing a thoughtful chin. 'You wouldn't care to try tackling that young woman on your own, would you?' Again he rolled expressive eyes to the ceiling. 'Girl talk, I mean — always said you have your uses, once in a while. It'd be a fine handle for the Civil Liberties crowd if *I* went barging in on her right now, but you — '

'Hang on, sir — listen!' Stone's keener

ears had heard something which made her catch her superior by the arm. She pulled him in the direction of the back door. 'Listen — I think it could be them . . . '

As Stone opened the door, the rich, pleasant aroma of autumn dampness wafted in, mingled with a swelling chorus of voices singing with lusty melody, more enthusiastic than tuneful. From the far side of the hedge, a small procession was advancing towards the house.

They were a long-haired, long-garbed group, whose gait suggested the sandalled state of their feet. There were three men, all with beards, though some were longer than others; and two young women, their faces bare of makeup. Everyone carried some bundle or bunch or bulky shape in his or her arms, and all had voices raised in song:

'They hired them men with scythes so sharp
To cut him off at the knee,
They rolled him and tied him about his waist,
They served him barbarously . . . '

167

Stone recognised the words, if not the tune. 'Sounds like *John Barleycorn*, sir — not that I'm surprised. It's one of those fashionably wholesome folksy tunes about planting grain and harvesting it and turning it into home brewed ale — '

Trewley groaned. 'Typical! Probably an illicit still in the cellar, as well.'

Stone restrained herself from reminding her superior that between them they had searched the whole house, and had found no sign of any cellar . . .

And the Phoenixes drew ever closer, singing as they came.

11

Their song faltered, then died, as they saw two strangers emerging from the back door of what — legally or otherwise — they had for some time past thought of as their home. Their feet stuttered on the path, and they came to a halt, their glances meeting, one with another, watchful, wary.

After a few moments, they moved instinctively closer together, and began to walk forwards again, ever more cautious as they drew near the house. By the time they were face to face with Trewley and Stone, who had advanced several paces to meet them, they presented a united defence.

There was a moment's pause, and then a tall, dark-haired young man, who had appeared to be leading the singing, stepped out of the group to stand alone in addressing the strangers. 'Greetings, friends — if friends, indeed, you are.

Your visit is . . . a surprise to us, but if you come in peace you are welcome.'

A general, though hesitant, muttering behind him appeared to confirm his words, and the tall young man, with a bow, looked expectantly at the strangers for a response to his little speech.

Trewley cleared his throat. For all his irritation with adolescent ideals, he hated to be the bringer of bad news. 'Umph. Yes, well,' and he rubbed his chin. 'Well, thanks for the welcome, but I'm not sure you'll be so pleased to see us once you know why we're here. You see — '

'Baldur!' The frantic whisper arose from the Phoenixes as they pushed past their leader to stare suspiciously at the intruders. 'It's Baldur — they've come to take him away! They must be social workers!'

'What?' Trewley was more than insulted. 'Bloody cheek! Do we — do we *look* like ruddy social workers?'

The very idea seemed to annoy him so much that he found himself unable, for the moment, to explain, and it was Stone who hurried to the rescue.

170

'In a way, I suppose you could say we are — social workers, I mean. At least, we work at making life better for people, as far as we can. We're — '

'Baldur!' cried one young woman, evidently less soothed by the sergeant's tone than the other Phoenixes, who had begun to relax a little as Stone spoke. 'Baldur!' wailed the young woman again. 'They've come to take my baby away — my Baldur! Oh, Apollo, you mustn't let them!'

With a quick look of apology for Stone, interrupted in the middle of her explanation, the young man — Apollo, the detectives deduced — moved across to put his arm about the shoulders of the girl, who was now sobbing, her hands over her eyes, her shoulders shaking.

'Star — Star, it's all right. Don't distress yourself — Baldur is safe. Nobody's going to take him away from us — it was just a — a misunderstanding . . . '

He glanced towards Trewley and Stone for confirmation. Both, after a pause, nodded. Apollo spoke again to Star, in a firm, clear voice, as one might speak

171

to a child. 'A misunderstanding, that's all it was. Baldur stays with us, his family, where he belongs.'

Sniffing, Star let Apollo coax her hands down from her face, which she raised at last to look into his eyes. Her own were red from rubbing, and there were tear stains on her cheeks. 'You — you promise?'

Apollo shot another glance at Trewley and Stone. 'Our baby — he won't be taken away from us? You're sure?'

For a second time, Stone nodded; but Trewley, wiser in the ways of the world, now realised he should have hedged his bets the first time round, and rubbed his chin without uttering a sound.

For Apollo, however, that was hint enough. 'Baldur is safe, Star dear. Now, to please me, stop upsetting yourself like this. Don't cry any more, Star. Don't worry, and let Ocean look after you for a little while — you'd like that, wouldn't you? — while I talk to our new friends to find out what they really want.'

Star gave a tremendous gulp, hiccupped twice, and knuckled her eyes as children

172

will, trying to hide all signs of their distress from the adults. A big, slow, fair-haired youth moved from the rear of the little group to stand beside her, and put his arm about her shoulders. At the same time, a small dark-haired beauty darted forward to stand on her other side, taking one of her hands firmly in her own and smiling up at her from reassuring eyes, talking softly to her while the blond giant said nothing. A red-haired, straggly bearded man neither moved nor spoke, looking from the little group to Apollo, and then at the two detectives, with obvious curiosity.

Apollo, too, was curious — but courteous, also. Before he would ask what these visitors wanted, he must explain the unfortunate effect their arrival seemed to have had on his friend. 'Star,' he told Trewley and Stone in a low voice, 'will be better soon, with Ocean and Flower to care for her. She is easily . . . upset by things, and she's particularly fond of Baldur. As the rest of us are, of course — he's our baby, he belongs to us all — but poor Star isn't — isn't as quick, sometimes, to understand what's going on as the rest of us. You said you had bad news, and naturally she feared . . . but none of us should have jumped to conclusions. We should have remembered that no harm can have come to Baldur because Breeze is with him — his birth mother. She came back to the house to feed him, you see.'

'We've met her,' Trewley told him. 'She's upstairs now, with the baby.'

'And Alpha,' said Apollo, with a smile that did not mask the relief he felt, 'is in the house as well, so it was indeed foolish to . . .'

Then he noticed the involuntary shake of Trewley's head, the shudder Stone, despite herself, couldn't prevent. With a frown, he fell silent for a moment. Then: 'Something's — something's happened to Alpha? It can't have!'

Trewley, with a nod in the direction of Star, tried to mute his normal rumbling tones. The attempt was only partly successful. 'If your — young friend there's the sort to fly up in the air over a baby, she's not going to like

174

what we've got to say at all, believe you me. Can you make 'em get her out of earshot for a while — until someone's worked out the best way of telling her? She'll have to be questioned about it at some point, but I'd rather do it without any highstrikes if we can avoid 'em.'

Apollo frowned, then shook his head. 'Star stays. If it's a family matter — and we are all one family now, the Family of the Phoenix — we must hear whatever you have to tell us while we are all together, so that we can support one another if the need arises.'

Trewley opened his mouth to argue, then shrugged. 'If you say so . . . ' He looked sideways at Stone, who was studying Star with the dispassionate curiosity of the doctor she had almost become. Sensing her superior's interest, she moved slightly, caught his eye, and nodded.

He turned back to Apollo, raising his voice so that his words could be heard by the whole Family of the Phoenix. 'Look, it's not about to stop raining in a hurry.

We'd — you'd — be better off indoors, for a start . . . '

Without waiting for a response, he turned, and led the way back up the path almost to the kitchen door, paused, and then headed round the side of the house to come in at the front. Only a sadist would allow these youngsters to see the chalk marks on the floor before they'd been prepared for the sight . . .

'We always — ' began Apollo, but Trewley ignored him, whisking his caravan onwards to the open door before anyone had time to notice the police cars on the other side of the hedge. With Stone bringing up the rear, he waited until the whole crew was safely inside, then signalled to his sergeant to push the door shut, and himself moved across to the staircase to stand on the bottom step. With another rumble, he cleared his throat.

'We're police officers, and I'm afraid we've got bad news for you. Your friend, the one you call — ' he made the effort — 'Alpha — I'm sorry to tell you that she's dead.'

176

It was not Star — who seemed to have been comforted into a near trance by the continued soothings of Flower and Ocean — who now exclaimed with shock and horror, but rather the rest of the little group. Flower — tightening her hold on Star's hand until, though still entranced, the girl cried out — stared at Trewley with eyes that suddenly showed deep, vivid green in a parchment-pale face. Sturdy Ocean blinked slowly at Star's side, and twice opened his mouth as if to speak, then shut it again without saying a word.

The superintendent's announcement had its effect on the other Phoenixes, as well. Apollo's dark eyes widened, his mouth dropped open, and he shook his head in disbelief, his face sickly white beneath his tan. The red-haired man moved awkwardly from one foot to the other, dropping his eyes as Trewley's gaze swept over the little group and observed how everyone was equally shaken by the news . . .

Or — were they? Stone's keen instincts, Trewley's experience, both sensed some reaction that was not what they would have expected — one quick start as quickly suppressed, so that neither could tell which of the Phoenixes had so reacted. Both, however, were sure that they hadn't imagined that reaction. The news of Alpha's death had been . . . of more than usual import to one Phoenix among the flock — yet at the same time, Trewley and Stone would have said, it had still been as unexpected to the individual concerned as it had been to the others . . .

'Dead,' repeated Trewley. 'And — murdered, I'm even more sorry to say . . . '

This time, he was ready, and raked each face in turn with his shrewd brown eyes: but too late, it seemed. There was nothing now to be seen in those faces except deeper shock, and greater horror, dismay and distress and disbelief — from everyone except Star, still blankly staring as Flower and Ocean gave her the support they looked as if they needed for themselves.

Apollo was the first to find his voice. All traces of his former confidence and warmth were gone. 'Are you — sure she's dead? She was fit and well this morning, when we left — she was happy and cheerful and busy — '

'She was going to make bread,' chimed in dainty, dark-haired Flower, winking back tears.

'Alpha makes the best bread of us all,' said Star, proud to pay compliment. Trewley winced; Stone shivered. Apollo looked at them.

'You spoke of — of murder. Can you be so sure of that? Perhaps it was an accident . . . '

'Perhaps,' said Ocean, with a sigh, 'it was . . . perhaps she did it herself. I mean — '

A hubbub of protest greeted this suggestion of suicide. Ocean knew all life was sacred — it was one of their basic beliefs! It would be a wicked, wasteful thing to do! Anyway, what reason could Alpha possibly have for wanting to commit such a sin?

Almost simultaneously, Apollo and Trewley raised their hands for silence. Trewley's was just a fraction slower.

Apollo, struggling to speak, said, 'Whatever — whatever has happened, we — we must accept it. Alpha's Fate was — was obviously Destined for its appointed hour, and . . . and the hour has duly come.' He coughed, and threw back his head, taking several deep breaths before continuing.

'Far back in her . . . unhappy past, Alpha spun — as we all have spun — the first of those threads that were doomed to be cut short today. We can — we *should* do nothing about our loss — although we can . . . grieve for one we shall not see again — '

'That's quite enough,' broke in Trewley, as Apollo's voice broke, 'of this damned defeatist talk! *Accept whatever's happened — nothing you can do about it —* I don't know when I've ever heard such a load of rubbish! It's feeble folk like you that make it a sight too easy for murderers to get away with it — and, what's more to the point, to think they can get away with it again. If there's a better recipe for trouble . . . Now, listen. I've already said this to your young friend upstairs with the baby, and I'll say it over to you lot so there's no mistake . . . '

As Trewley paused to draw breath, Star stirred, perhaps woken from her trance by his mention of baby Baldur. For the first time, she paid full attention to what was going on about her.

The superintendent leaned forward. His tone was grave. 'You just listen to me. Whoever this chap is who's killed your friend, he could well be thinking of having another go, so until we've caught him you could all be in danger — and never you mind believing in fate and destiny and heaven knows what. *I* believe in the law of the land that says people who go around killing other people have to be caught, and stopped. And if,' he added, raising his voice above the ensuing protests about vengeance and karma, 'the only way of stopping them's to put all their likely victims into protective custody, then that's exactly what I'll do!' He drew himself up, folded his arms, and favoured his audience with his most stubborn bulldog glare. 'And don't think I won't, if I have to . . . '

There was a pause, long and pregnant. Flower, her green eyes wide, looked pleadingly at Stone, who nodded confirmation of her superior's threat. She sighed, and was silent.

In the end, Apollo broke the silence. 'Then,' he said sadly, 'I suppose . . . we'll have to help you . . . '

Their leader had spoken, and the Phoenixes, murmuring, did not noticeably disagree with his judgement. Trewley was observed to relax his frown into something like a smile . . .

There came a flicker of movement at the head of the stairs behind him. Star's face was at once alive as Breeze, with Baldur in her arms, appeared on the top step and began, slowly, to descend. From her expression, it seemed that she must have listened to everything that had gone on since her fellow Phoenixes had been brought by Trewley and Stone into the front hall of the North Lodge. She said nothing, however, as she passed the superintendent, who moved aside to let her by, watching with interest as she went up to Star — smiling broadly now — and offered her the swaddled bundle that was Baldur.

'Would you like to hold him?' she enquired, and Star was only too happy to do so.

'My Baldur,' she crooned, rocking the bundle to and fro, gazing at the two police officers from wistful eyes. 'My own darling Baldur, nobody's going to take him away — not even the cross old lady who doesn't like Alpha — Apollo's promised, and so have they . . . '

She began to drift down the hall towards the cosy warmth of the kitchen. Stone sprang into action, guiding her into the dining room with its cushions on the floor, its posters on the walls. The other Phoenixes automatically followed and Stone was about to join them when Trewley, beckoning to her, waylaid Apollo and asked the question that had been worrying him.

'That girl — Star,' he said urgently. 'Just how simple — barmy — would you say she really is?'

12

'Or is she,' put in Stone, as Apollo seemed more than a little startled by this plain speaking, 'just very . . . preoccupied with what directly concerns her, and not much bothered about anything else?'

He turned to her with a smile. 'Preoccupied, that's the very word for it! She's — well, like a child in some ways, except that children are always very *self*-centred, and poor Star . . . isn't. When something is important to her, she'll make more of an effort to — to *focus* properly, to relate to it — but the rest of the time . . . '

He shook his head, sighing. 'She — comes and goes, if you like — the results of a bad trip some time back . . . oh, long before she came to us,' as the two detectives looked at him. 'We in the Family of the Phoenix will have nothing to do with drugs' — his voice was throbbing with sincerity — 'because we've all seen too much of what can go wrong, and there are those of us who were luckier — who were better Fated — than others. Poor Star is . . . almost normal sometimes, if 'normal' has any real meaning in the world, but even when she . . . isn't, she is good-hearted and loving, without an ounce of darkness in her soul. And it is for this reason that we consider her presence among us a blessing, not a burden. Nobody ever minds doing their bit by taking care of poor Star . . . '

Trewley gave him another sharp look. 'The voice of experience, by any chance?'

Slowly, Apollo nodded. 'Long ago, I dabbled — and more than dabbled, in my stupidity. I know better now — but I also know,' firmly, 'that it's not me you're interested in, but — but Alpha. I suppose I must — I should — tell you, before you find out in some other way and wonder that I did not tell you myself . . . I knew Alpha from way back, you see. We . . . we went through some bad times together, and when we finally decided it was a scene we both wanted

185

out of, we helped each other over the worst . . .'

He shuddered, perhaps at the memories flooding back, then forced a smile. 'I'm probably the only person around who knows her name — the one she was christened with, I mean. When we founded the commune we said we would discard all traces of the past, especially those which had been forced on us by others. We chose new names — so Angela O'Neill elected to become Alpha, the beginning, to symbolise the beginning of her reborn life.'

Trewley said nothing, but rubbed his chin and waited for more, hoping something useful would come out of the morass of high-blown twaddle Apollo was handing him . . .

Apollo — *that* couldn't go on, for a start. He abandoned his resolve to be silent and encouraging. 'So she was Angela O'Neill when you first knew each other, was she? And who were you?'

'Myself,' Apollo told him simply, then winced at the superintendent's look. He soon rallied, however, and began trying to reason with this product of an older, hidebound generation. 'Names are strange things, my friend. In your world, nobody has any say in what he is called — his parents have him baptised, his great-great-generations-back-grandfather originated his surname — which is no more than a label, a classification, a pigeonhole of prejudice we, with our own chosen names, have tried to escape.'

Stone, to cover Trewley's sounds of wrath, said quickly: 'You mean that someone admitting to, oh, Peregrine de Courcy might be a runaway duke — and Percy Clutterbuck might be a dustman — but nobody need ever find out?'

As Apollo congratulated her on having grasped the principles of Phoenix nomenclature, Trewley muttered quietly at her side. There was an element of mirth in the superintendent's response: in his experience, only con men, fashion designers of dubious gender, or pop stars ever saddled themselves with a handle like Peregrine de Courcy — in fact, they would probably change such a handle to Percy Clutterbuck in the interests of street credibility. There was some sense behind Apollo's daft notions, though. If these youngsters could manage to keep themselves anonymous while they lived this lunatic life, they'd be only too glad, once they grew up and settled down sensibly, that they'd taken such an elementary precaution.

But all that was in the future: he'd got the present to worry about. 'Let's assume,' he said grimly, 'that your name *isn't* Peregrine de Courcy — but whatever it is, we need to know it. We'll promise not to laugh, if it'll help the confession,' he added, as Apollo began to look mutinous.

There was a pause. 'Arthur Payne,' admitted Apollo, and — having made the admission — bowed from the waist, and gave a practised social smile. 'Not very exciting, is it? Are you going to force everyone else to make similar confessions in front of the others?'

Trewley rolled his eyes. 'I thought the idea behind all these communes was to share *everything*?'

Apollo bowed again. 'Touché, Mr. — I'm sorry, I didn't catch your name — either of your names,' with a smile for Stone, who had produced her notebook and pencil. He paled, and turned serious at once, repeating the detectives' names as Trewley made the introductions Stone hadn't finished out in the garden, nodding as the superintendent insisted that his questions must be answered.

'You say you knew her best,' said Trewley. 'Tell us about her, then — Angela O'Neill.'

'Or Angelique Royale, as she was when I first met her,' said Apollo, with a faint smile for Trewley's look of sudden exasperation. 'She'd been a model, though I don't think she can have been very good — she was attractive to look at, and moved well, but she was . . . impatient, I suppose you'd call her — too restless for all the palaver of the catwalk, the changing costumes every five minutes and always having to smile — she preferred photographic work, where she could get it over and done with in a couple of hours and be free for the rest of the day. But word gradually got around that she — wasn't the easiest of people to work with. She wasn't anywhere near the top of the tree, and it was easy to see she was unlikely to reach it if she kept on as she did — but she didn't care, because . . . '

'Because?' prompted Stone, as Apollo's eyes flicked in her direction, and his lips twitched. Trewley glared as the young man hesitated.

'My sergeant's unshockable, for heaven's sake, if that's what's eating you. Why didn't Angela care about not making it as a model? Other fish to fry, had she?'

Apollo, after a brief hesitation, nodded. 'It was still modelling, you could say, but more in your line — I mean the police — than anything a — a reputable fashion house would want their girls doing in their spare time. You must know better than I do the market there is for — for that sort of photograph . . . ' It seemed odd that one so professedly uninhibited should blush, but there could be no doubt that the former Arthur Payne, now Apollo, was undeniably turning pink — and turning from pink to red — as Trewley and Stone (particularly Stone) regarded him with interest.

He coughed, and struggled on. 'Angela was good, you know — very good. She had a wonderful body — that's why she lasted as long as she did on the catwalk — but then . . . '

Again he fell silent. The redness of his sunburned cheeks showed no sign of fading, and Trewley shot a look at his sergeant, whose presence seemed to have so dramatically affected the witness. Stone said cheerfully: 'Then she decided to let her natural talents blossom by turning from photographs to films, did she?'

She suppressed a chuckle as Apollo stared. 'I'm rather afraid,' she told him, 'it's not an uncommon story, you know. Is that when you met?'

He blushed even more. 'I was always keen on photography at school,' he muttered. 'The camera club — spent my pocket money on new equipment . . . '

Stone studied him closely. Under the bulky homespun of his attire, Apollo's physique was not unpleasing; his features behind the beard were regular and clean-cut. Had he been something more than a mere recorder of the pornographic scenes in whatever squalid studio they had taken place? She guessed that probably he had — that he and Alpha had shared more than an employer in the past they had later been so anxious — understandably — to escape.

'Drugs next?' she enquired, with some sympathy. 'To make the whole business more bearable — that's what usually happens,' as again his look expressed surprise. 'No wonder you both wanted out. How long ago was this? And where?'

Apollo frowned. 'I've tried so hard to forget . . . but two years now — two years of trying to stay clean — to forget the filth of London, the degradation — to start again with a fresh identity, a new life — '

Trewley couldn't help it: the interruption almost burst from him. 'A new life? And what on earth made you start it in Campions Crest, of all places? I mean, what made you arrive here when you did?' remembering that, if Apollo spoke the truth, the Phoenixes had been in flight from London for some time past. 'Why *now*?'

Sergeant Stone, whose holiday weekend had been ruined, stirred, but said nothing. Trewley groaned as the realisation suddenly hit him. 'You've come for the equinox festival, of course.'

'Equinox? Oh, that.' Apollo's dismissive tone was almost believable. 'Childish nonsense, and not for us, even though Sirius has done his best — '

'Sirius?' Trewley affected not to notice Apollo's quick silence, his closed lips. Loyalty was all very well, but in a case of murder . . . 'Sirius? He'll be that red-headed type who hasn't said anything yet, just lurked in the background looking a bit off-colour. Not been with you long, has he?'

Apollo's eyes widened at the accuracy of the guess. 'You're absolutely right, he hasn't. He joined us a matter of days ago — that is, time has no real meaning for us, but no more than a month,' he enlarged, as Trewley looked on the point

193

of exploding. 'Perhaps a fortnight,' he hazarded, and — after pondering the matter — reinforced this third guess by repeating it.

'Two weeks,' Trewley said. 'Tell me what you know about him — if anything,' he added grimly. 'Seems a twitchy sort of bloke, to me. Withdrawal symptoms, perhaps? Seeing you say your lot don't hold with drugs.'

'We say so, and it's true,' said Apollo. 'You are at liberty to search the house, if you want — you'll find no drugs here, believe me. As for Sirius, his past is his own, and his present is ours, for as long as he chooses to share it with us. We know nothing of him beyond the name he gave us, and the fact that he came seeking us on the road as we walked. We move from place to place in search of a home . . . He learned of our current whereabouts in the way one does, I suppose, and followed from Grant's Tey, and found us. More than that I can't tell you, I'm afraid.'

'Umph.' Trewley regarded him thoughtfully for a moment then announced that, if there was nothing more for the moment, they might as well go along and see what the rest of the gang had to say for themselves . . .

The Phoenixes had gone to roost in the sitting room, the cushions and rugs heaped more closely together than they'd been when Stone saw them earlier. Star, cradling Baldur in her arms, sat smiling and oblivious on the floor, cocooned by swathes of fabric; Flower and Ocean were nearby, holding hands. Breeze and the ever-silent Sirius lurked about the edges of the little group. Breeze had her attention focused on the baby and Sirius . . .

Sirius. Once again, it was no more than an impression, but Trewley and Stone, coming upon the scene a little sooner than their footsteps along the hall had hinted, each thought that Sirius was not as much in tune with his fellow Phoenixes as he might hope to suggest. He seemed, for all his superficial resemblance to the others, to be something of an outsider. The impression vanished as everyone — except Star — turned to the open

195

door, but there had been something about his face, his eyes, the way he sat tense and watchful while the others were merely tense . . .

A general murmur greeted Apollo, who smiled reassuringly at his friends. Everyone except Star and the baby scrambled to their feet, but Trewley, knowing the advantages of the high ground, waved them back to their cushions. Apollo, before joining the others, manoeuvred one of the larger cushions to the centre of the floor, when he invited the two detectives to seat themselves in relative comfort while they asked their questions.

'Questions?' said Breeze at once. The rest echoed her surprise. Trewley, psychologically — and physiologically — incapable of accepting Apollo's invitation, leaned against the wooden half-pillar of the fireplace, and nodded.

'Questions,' he said. 'I hope that by now you've got over the first shock of your friend's death, because we'll be wanting answers to quite a few questions, one way or another. We have to find out who killed her. Young, er, Apollo there has already helped us a little, and we're looking to the rest of you to help us some more. We'll talk to you all together first, and take things from there if we think they need it. All right?'

More murmuring. Ocean, frowning, turned to Apollo. 'So you've gone against the hand of Fate after all, have you? You don't think it wrong to help these — these officers of a corrupt system to pursue their scheme of vengeance — when it can be of no possible use to Alpha?'

'If you choose to put it that way,' Apollo told him, 'I have, and — yes, I do. I knew Alpha longer than any of you. Oh, I agree that we've all been reborn into one family with a new life, but there are some things about the past it — it isn't that easy to forget. What Alpha and I . . . have been through . . . made us extra close, and I feel . . . '

As he suddenly choked: 'And so do I,' chimed in Flower, to Ocean's evident surprise. 'I'll help in any way I can, now I've had time to — to get over the

197

first shock and think about it clearly.' Having removed her hand from Ocean's to describe a graceful, pleading gesture, she slipped it back again, and squeezed in silent apology. 'It isn't . . . vengeance I want, any more than I think Apollo does. What I want is to — to say thank you, I suppose. I can't help it, when I remember how Alpha and Apollo helped me — and especially Alpha. I can't bear to think of someone just — just wiping her out of the world as if she'd never lived — I'd simply hate it if she thought I'd forgotten what she did for me, that I was — that I am — ungrateful, that I don't care . . . because I'm not, and I do!'

'We're all,' said Ocean sadly, 'supposed to care for one another, I thought. Equally — everyone for everyone else, sharing everything. Isn't that why Baldur's so special?'

All eyes turned to Star, rocking the baby in her cushioned nest. She blinked, smiled, and nodded. 'Oh, yes, my own darling Baldur — the most precious baby in the world — of course we all love my baby!'

Trewley had to get to the bottom of this, once and for all. 'I thought — ' he began, looking from Star to Breeze, then on to Flower, nodding and smiling her beautiful smile. 'Whose child is that, for goodness' sake?'

'Breeze,' explained Apollo, as the rest looked to him to explain, 'carried him within her, and nurtured him, and bore him — but she did this with the assistance of each and every one of us, except Sirius, who has not long been a member of our family. Flower and Star are as much Baldur's mothers as Breeze is — just as Ocean and I are his fathers, and as Sirius will become, in time. Neither of us knows which planted the seed which has become the fruit — the work of creation was, and is, shared by everyone.'

Trewley was speechless. Stone, in some circumstances rather more robust than her superior, took over. 'Talking of the baby — there was some mention earlier of 'a cross old lady' who didn't like Alpha, who wanted to take him away. What can you tell us about her?'

'We *aren't* cruel to him!' burst from

Star, as the others regarded one another gravely. 'You mustn't believe her — it isn't true — we love him, our own Baldur!'

'We can see that you do,' Stone told her kindly. 'And he seems to love you, too,' as Baldur opened his eyes at the outcry from his devoted nurse, and blinked, and gurgled in her arms. 'What made the old lady say you didn't?'

Star's attention had drifted back to the baby, and only after some moments did she look up, smiling with vacant eyes in the sergeant's direction. 'A cross old lady,' she said at last. 'She doesn't like Alpha, you know — and I don't think Alpha likes her, either. They were angry, you see, and shouting — yesterday, on the front step.'

She frowned. 'We don't use the front door — Apollo said not to, so we don't. But I suppose the old lady didn't know what Apollo said, and she came to the front, and Alpha was talking to her — they were ever so cross . . . ' She shivered. 'I didn't like to hear them, and neither did Baldur. *She* said we were

200

letting him cry, but we weren't — I wasn't I was looking after him — Breeze said I might, before she came back — if she hadn't woken him up, he'd have been so happy with me until she came . . . '

'He's very lucky,' said Stone, 'to have you to care for him as well as Breeze. Were you — was Breeze with you when the old lady was so cross, or just Alpha?'

But Star was rocking the baby in her arms, and Stone had to look to Breeze for any intelligent response. Baldur's birth-mother frowned.

'It wasn't my duty day yesterday, so I didn't need to be indoors much. It's easier to leave Baldur behind than to take him out with me, but of course he still needs feeding.' She shot a triumphant look in Trewley's direction. 'When I came back, I couldn't help wondering why there was nobody around, even though I could hear Baldur crying, and voices — I was afraid there must be something wrong . . . '

As she hesitated, Stone said: 'Voices from the front of the house?'

Breeze scowled. 'We don't — Apollo

advised us not to use the front, because that would leave two doors unlocked for the legal types like you to come in and evict us. If the front's always bolted — anyway,' recollecting herself, 'when I went to look, the front door was wide open, and Alpha was watching an old woman go down the path — one of the tweedy sort, with a face like a horse and a plum in her mouth, but very cut-glass, you know? Star must have taken Baldur upstairs to hide him as soon as she heard her — she can hardly have missed hearing her. She was probably afraid the old woman was a social worker — we've all seen enough of those to know what they can be like.' The scowl returned. 'Perhaps she was, I don't know. Alpha never said — she just slammed the door, and the old woman went away.'

Trewley coughed. Not one of the Phoenixes could be so much as thirty, and he was sensitive about other things than his weight. 'You keep saying she was old. How old's that?'

'Oh!' Breeze seemed puzzled by his challenge. 'Well, just *old*. I mean, she had grey hair, wavy in a sort of bun — and a hat, of all things, when it isn't even October — and tweeds, like I said. Walked with her nose in the air — but not tottery. Her sort never are. Oh, and her car — I could just see the top of it over the hedge, and it was a Morris — fawn, grey, something boring like that. If all that doesn't mean *old*, then I don't know what does . . . '

Which remarks made Trewley and Stone wonder what make of car was driven by Miss Melicent Jervaulx, of whom Sergeant Pleate had told them; and they also wondered what — if the mysterious visitor had indeed been the cousin of the former squire — had been Melicent's purpose in calling on the Phoenixes in the first place . . .

13

'Right,' said Trewley. 'So you're telling
me that . . . ' He couldn't bring himself
to say it. 'That your friend,' he said,
'didn't say who this old lady was, or
what she wanted with her — with you.
You mean she just shut the door, and
said nothing about it at all?'

Breeze managed to smile. 'She told
me she was a . . . a silly old woman,'
she said, obviously giving the censored
version.

He might have guessed as much. 'Apart
from all that, I mean. She must have said
something to explain the shouting that
seems to have upset young — young, er,
Star.' He felt Stone's eye on him, and
scowled. 'You don't shout at someone
without good reason, even if it doesn't
seem that good to other people.'

At this, Star whimpered, holding
Baldur close. Flower reached across
with her free hand, and gently patted

her on the shoulder; Ocean, smiling, leaned over to take her other hand; and Baldur blew quiet bubbles.

Breeze, ignoring her son, appeared to be making a great effort to recall the events of the previous day.

'Not really, no, I don't think she *did* say what it was all about — though it must have upset her, as well as Star. But she was in a funny mood for the rest of the day — restless, wasn't she?' Breeze appealed to her friends. 'She couldn't settle to anything, could she?' And, as the Phoenixes agreed that this had been so, she went on.

'That was why, after she'd been out for her walk and it hadn't seemed to do any good, I didn't mind changing my duty day with her when she asked me. Sharing — '

'What?' Trewley almost barked the word. Here, slipped calmly into the casual statement of one who had proudly confessed to dropping out of civilised society in order to live a life untrammelled by timetables and routines, came news of an unexpected change in the basic routine she and her fellow dropouts had — for all their fine talk of freedom — adopted (so Trewley guessed) out of sheer self-preservation. 'Asked to change her duty day, did she? Why?'

Breeze blinked at him, opened her mouth, and shut it almost at once. Apollo came to the rescue as she seemed quite unable to find a sensible response.

'The girls take it in turns to stay at home to care for Baldur — a day each, usually. But we — they — sometimes,' with the hint of another blush, 'there are good reasons why they prefer to stay in the house rather than come into the fields with the rest of us.'

The delicacy of his approach was wasted on the father of three teenage daughters. 'And *was* today the wrong time of the month for her? Surely,' as the Phoenixes gazed at one another in some bewilderment, 'You're bound to know *that*, with sharing everything the way you say you do?'

But nobody could confirm for the superintendent whether or not Alpha had good reasons for wanting to stay close to proper plumbing on that particular day; and he observed Stone writing in capital letters at the top of a fresh page in her notebook.

Breeze had made the same observation. 'I'm sure I don't know why she wanted to change, but I know why she asked me instead of either of the others: because today was my day. Flower's is tomorrow, and Alpha shared with Star yesterday.' Had there been an overemphasis on the *sharing* as she gave this explanation? 'We don't have to provide each other with chapter and verse for everything we do — that isn't sharing, that's being made to feel guilty. And the last thing any of us would want is to upset anybody like that.'

Trewley gritted his teeth, and succeeded in sounding relatively calm as he enquired: 'So would — would Alpha have been upset if you'd refused to change?'

Once more Breeze blinked at him. 'But I didn't refuse — why should I? Nobody ever does. Alpha would have changed back with me some other time — that's how we work together, sharing

207

everything equally. It would have evened out in the end — but if it never did, I wouldn't have known, because who'd be counting? None of us!'

'Besides,' interposed the gentle Ocean, with his kindest smile, 'I think Breeze would be the first to admit that of all of us, Alpha makes — made — the best bread, while yours, dear Breeze . . . '

Trewley and Stone suppressed shivers — nobody had yet been told how Alpha had died — and watched as, despite the grim purpose of their assembly, laughter rippled round the youthful Phoenix faces in front of them.

Breeze was able to laugh with the rest. 'Poor Alpha tried so hard to teach me, but some people have the knack, and some haven't. She always made bread on her duty days — to make up for when my turn came, I suppose! Nobody could make bread as well as Alpha — mine always sinks, and hers always rose — and it tastes — tasted — wonderful, too.'

'She took such care of us,' said Flower, her beautiful green eyes filling with tears. 'Her bread, her cooking, the way she found us this house — she could sew, and — '

'House?' Trewley was barking again. 'She found this house? What exactly d'you mean by that?'

Flower winked away her tears, and managed a chuckle. 'Oh, those lovely fish and chips — I can still taste them!' She smacked her lips, and smiled. 'Of course, I suppose it was all thanks to Ocean, really . . . '

'And how was that?' enquired Stone quickly, as Trewley's face darkened. She nodded to Ocean. 'Fish and chips? Very fitting, in the circumstances, I should say,' and she forced herself not to comment on this apparent lapse from the vegetarian lifestyle she'd understood the commune to follow.

Ocean smiled at her feeble joke, but said nothing. It was Apollo who answered. 'Ocean,' he explained, 'knows a great deal about fruits and berries and living off the land — at this time of year there are any number of free foods, if you know what to look for. Walnuts, cobs, sweet chestnuts — hips and haws and, oh, all sorts.'

He glanced at Trewley, hesitated, and went on: 'Before we came to live here, we were in a — a squat over at Grant's Tey. It was a hotel that had gone bust, and while the lawyer types all argued about what to do with it we — well, we just moved in. We patched it up where the damp was getting in, and took pretty good care of it, all things considered. But of course we knew they were going to get us out in the end, and that's why we came here — the workings of Fate, I suppose . . . We were out foraging one day, and Ocean ended up near a bunch of people from the town who obviously had no idea what they were doing. He was just in time to stop them going off to cook some mushrooms that weren't — mushrooms that were toadstools, I mean.'

'Blushers,' murmured Ocean, as Apollo gestured for him to take over the story. 'They'd picked a whole basketful.' He smiled. 'Not that blushers are exactly poisonous, but whoever ate them would have felt . . . very uncomfortable, for a while.'

'So he showed them the safe place where we'd left enough mushrooms for others to share and enjoy,' went on Apollo, as Ocean fell silent, 'and they were so grateful they tipped him a fiver — with which we bought one portion of cod, and enough chips to go round.'

Ocean smiled again. Trewley glowered. 'I don't see — '

'The fish and chips,' said Apollo, with a little cough, 'were wrapped in newspaper, of course, round the greaseproof paper inside — and before we, er, recycled the newspaper, we read all of it we could. We wanted to find out whether anything had been decided yet about our home — about the hotel. We knew all the current planning applications would have to be listed, and we knew we'd have to find somewhere else to live before the bailiffs and the bulldozers moved in.' He coughed, a little more loudly than before. 'It was — it was Alpha who spotted the writeup about Campions Crest having been sold when the squire left, and being bought by a conference centre firm — there was a long article about their future plans — and she laughed, and said she had a — a lucky feeling . . . '

He could not go on. Flower sniffed. Ocean sighed. Breeze said at last, in a low voice: 'She said it was — the hand of Fate. Fated — that's what she was, in the end . . . '

Apollo forced himself to continue. 'She hitched over here one day, to see what the place was like. She found one of the four lodges was empty — some talk about a ghost . . . '

'So we moved out,' said Breeze, as once more he stumbled to a halt, 'before they came to evict us — and we've been here ever since. We haven't done any damage — we've taken care of the house, it's our home — we haven't done any damage, no matter what people say in the village. We work, if they let us — we collect firewood to sell, or the boys offer to dig gardens in exchange for produce . . . '

'Every day?' If Alpha had deviated from the (admittedly casual) routine the Phoenixes had evolved, Trewley wanted to know just how casual that routine was.

'Every day?' They looked at one another, pondered for a moment or two, and then agreed that (as far as possible) every day was much the same as the rest. They woke with the sun, and ate a hearty breakfast, after which everyone not on Duty Day within the house went out to glean, to forage, or to call on local houses, looking for work. They carried food with them, and did not — unless, as today, the weather was against them — normally return until dusk.

'The same every day?' persisted Trewley. 'This last week in particular?'

'This last two years,' said Apollo, as the others nodded. 'Which is how we like it — why we opted out in the first place. Nothing and nobody but ourselves — '

Flower said suddenly: 'Oh!' She looked at Star, and spoke in a coaxing voice. 'Do you remember, Star — the man in the suit? Our last duty day together, just a few days ago — you answered the door, and it was someone wanting to know if he was right for Allingham, and you weren't sure of the directions, so you called me.'

Star, with a little more coaxing, agreed that she did remember; but it occurred to both Trewley and Stone that she was such a biddable girl Flower could easily have invented the story of the mysterious, lost, suited stranger for some purpose of her own, relying on Star to support her. Yet what that purpose might be they couldn't begin to guess, and the girl had appeared (they admitted to themselves) genuinely upset on hearing of Alpha's death . . .

Flower and Star together were unable to produce a worthwhile description of the man in the suit. They had (they told Trewley, when questioned further) told him what they knew of the local geography, and he had driven off. No, they hadn't noticed his car — it would be difficult to see more than the roof over the top of the hedge unless you were as tall as Breeze (which neither of them was) or unless you stood on the front step and looked down the path, which they had been too busy — going back inside to lock the door, as Apollo had instructed — to bother doing.

'Umph.' Trewley's wrinkles twitched with annoyance. 'Has there been anything else out of the ordinary routine, then — before yesterday, I mean?' Heads were shaken, denials murmured. 'How about this walk Alpha took last night? Wasn't it out of the ordinary for her to go off like that, by herself, in the dark?'

The expression on their faces gave him the answer before Apollo had finished putting it into words. 'Why, we often go for a walk in the evenings, once our appointed tasks are over for the day. We like to feel closer to nature — the twilight peace of the countryside, the scented freshness of a drowsy wood — it's nothing at all out of the ordinary for any of us to go outside after our final meal, whether alone or with some of our friends.'

'Alone's a bit risky, wouldn't you say? In the middle of nowhere as this place is . . .'

Apollo's eyes were sad. 'Alpha came to no harm from the creatures of the night, Superintendent. Your presence here now bears witness to the fact that it was her own kind who harmed her, and in broad daylight — no, I can't agree that walking alone is risky. We all need our personal space, and Alpha was no exception. She asked none of us to accompany her, and that was her privilege — and none of us suggested following her when we all went out a little later. We also need our personal space, you see.'

This sentiment did not appeal to Trewley, who smothered a groan with some difficulty. 'You all went out later,' he repeated, in a monotone. 'By yourselves, of course — with nobody noticing where anyone else went, or what they did — or whether Alpha happened to bump into the old lady again, or the man in the suit . . . '

He hadn't voiced it as a question; he could guess what the answer would be. He was not in the least surprised when everyone said that they had, indeed, all gone outside separately — apart from Star, who stayed to sing Baldur to sleep after Breeze had fed him — and had drifted back to the house later without noticing how long any of them had been gone. Trewley rolled his eyes, and muttered under his breath. Alpha could have made a dozen assignations, could have issued a dozen invitations to people — including her killer — to visit her next day in the house alone —

Although he had no idea why she should want to.

Suddenly, he found everything about this case too much for him. 'I need to *think*,' he announced, gruffly. 'Sergeant Stone, you take down a few details of our friends, will you? I'll be outside. It isn't only you lot,' he growled, marching in the direction of the door, 'who need your bit of *personal space* . . . '

* * *

When Stone emerged from the lodge twenty minutes later, she found Trewley sitting by himself in the car, his eyes blankly following the wipers as they lashed in rubbery rhythm to and fro across the windscreen. Of Hedges, and the other car, there was no sign.

'You'll flatten the battery if you're not

careful, sir. And where's everyone else?' Stone climbed into the driver's seat, and switched off the ignition. 'If it wasn't so wet, I'd think we were on a desert island.'

Trewley muttered something about batteries and damnation, then said aloud, 'I've sent Hedges to find out just how far we are here from the other three lodges — especially from the West Lodge, where Miss Jervaulx lives — and how long it takes by car.' He began to look rather more cheerful. 'Young Benson turned up a few minutes ago, soaked to the skin and telling me he hadn't found the hippies. I told him why. And then, well, the lad couldn't possibly be any wetter, so I've sent him on foot up to the big house, to see how long *that* takes. Now,' as Stone shifted on the seat beside him, 'I know it hasn't sounded yet as if this case'll be one of the alibis-and-timetables sort — but that doesn't mean to say it won't, once we've dug round a bit.'

Stone was used to his odd flashes of inspiration, and nodded. 'It's not so much the time of death we're trying to

218

pinpoint, though, is it, sir? We've already established there are too many variables — the yeast, the room temperature, her own — ugh. But if we can somehow work out when the attack took place — and if we find someone with an alibi for that time . . . '

'Someone who's trying to be a bit too clever,' Trewley snarled. 'Timetables, indeed!'

Stone ignored his outburst, as over the years she'd had practice in doing. 'If we find an alibi,' she persisted, 'then I agree that to break it we'll need to know all the likely times, and even some of the *un*likely ones . . . '

'I don't know how many folk are taking this ridiculous Course,' said Trewley, after a pause, 'but they needn't all have come by car. And if one of the carless ones vanished for, oh, however long it'd take, this morning, and acted out of breath when they reappeared . . . '

'He'll probably say he'd been jogging,' said Stone, 'or doing press-ups, or swimming a few lengths of the pool they built on the back, according to the

Argos report. If, that is, he exists at all, sir.' She reached for the ignition. 'Shall we go and find out?'

Trewley grunted. 'Told those young noodles in there not to make a run for it, did you?'

'Yes, sir.'

'Get anything useful out of 'em?'

'Their life histories.' After a moment, she sat back, and tapped her notebook. 'Plus — after a fair amount of cajolery on my part, I admit — their original names, which means we can run checks on them if we want — if we think they've told me the truth, that is, which I wouldn't fancy swearing to, in some cases. I can fill you in on the way up to the house — but at first glance there wasn't anything particularly remarkable about any of them, except . . . '

She leaned forward again, and turned the key; the engine fired, she released the brake, and the car moved slowly away from the North Lodge. 'Breeze, she says, is a failed nun.' Trewley spluttered, but once more she ignored him. 'Says she couldn't cope with the strict convent life, and asked to be . . . not discharged, she used a different word, but I'm afraid I've forgotten it until I've checked my notes — sorry, sir.' She coughed. 'Anyway, Ocean is a carpenter by trade, and met up with the others at a Crafte Fayre.' She spelled the words letter by letter. Trewley snorted.

Stone grinned. 'Flower,' she went on, 'ran away from home because her stepfather messed her about, and fell in with the same lovely film crowd where Alpha and Apollo met — he's a university dropout, he says. Philosophy and sociology — yes, I know,' as Trewley snorted again. 'My reaction too, sir. Star is another college dropout — a friend of a friend, they told me, who had a bad trip she never really recovered from, which is at least consistent with what Apollo said earlier. But Sirius . . . '

'Yes,' said Trewley, and sat up. 'Struck you the same way, did he? Whatever he told you, it won't have been the truth — not by a long chalk, it won't.'

'He told me,' said Stone, 'that he'd gone to college and dropped out like the others — but, sir, that was *after* he'd listened to everyone else rehearsing their stories. It's not too hard, I'd suggest, to work up a background like that if you're sufficiently quick-witted — which I think friend Sirius is. There was a look in his eye . . . '

'Watching them, wasn't he?' agreed Trewley. 'Like specimens in a jar — like potential victims . . . or customers, perhaps. Could be he's a drug dealer looking for a fresh market — gone into hiding after a deal went wrong . . . '

'He's a twitchy sort of chap, that's true,' said Stone, thinking back to her student days. 'And dealers at the lower level are often users themselves — but I'm not sure, sir. There's something about him I can't quite make out, even if we think along drug lines . . . I suggest we run a computer check, just in case he's told me the truth about his proper identity — but if it turns out he's been lying, it won't be any great surprise.'

'Umph.' Trewley peered through the driving rain. 'That young Benson up ahead? And there's the house. Hardly

222

worth letting him in, to make the back seat all wet — we'll sweet-talk the butler or whoever to dry his clothes in the pantry. Give him a chance to get the dope on the backstairs view of these Attitude Analysts . . .

'Because, if we're on the lookout for anything odd, to go by what we've already heard those blasted hippie squatters certainly aren't the only odd folk around here . . . '

14

Banter's well-trained eyebrows expressed little surprise at the arrival of two detectives on his doorstep: Simeon Gotobed hadn't been exactly reticent on the matter of his discovery in the kitchen of the North Lodge. The butler had inveigled the young man into his own kitchens, plied him with coffee, and thoroughly picked his brains before letting him loose on the Course delegates: Banter had been a bewildered eavesdropper of the morning's proceedings in the attic, and wanted to know what on earth it had all been about. Having learned as much as Simeon was able to tell him, the butler promptly withdrew his support and abandoned Mr. Gotobed to his fate, reasoning grimly that the Unexpectedness of his encounter with the suffocated corpse was neither more nor less than the Attitudes Analyst deserved.

'We've been waiting for you lot,' he

informed Trewley and Stone, leading the way along the hall towards the salon where everyone had assembled. 'So I've kept the staff hanging about in the kitchens, when by rights they ought to be getting on with their work — try to make it snappy with the nobs, won't you?'

He then cleared his throat, flung open the door, took two steps over the threshold and, in professionally clarion tones, announced: 'The Police!'

Everybody jumped — and jumped again, as Banter slammed the door shut behind Trewley and Stone without bothering to say anything else. Trewley scowled, but Stone smothered a grin: a butler of Banter's character switching from conventional to unorthodox behaviour and back in the blink of an eye, must be ideally suited to his employers' crazy theories about Expecting the Unexpected . . .

For a group with so paradoxical a motto, the Attitudes Analysis students and tutors were a sorry bunch. The late — unduly late — appearance of Simeon Gotobed, babbling of dead bodies as he burst into the attic, had shaken everyone: especially Andrew Ryan, who turned an interesting shade of chartreuse, and had to be fanned, and fetched glasses of water. He was eventually helped downstairs by former Girl Guide Geraldine Burghley, whose fingers itched to slap his ghastly cheeks, but who restrained herself because of the number of witnesses.

By unanimous consent, everyone else abandoned the attic at the same time. The shock of Simeon's news demanded strong black coffee, which for once appeared in proper cups, with saucers and silver spoons; and Banter made sure there were unlimited amounts of sugar. Simeon drooped on the sofa beside Andrew, both young men trying to restore their shattered nerves, and both less than successful in the attempt.

Sir Lionel Tobias surveyed the ebb and flow of excited chatter with interest. If the main aim of the Attitudes Analysis Course had been to jolt his employees out of their narrow-minded approach to life, then jolted they most certainly had been. Braziers and Allshires hadn't co-existed in such harmony for decades, but it seemed rather a drastic way of achieving so unexpected (he smiled) a rapprochement, and moreover was (he hoped) unrepeatable as a method for regular use. His eyes, unnoticed by any of his employees, met those of Archie Brazier as the turmoil of speculation and surmise surged around the room. Acute observers might have seen Archie's left eye flicker in a knowing wink.

Both men turned their attention to the Course tutors, huddled miserably together, proving — to the cynic — that the theory of Attitudes Analysis was a dismal failure. If exposure to the Unexpected did indeed ginger up the mental processes, then Andrew and Simeon should have been foremost among the excited speculators — but they weren't. Simeon was grey, Andrew still green, and neither of them seemed to have any stomach for the sugared coffee Geraldine and one or two others were urging them to drink.

When Banter ushered in Trewley and Stone, Andrew leaped like a startled virgin, spilling coffee in his saucer, and fell back against the sofa cushions with a groan. Simeon, recognising officers he had already met, managed a feeble smile, though his legs were still too shaky to let him clamber to his feet.

'Good afternoon.' As Trewley went on to introduce himself and Stone, his eyes scanned the crowd of assembled Analysis victims to see if any of them were known to him; and it came as no surprise when — given his local reputation as a civic worthy — Sir Lionel Tobias, after a moment's uneasy silence, took it upon himself to reply.

'Good afternoon, Superintendent, Sergeant. We've all been, ah, expecting you since we learned of the . . . the unfortunate incident at the lodge from Mr. Gotobed here.'

Trewley now permitted himself to notice Simeon, gulping with apology at Andrew's side. 'I — I'm sorry, Superintendent, if it was wrong of me, but I — I couldn't help it — having to explain why I was so late, you see, and you said — you said you'd be coming here after you'd . . . finished . . . '

'That's all right, sir. I wouldn't have *expected*' — and Trewley paused to savour the word — 'you to do anything else — not when I'd asked you to let everyone know we'd be wanting to have a word with 'em before long, if you remember.'

'Oh,' said Simeon, faintly. 'Yes, of course. I was so — it was all so — I forgot . . . '

At his side, Andrew shuddered, and licked his lips with an audible gulp. Simeon hurried jerkily on.

'It was all so awful — just awful! It only really hit me when I got here, and . . . I haven't told anyone . . . exactly what happened, Mr. Trewley — I couldn't, not to save my life — but I had to tell them something, to — to warn them to expect you, and . . . '

'Your expectations,' Trewley assured him gravely, 'have been fulfilled, Mr. Gotobed.' The phrase had popped into his head: he'd found it irresistible. He heard Stone choke quietly close by, while audible snuffles arose from Sir

Lionel Tobias — and from another man, whose dark Casanova face he thought he recognised, though he couldn't immediately place him. Their eyes met: there was a decided twinkle in those of Casanova. *So you think all this is a load of rubbish as well, do you!*

Trewley, mentally filing this twinkled communication for later consideration, now sobered. 'Suppose,' he suggested, 'we start with a few general questions.' Stone pulled out her notebook, and moved to a seat convenient for the table. The superintendent chose the most imposing armchair he could find. 'If you'd all be kind enough to tell us who you are, and where you were earlier today — say from around eight o'clock until half-past one?'

Breakfast had been gonged at eight, and everyone was in the dining room by about five past —

'Except Mr. Ryan,' somebody said quickly. The rest of the delegates at once murmured confirmation of this exception. Trewley glanced towards the sofa, but Andrew's eyes were closed: he

230

gave no sign of having heard a word.

Trewley rubbed his chin, and frowned. Stone made another note as Trewley signalled for the statements to continue.

' . . . Heard the gong, and waited until I heard people moving about, then I came downstairs . . . '

' . . . Hungry — didn't know what to expect after last night, so I wanted to make sure I stoked up in case there wasn't a coffee break . . . '

It was generally agreed that, by nine o'clock, breakfast had been over, with the Course attendees waiting for Andrew Ryan to put in an appearance. Trewley glanced towards the sofa again, and observed Simeon's nod of approval as well as Andrew's continuing silence. 'And after breakfast?' demanded the superintendent, silently marvelling how theorists could be pleased by the most peculiar things.

As soon as it was established that the first session of the Course had opened at nine-thirty sharp, Trewley sat up. Everyone was agreed that breakfast had finished by nine: could this have been time enough for someone to slip unnoticed down to the lodge? What had people done with their free half-hour?

Some had returned briefly to their rooms, then had come straight back to the coffee lounge to await developments. Nobody had paid much attention to anybody else, or was able to confirm times to within more than a few minutes; but it seemed that few of the Course attendees had been out of sight of one or more of their fellows for very long.

'I'm one exception, I know,' said Sir Lionel cheerfully. 'That is,' as the bulldog face turned towards him, 'an exception in that I can't claim any of my, er, colleagues as an alibi — oh, don't misunderstand me. I was certainly with *somebody* for much of the relevant time, but it wasn't anyone on the Course, exactly. It was Banter.'

'The butler?' Trewley sighed. Even that brief encounter they'd had in the hall had left him with the impression that Banter's mind was of a sort to enjoy running rings around the police just for the hell of it, thinking up alibis on the slightest provocation. 'An odd sort of bloke,' growled the bulldog, suspecting that it had been Banter's unpredictability — in other words, his Unexpectedness — when showing potential buyers around the house which had so appealed to the Attitudes Analysts that they had resolved to offer him his old job back.

'The butler, indeed,' said Tobias. 'I'd intended to go for a stroll about the grounds, but on my way out I bumped into him in the hall. We fell into conversation. The chap has a — an original turn of mind, and he insisted on accompanying me on my stroll to propound the theory of Marxist doctrine — in a purely academic sense, naturally.'

'Naturally,' echoed the superintendent, sighing again. It wasn't enough to have a gaggle of Sixties leftovers and a house full of lunatics in the case — now he had Reds under the Beds, as well. 'The pair of you, er, strolled about . . . propounding until half past nine, did you?'

'Until almost half past, yes — for as long as it took each of us to smoke one of my cigars.' Sir Lionel chuckled. 'An example, so Banter explained, of socialism in practice — this after having spent a good ten minutes on the theoretical side. He took my cigar, and in exchange gave me a history of this estate — most interesting.' He turned to Simeon. 'Spare ten minutes to talk to Banter, Mr. Gotobed, and you'll soon learn how you came to make the evidently common error of believing that the North Gate is the main entrance to Campions Crest . . . '

Centuries before, plain Jolyon Jervaulx, gentry-born but not as yet ennobled, had supported Charles I during the Civil War, as a result forfeiting his estates to the winning Commonwealth side. With his young bride, Jolyon fled into France, loyally joining the murdered King's heir in exile. Araminta Jervaulx was an eighteen-year-old beauty married, for purposes of policy and inheritance, to a husband older by some two decades than herself. Jolyon, whom a sword-thrust sustained in the course of duty had rendered less than satisfactory in certain respects, was a fervent monarchist. The younger Charles, with his roving and appreciative eye, was in peak physical condition . . .

In such circumstances, it became inevitable that the three exiles should arrive at a discreet arrangement beneficial to all concerned . . .

The Restoration found both Jervaulx (now Sir Jolyon and his Lady) once again living at Campions Crest, with Charles (now crowned King) in London, looking for other married couples as accommodating. He found them, by the score; but the Merry Monarch never forgot his friends. From time to time he would visit Campions Crest, and when even Araminta's beauty faded she would, for old acquaintance' sake, procure for the royal embrace whatever was required in the persons of abigails, filles de chambre, or distant female relatives: prudence, and the biblical ruling on incest, denying the daughters of the house — just in case.

The King was much gratified by these tireless demonstrations of undying loyalty to the crown, and cheerfully passed the word around his intimates that the faithful family could always be trusted for tact and discretion in the deflowering of pubertal princelings, viscounts, honourables, and other sprigs of the aristocracy . . . and it was in this manner that the Jervaulx, and their descendants, established a unique place in Society over the years.

Queen Victoria, however, heartily deplored this benevolently carnal tradition, age-old though it might be, and as soon as matrimony had opened her eyes to what was going on in Allshire she brought herself to Speak to Mr. Disraeli about it — in terms so very obscure that he almost failed to understand what really troubled his sovereign. Had it not been her own idea to marry Prince Albert? At last, however, he grasped that Her Majesty considered it his plain prime ministerial duty to Speak To the Jervaulx about the way in which blue-blooded young males visiting Campions Crest could be too easily observed by the working classes as they entered the estate through the mansion's main gate — a sight very likely, in the Queen's ultra-respectable opinion, to lead to the corruption of the vulgar, and, as a consequence, one which simply Would Not Do.

'So it seems,' concluded Sir Lionel Tobias, with a nod and a regrettable wink, 'that they simply changed the names — road, gate, and all. The North Gate might have been *built* as the main gate — huge stone lions perched on pillars, and wrought-iron whirligigs for decoration — but nobody called it that any longer. Every visitor on what we may term acceptable business now goes round the side, as it were, and enters officially by the East Gate — where I believe one of the family retainers still lives. The Victorians added some twiddly bits to make the east archway rather more imposing, I understand, and gilded the gates and so on, although Edward VII and his cronies still sneaked in by the North Gate, of course — it's much more convenient to the main Allingham road, despite the altered geography. Still, so long as none of the peasants could ever say they'd spotted 'em using the main entrance, propriety was satisfied.'

Trewley rubbed his chin, trying to decide whether Sir Lionel's or rather Banter's, remarkable story (remarkable, all right, but certainly plausible — everyone knew about Charles Two's wenching) was true, or not. For himself, he hadn't been much of a one for history at school, but being Allshire history he had a feeling this tale rang a few vague bells with him — and it would certainly explain why Gotobed had made the mistake of turning up at the wrong gate when he'd been looking for the main lodge, which of course it hadn't been for years . . .

He shook his head. Could Gotobed's three-nines message now really be considered proved to have come from a stranger knowing nothing of the Main Gate conundrum? Surely he must have visited the place before, and heard its history? Had he forgotten in his panic — or never listened to begin with — or had he tried a piece of monumental double-bluff, hoping to prove he'd never been to the North Lodge before and consequently hadn't any idea the hippies were there? Or . . .

Stone stared at her chief in some alarm as he groaned, the bloodhound jowls vibrating in unison. She coughed, and every head turned towards her.

'After Mr. Ryan made his appearance at nine-thirty,' she said, 'were you all together from then on?'

It was, of course, too much to expect that such had been the case, but Trewley and Stone were rapidly becoming accustomed to having their expectations overturned. The depressing thought occurred to both of them independently that perhaps there was something in Attitudes Analysis after all . . .

'No,' said Archie Brazier. 'I, for one, didn't care to stay on the Course all morning — I needed a stiff drink, and when Mr. Ryan announced that we'd be having a coffee break after all, I, er, made my escape. When I bumped into the butler on my way out of the attic, I found myself invited to his pantry — to sample one or two choice items Sir Joyce didn't think to take with him — or

239

didn't get the chance to,' he added, with a knowing wink.

Stone grinned in sympathy. 'And did you,' she enquired, 'manage to tear yourself away from the delights of Banter's cellar in time to join the others in the attic later on?'

Archie, the former playboy, shook his head, and chuckled. 'Like Sir Lionel, I, too, became embroiled in political discussion. Our friend Banter has definite Revolutionary tendencies, and the more we drank the more definite they became; especially his views on the redistribution of wealth. He says — this is hearsay evidence, of course,' in a mischievous aside, 'he says he'd like to commit the perfect business fraud, by diverting the funds of . . . certain ideologically unsound conglomerates into his personal banking account by the application of some technological wizardry. He lacks, however, the requisite skills. The only reason he agreed to come back here to work for the conference syndicate was because he expected them to use computers as part of their training programme. Which they don't, of course, or at least they haven't so far. Banter is a disappointed man, I fear. He's been eavesdropping like mad since we arrived here, and all he's heard is a load of . . .'

Brash Archie Brazier paused. He grinned, showing his teeth. 'Nothing that's likely to be of any use at all,' he said.

15

Simeon Gotobed opened his mouth to emit a startled bleat. 'Oh, I say . . . '

As a protest it lacked, perhaps, a certain degree of force. Trewley's glance flicked across the pouting Attitudes Analyst, then back to Archie Brazier — just in time to catch the tail end of an unfathomable exchange of looks between the lapsed playboy and the clothing tycoon. The superintendent rubbed his chin in a marked manner, and frowned. Instead of asking his next question of Archie, he turned — unexpectedly — to Tobias.

'Would you go along with Mr. Brazier's point of view, Sir Lionel? That what you've all been doing this weekend's not been worth the bother?'

A gleam — of amusement? Trewley couldn't tell — showed for a moment in Sir Lionel's eye before he said that, on the contrary, he set the highest value on his recent activities. Simeon

Gotobed sighed, looking relieved and much gratified by the commendation. However, Sir Lionel quickly added, all new theories had their teething troubles. Once those troubles were sorted out, he saw no reason to doubt that the Campions Crest Conference Centre would serve a useful purpose in the business training world . . .

Archie Brazier spluttered. Trewley swung round to glare in his direction. 'You've got hopes for the future too, Mr. Brazier, have you?'

'I certainly have! That is . . . ' Archie recollected himself hurriedly. 'I agree with Sir Lionel — I'm not sure the Analyst theory works quite as well as we'd, er, expected. I don't see how it can be right to leave everyone to their own devices for hours on end — '

'Only until half past nine!' Simeon's protest was louder this time. 'Good gracious, that's all part of — '

'And last night as well,' broke in Sir Lionel, backing Archie Brazier every inch of the way. 'No doubt you'll try to claim that Mr. Ryan's disappearance had the desired effect of making us all talk to one another — which probably does as much good in improving company morale than half a dozen of your fashionable psychological tricks. But — '

'Hang on a minute!' Trewley's roar silenced everyone before the argument could grow even more heated. 'Let's get this straight. Are you telling me, Mr. Brazier — Sir Lionel — that Mr. Ryan disappeared and left you all to your own devices for some hours *last night*?' Last night, when Alpha had walked by herself in the lonely dark . . .

Or perhaps not so lonely.

The shrugs and confirmatory murmurs of Archie and Sir Lionel were mirrored by almost everyone else in the room . . .

Everyone except the two Attitudes Analysts. Everyone except Simeon Gotobed, who stared . . .

At Andrew Ryan, who flapped his hands despairingly in front of his face, tried to struggle up from his cushioned silence on the sofa, gave a weak little cry . . .

And slid to the floor in a faint.

★ ★ ★

'Drew!' Simeon leaped from the sofa and fell to his knees at his stricken henchman's side. 'Drew!' He clutched Mr. Ryan by the hand, and shook him urgently. 'Oh, Drew . . .'

Stone had dropped her notebook, and was across the room in an instant. 'Here, let me — I trained to be a doctor.' She pushed Simeon — who seemed likely to go burbling on forever without achieving much — out of the way, and tugged at the open neck of the shirt beneath Andrew's sweater. She slapped him once or twice around the cheeks, and saw signs of life returning.

'Mr. Ryan?' Andrew let out a little moan. Simeon began burbling again. Stone shot him an impatient look. 'Help me sit him up, and then we'll shove his head between his knees. Gently, now . . . Good . . . Prop his back against the sofa, and let him breathe — and could someone fetch some water?'

'How about black coffee?' enquired Geraldine Burghley, former Girl Guide.

Stone said coffee would do, but she preferred water, if possible. Trewley, who knew his sergeant well, chortled. Stone was quite capable of dashing a glass of cold water in Andrew Ryan's face if he decided to go into hysterics — though on second thoughts perhaps that would be unwise. Best not let her get carried away . . .

He wandered over to the busy little group, and scowled so fiercely at Simeon Gotobed that he dropped Andrew's hand, blushed, jumped to his feet, and retreated to a far corner of the sofa — though it was noticeable that he kept his eyes firmly on Andrew's face, where the colour was slowly returning. Andrew sipped water, and shivered. Trewley peered down at him with some interest, checked with Stone in silent communion, then said:

'Let's have you a bit more comfortable, Mr. Ryan, shall we? That's a draughty floor you're sitting on.'

With the assistance of his sergeant — who whispered one quick warning about blood pressure and then thought better of it — Trewley heaved Andrew

Ryan's flaccid form up from the floor to the opposite end of the sofa from Simeon. He stood dusting off his hands, hardly panting at all, preparing to throw Stone a triumphant life-in-the-old-dog-yet look, when:

'We-e-e-ll-a-a-aarf!' A massive sneeze erupted from his throat. 'Aaarchoo!'

As he delved in his pockets for a handkerchief, the look he directed towards Andrew Ryan was thoughtful indeed. Another convulsion of sneezing struck before he had time to move out of range; but between spasms he managed to gasp one word which had Stone's fingers twitching for her notebook, and Andrew's nerves jangling.

'Joss!'

'Oh, my goodness,' breathed Simeon. 'Oh, Drew, no . . .'

Sir Lionel Tobias frowned. No wonder Ryan had acted the part of an incompetent so well — he hadn't needed to act it. He said sternly: 'Young man, you shouldn't mess with these heathen pursuits. Incense — pah!' Then his tone changed from disgust to pride. 'My boy Michael,

247

now . . . ' Few people in the Allingham area remained ignorant for long of the fact that Tobias had a doted-on adopted son. 'He's only ten, but he's a real little fresh air chap, camping and Cubs and good healthy pursuits . . . ' He caught Trewley's look — the superintendent's sneezing fit was over — and subsided.

Although there were hundreds of routine questions that ought to be asked, if a lead jumped out at Trewley he wasn't one to tell it to get back in line. He said:

'Mr. Ryan, let's think about this, shall we? You're not going to try telling me you didn't disappear last night for a few hours, are you?'

Andrew gulped. Simeon seemed on the point of renewed lamentation, but was quelled with one of Trewley's fiercest bulldog scowls.

'No,' said Andrew at last, sweeping back the blond forelock which had drooped over his pale brow in the excitement of the moment. 'No, I'm not — I can't. Could I — could I talk to you alone, please?'

★ ★ ★

They ended up in a small side room off the hall, with Andrew no less pale than when he'd made the request for a private interview. Simeon Gotobed had stayed, reluctantly, with the others, sipping coffee from a cup which clattered every time he set it down on its saucer. Nobody knew what to say to him, and so said nothing . . .

'Nothing to say for yourself after all, Mr. Ryan?' Trewley glared at the reluctant witness. 'Here's my sergeant gone and sharpened her pencil specially, and you sitting like a — well, I don't know what, really, but someone that doesn't like talking. And that's a pity, when me, I'm such a good listener. Suppose,' he turned from introduction to accusation in a second, 'you tell us just what your business was with the dead girl yesterday, Mr. Ryan. And don't try to fool me you didn't meet her, because I'd find that hard to credit. Very hard.' He pulled out his handkerchief again, and trumpeted into it in a meaningful fashion.

249

Andrew gulped. 'The — the dead girl,' he said, with a visible effort. 'Simeon only said — he didn't tell us — but I just had the most awful feeling . . . '

'That you knew her?'

Dumbly, Andrew nodded.

'But there's more than one young woman living in that commune, as you probably know very well without me telling you,' Trewley said. 'So why should you think the one we're interested in's your friend?'

'My — my sister,' said Andrew, in a low voice. 'I'm so afraid . . . Simmie said she — she had long dark hair, and — and Angela . . . '

Anxiety had sharpened his senses. Trewley shifted just a little on his chair, Stone's hand tightened in sympathy on her pencil, but Andrew needed no stronger hint. He groaned, and buried his face in his hands. 'Oh no — Angela . . . '

Trewley cleared his throat. 'I'm sorry, Mr. Ryan, but if your sister was calling herself Alpha — previously known as Angelique Royale and Angela O'Neill,

250

then I'm afraid — '

'No!' A muffled sob interrupted him, and Andrew's bowed shoulders shook. Trewley and Stone exchanged glances. The sergeant nodded, jumped to her feet, slipped from the room, and was back in a few moments with another glass of water in her hand.

A few shuddering gulps, and Andrew Ryan was more composed. He tried to square his jaw, to stop his mouth from wrenching sideways; and he sat up straight, prepared to tell his story.

'I just knew — when Simeon described . . . She wasn't my real sister, Mr. Trewley, she was adopted — foster . . . They always said she'd come to a — to a bad end, and now . . . She ran away from home after we — after our parents found us . . . We'd been to the cinema . . . Dad's cousin was the manager of our local.' Andrew blinked. 'He used to give us free passes — Angela was always going. She was a really lovely girl to look at — she wanted to be a model, or an actress, she couldn't decide which — she saw everything over and over, she went to all the retrospectives . . . '

There was a long pause. Trewley rumbled deep in his throat, and Andrew blushed.

'She — she dragged me to see *Love Story*,' he said, forcing the words from an obviously reluctant mouth. 'She was wild about Ryan O'Neal — it was partly the name, I suppose, but she said she wished . . . We went to the pub after the film, and I suppose we — we had . . . I wasn't as used to drinking as Angela was. She looked older than she really was — she used to buy bottles for all her friends at the supermarket, and if anyone ever asked she said it was for our — our parents . . .

'They — they came home earlier than we'd expected.' He shuddered. 'They — they were furious when they — discovered us together — but it wasn't as if we were really brother and sister, was it?' This was clearly an argument he'd rehearsed over and over again, trying to convince himself. 'Angela is — was — three years older than me.

My parents thought they couldn't have children — they hadn't completed the adoption process before I came along — and then they went ahead with it anyway . . . oh, I wish so much they hadn't!'

As Andrew buried his face in his hands again, Trewley said, 'Did you resent her, then, Mr. Ryan?'

Andrew's head jerked up as he uttered a horrified cry. 'Resent her? Of course I didn't — I adored her! She was so — so pretty, and such fun — so lively — she spoiled me rotten, even more than my — my parents did . . . we went everywhere together — we'd egg each other on to sneak cigarettes and drinks from the sideboard to take to our den, and we'd hold each other's heads when we were sick . . . I'm teetotal now.' Once more he blinked, and brushed his forelock back. 'After that — that dreadful evening . . .

'My mother was sick,' he said, in a whisper. 'I mean physically, down the loo — she just stood and screamed at us and rushed away to be sick — and my father . . . took a strap to us, Mr. Trewley. Both of us — I tried to stop him beating Angela, but he — he blamed her . . . '

'It takes,' the superintendent pointed out grimly, 'two, Mr. Ryan. Always has done, always will.'

'He said,' groaned Andrew, 'that it was all her fault — she was three years older than me — but not blood relatives, Mr. Trewley . . . Angela ran away the next day. She left a note — she said if that was how they treated her, she'd be better off somewhere else . . .

'And I didn't see her for more than ten years. Not until yesterday — and now she — she's dead!'

Trewley rubbed his chin. 'She's dead, yes, I'm sorry to say,' he told Andrew, who was again overcome with emotion. 'And it's my job now to find out who killed her — and why. Somebody suffocated your foster sister, Mr. Ryan. He shoved . . . something — in the poor girl's mouth, almost as if he wanted to stop her talking. As if he didn't want to hear what she had to say — or didn't want anyone else to hear it. Your friend Mr. Gotobed, now.' Trewley clicked his tongue. 'He's the chap who reported finding her dead — already dead when he found her, so he says. But what does your Mr. Gotobed know of what you've just told us about why Angela left home? I daresay he could be pretty upset to find out something like that about his friend out of the blue when — '

'No!' Andrew bounced upright from his exhausted pose. 'I swear to you, Simmie didn't — doesn't — know anything of what happened that night — nobody except my parents knows. They put it about that Angela had gone to dramatic school, it was too — too shameful for . . . Fourteen,' he said, with a gulp. 'That's all I was — and she was seventeen . . . And she — she had to have an abortion . . . '

'How,' demanded Trewley, 'could you have known about her abortion if you never saw her from the time she left home? Are you *quite* sure you two didn't keep in touch, or have any dealings after you'd — taken up with Mr. Gotobed?'

'She — she told me last night,' confessed Andrew, twisting his hands together in front of his trembling mouth. 'It was — horrible! She — she accused me of — of . . . She was so — so hard, not like before. She said it was all my fault she'd ended up the way she did — and she'd been so . . . different, not so cruel, when I saw her before, I could hardly believe it was the — the same person . . .'

His voice trailed away, but too late. Trewley said: 'You saw your sister *twice* yesterday, then, Mr. Ryan? From the way you talked earlier, I understood it was only the once.'

'Oh!' Andrew would have collapsed, had the superintendent's stern eye not silently forbidden him to be so self-indulgent. He licked his lips; his voice emerged in a squeak. 'I — I'd forgotten — before lunch, after my drive — I went for a walk. The butler had told me there were . . . squatters in the lodge — hippies . . .

'He — he only mentioned it to see what I'd say, I think. He said they weren't doing anyone any — any harm, and to his mind it was a crying shame the house should stand empty when there were people around without a roof over their heads . . . He was — was sneering when he said he supposed I was technically his employer, and I ought to know about what was — I ought to know about them . . . So once I'd unpacked, I walked down to the lodge to see for myself . . . '

'You walked. Why not go by car?'

'Someone had put my car round the back of the house, and after the drive from London . . . besides, I was looking forward to seeing something of the estate — I'd only heard about it, you see, from Simmie — Mr. Gotobed . . .

'I was curious, when I arrived at the — the commune. It wasn't at all what I'd imagined, it was clean and tidy and — and Angela opened the door when I knocked . . . ' He clapped a shaking hand over his mouth, and swallowed twice. 'After more than ten years . . . She said there was another girl in the house with her. A bit — a bit simple, Angela said,

257

but we still couldn't talk. I *needed* to talk to her, I simply had to know what had happened since — since I'd last seen her — since we'd been sent to bed with nothing to eat after the — the beating . . .

'I was in such a state, I forgot all about having to get back to the house to greet the first arrivals, but Angela — she got rid of me by saying we'd have to meet later on — in the evening, in the woods . . . I agreed — she was expecting another visitor, I saw a car turning from the road into the drive as I walked away . . . '

'A car?' Trewley sat up. 'What sort of car?'

'Oh,' said Andrew, screwing up his swimming eyes to look back into the past. 'Oh, I'm not sure — something pale. It was grey, or fawn — a Morris Minor, I think . . . '

As reputedly driven, Trewley could hardly help recalling, by Miss Melicent Jervaulx.

16

'Did Angela,' enquired the superintendent, 'tell you she was expecting this visitor, or did you just assume she was from seeing the car?'

Andrew stared, then shook his head. 'I — I can't really remember. I think I just assumed . . . it stopped outside the lodge, you see, and where else would she have been going?'

'She?'

'The driver — a woman. An elderly woman, I think — she was wearing a hat, and tweeds — that sort of thing, anyway. I only caught a glimpse of her through the windscreen as I was walking away, so . . . '

'About what time was this, Mr. Ryan?'

There was a pause. Andrew's smile begged for understanding. 'I don't know — I'm sorry. Before lunch, that's all I can tell you . . . I was too — upset, I suppose, to take much notice, and then

I was . . . rather worried about — about having to meet Angela later . . . '

'Later that evening,' supplied Trewley, as Andrew's voice quavered to a halt. 'You met her, in the woods, the way she told — asked you to. So then what happened?'

Andrew lowered his eyes, the lashes sweeping dark shadows across his ghastly cheeks. 'She . . . told me about . . . the baby,' he admitted, so quietly that the two detectives had to strain to hear his words. 'She blamed me for — for the filth and the horror and — and . . . A ghastly old woman in a — a blood-stained overall . . . '

Stone caught Trewley's eye, and mimed surprise. Angela, it appeared, had over-dosed on the old movies. Needles and buckets and back-street hags had gone out years before . . .

Andrew's voice was still barely more than a whisper. 'She — she said it had all been my fault, and that now I had to — to make up for what she'd suffered. She said I had to persuade Simeon — Mr. Gotobed — to talk to the syndicate. She said I must make sure they — the commune — weren't evicted from the lodge . . . she didn't even want them to have to pay rent . . . '

'And could you,' Trewley asked, 'have arranged everything the way she wanted, d'you suppose?'

Andrew stared — shook his head — nodded . . . and stared again. 'I don't know, but I — I'd have tried, Superintendent. It would have been a — an obligation — a recompense — an atonement . . . '

'A bit of bad luck, your sister turning up on the doorstep after ten long years,' was Trewley's comment. 'The hand of fate, I daresay she'd've called it.'

'Oh, no.' Andrew shuddered. He'd evidently been treated by Angela to enough of the Phoenix philosophy to recognise the superintendent's prompt. 'No, it was the local paper — there was a big write-up about the Centre, and the Attitudes Analysis, and — and photographs . . . '

'Umph. A bit of bad luck,' said Trewley again; and Andrew nodded. Trewley said,

'It really was in your interests to shut her mouth, wasn't it, Mr. Ryan?'

Andrew's mouth dropped open. He stared. He went whiter than ever — and fainted again.

'We'd better,' said Stone, 'shove his head — '

'In a bucket of water!' snapped Trewley, who'd had more than enough histrionics for the time being. 'Oh, take care of him while I yell for Gotobed, will you? They can fuss round each other to their hearts' content . . .

'While we,' he said, once messages concerning Mr. Ryan's welfare had been duly passed on, 'do our sums, Stone — and don't start telling me you had to be coached through 'O' Level maths. Even you must have spotted that young Andrew's supposed to have had his tumble in the hay with Angela about ten years ago — and there's Sir Lionel Tobias rabbiting on about his precious only son, who we all know's adopted — and who's nearly ten years old . . . '

'And,' said Stone, 'Angela's ideas about abortion are just a little hard to swallow, sir. Suppose she invented the whole story on the spur of the moment, to bamboozle Andrew into feeling so guilty he'd promise the moon to keep her quiet? Suppose she actually had that baby ten years ago, and put him up for adoption?'

Trewley rubbed his chin, and nodded. 'Tobias manages to find out more about the kid while he's adopting him than the authorities usually let on — his mother's name, at least. With his money and connections, that wouldn't be too difficult — the man's always been active in all sorts of welfare-type organisations, not just the Scouts. The tycoon with the social conscience, the papers call him, don't they? And his sort don't change — he's bound to have taken an interest from the start — only he won't have been that bothered about acting on the information, just interested, until he bumped into the girl here. Somehow or other he realises who she is and gets rid of her — not just for being the boy's natural mother, but because she's turned out barmy with it. He'll be one of these heredity people, probably, scared

263

his precious son'll grow his hair and drop out to sniff incense — or worse — by the time he's in his teens.'

'Nature,' murmured Stone, 'or nurture? Nobody's ever been able to prove anything definite . . . Or perhaps, sir, it was one of those informal arrangements, and he doesn't have a legal leg to stand on because it wasn't a proper adoption, just a — a welfare-type thing . . .'

Trewley grunted. 'It's all very well speculating, and we'll check it out, of course, but I've a nasty feeling it's not going to be quite as straightforward as we'd like, my girl. Tobias made it pretty clear he's spent most of his time hobnobbing with other people, didn't he? Especially hobnobbing with that blasted butler . . .'

He sighed, then brightened enough to produce a slight chuckle. 'Still, young Benson's no doubt doing his own bit of hobnobbing right now, toasting his toes and swigging port — for medicinal purposes only, naturally. We'll hop along this minute to Banter's hideout and find out what he's got to say — and find out if we think we can believe him,' he added, sighing again. 'He's the sort'd happily take a backhander to say whatever anyone asked him to — or else he'd say it just for his idea of a joke, if he thought he could get away with it.'

'Perhaps,' suggested Stone, as they set off towards the green baize door behind which lurked the butler's pantry, 'it was Banter who killed Alpha, for a fee — though I admit, sir,' as he uttered a groan, 'it's not very likely.'

'Umph.' Trewley shot her a suspicious glance. In all his years of murder investigations, he'd never yet come across a case where the butler did it, but . . . 'There's always a first time, my girl, remember.' To which Stone responded with a chuckle of her own.

They found not only Benson with Banter, imbibing port, but Hedges as well, drinking what looked like fruit juice. Both constables would have leaped to their feet with embarrassment at the unexpected entrance of their superiors, but Trewley waved them down again with a growl. What (he demanded) had

265

they got to say for themselves? About the time it took to wander round the blasted estate, not about the way they were trying to stave off influenza . . .

Hedges produced neatly written notes. It had taken five minutes to drive between the North Lodge and the West, this to include starting the car and stopping it properly at the appropriate ends of the journey. He'd then driven on from the West to the South, from the South to the East, and back to the North again, all of which had taken longer — he was not, of course, familiar with the roads. If the superintendent would care to examine his timetable for this boxing of the Campion compass . . . ?

Trewley glanced at the paper, grunted, and passed it to Stone, who quietly folded it into her notebook.

'Another question, lad. Notice any cars parked outside any of the lodges on your travels?'

Hedges had not. Banter's ears pricked up. 'Any car in particular you want to know about?' he enquired, pouring port for himself in a manner which had Stone automatically assessing the probable state of his liver.

'Mr. Smith, for one,' said Trewley, recalling the whimsical behaviour of the East Lodge's leather-waistcoated inhabitant. 'Well, all of 'em, really. You'd know, of course, being local.'

Banter nodded. John Smith (he reported) didn't have a car; neither did Squadron Leader Kempshott; and he doubted whether the hippies possessed such a thing. He believed they'd brought their belongings to the lodge in a handcart, though the superintendent was bound to know more about that than he did . . .

He quirked an eyebrow in Trewley's direction, and paused expectantly before continuing: 'Miss Jarvis, now — she has a car, a grey Morris Minor. Had it years, and never gone farther than Allingham in it twice a week — regular collectors' item, it must be by now.'

'Thank you, Mr. Banter. And what about you, Benson?' Trewley was giving nothing away. 'How long did it take you to end up looking like a drowned rat?'

267

PC Benson looked hurt that his earlier hippie-hunting efforts had been forgotten. 'I was already wet through when I started, sir — remember? That's why — er, ten minutes, sir.' he said, as the bulldog growled softly at him to stop wasting time feeling sorry for himself.

Stone was flicking back through her notebook, doing calculations, wondering whether the result would eliminate anyone. With a frown, she concluded that the field was still wide open. Glumly, she stabbed her pencil into the paper, and then had to fish in her pocket for her penknife keyring to sharpen the broken point.

Trewley had been thinking. With a warning frown to Benson and Hedges to keep quiet, although in the latter's case this was hardly necessary, he pressed Banter to describe in as much detail as possible his movements for the past two days, concentrating on the previous evening and the whole of that morning. The butler reeled off a list of names — including (perhaps rather too promptly volunteered) those of Sir Lionel Tobias and Archie Brazier — belonging to people he insisted would vouch for his probity. Trewley scowled, and asked to speak to the rest of the domestic staff. With no apparent hesitation, Banter made him free of the entire region behind the green baize door. Campions Crest was Liberty Hall, the butler cheerfully told him.

Trewley ground his teeth, thought of his blood pressure, and forced himself to thank Banter for his co-operation . . .

'But I'll leave that side of it to you two, once you've sobered up,' he informed Benson and Hedges. Benson blushed; Hedges pursed his lips. Trewley glowered. Unless the butler was trying a monumental double bluff, it sounded — for the moment — as if he could well be out of the running. In which case, there were more important witnesses to see than a load of giggling girls agreeing that their boss — if Banter, indeed, was the boss: Trewley was unsure of below-stairs etiquette, and had no intention of asking — that their boss hadn't been out of their sight for more than five minutes since breakfast — something the superintendent felt gloomily sure they'd say.

'We've a few more people to see outside,' he said, nodding to Stone. 'Get on with it, you two!'

Stone closed her notebook, and hurried in Trewley's wake as he stamped out of the pantry and made for the hall. 'Are we going to have a word with Sir Lionel, sir? This adoption business — it's a pretty strange coincidence — '

'Not yet,' he told her, hurrying towards the main door. He cast an anxious eye in the direction of the little room in which Andrew Ryan had last been seen, surfacing from hysterics. 'Not until we've checked . . . Tobias will keep. He won't run away, that type doesn't, and we know we can always lay our hands on him if we need him. Besides, if he did it, it'll do him no harm to pickle for a bit, wondering exactly what we know . . . but I do like the sound of that grey Morris, girl. Talk about coincidence — that's far too much of a one for me. I reckon we ought to have a word with Miss Jarvis before very much longer . . . '

The rain had eased off while they'd been in the house, and when they arrived at the West Lodge they could see Miss Melicent Jervaulx pottering in her garden, with a sensible mackintosh over her tweeds and grey galoshes on her feet. She glanced up with an expression of genteel distaste as the police car arrived from the direction of the former manor, then rearranged her aristocratic features to show no more than surprise when the doors opened and two strangers emerged, heading for her front gate.

Moving swiftly, Melicent was before them, blocking their entrance. 'I'm afraid,' she said, 'that if you are looking for the Conference Centre, you seem to have driven straight past it. If you turn your car round, and — '

'We've just come from Campions Crest, thank you, madam — er, miss — Jarvis,' Trewley brought out, feeling unaccountably awkward. 'It, er, *is* Miss Millicent Jarvis, isn't it?'

Melicent Jervaulx flinched, very discreetly, and agreed that it was.

'We're police officers, Miss Jarvis, from

Allingham . . . ' He produced his warrant card, and held it out. Melicent did not take it; nor did she give him time to make proper introductions. Her eyes gleamed.

'Why, this is most gratifying — and most welcome, after my — I have to confess it — *disappointment* with the behaviour of the officer I spoke to yesterday! Some kind of — of public relations exercise, no doubt — your visit,' she went on, smiling, preparing to unlatch the gate. 'I'm delighted to see that you have decided to take my warnings seriously. Those *dreadful* hippies — something really must be done about them, and if I can help in any way . . . '

'You can certainly help,' said Trewley, as she led the way up her neatly paved path. 'For instance, would we be right in our understanding that you paid a call on the — the commune yesterday after you'd spoken with Sergeant Pleate?'

'Was that his name?' Melicent frowned. 'Hardly what I should call an *example* to the younger officers,' with a nod in the direction of the youthful Stone. 'However, it is my view that, if an example is expected, then it is only right that an example should also be set, by those best able to do so.' She drew herself up to her full height. 'I called on the — the illegal occupants of the North Lodge early yesterday afternoon, and I'm not ashamed to admit it!'

'No need to be ashamed at all, Miss Jarvis.' Trewley was shaken to hear himself trying to pacify her. She reminded him horribly of the schoolma'am who'd kept his entire class under control with one flash of her gold-rimmed glasses, and he had an uneasy vision of himself kept in at break for talking in the Arithmetic lesson. Suddenly he had the ridiculous desire to plead — as he'd pleaded all those years ago — that he'd only been asking for help . . .

He coughed, and dragged himself back to the present with a noticeable effort. Both Melicent and Stone stared at him with some interest. He said:

'Nothing to worry about, Miss Jarvis — depending on what happened when you called on them, that is. Because we're investigating a — a recent incident at the North Lodge, that happened around lunchtime today, and — '

'Yesterday,' Melicent corrected him sharply. 'I visited these *squatters* yesterday, just before luncheon — I consider it most unwise to rush one's meals. They should be taken at regular intervals for the benefit of the digestion — with the intention of speaking my mind about such conditions as I found there. I spoke to a young woman, who had a most *abrupt* and lamentably *discourteous* manner. She refused to let me in — despite the fact that there was a baby in the house, clearly distressed. I could hear it crying, although another girl, of a — a regrettably *simple* type, tried to assure me that the child — which she referred to by an outlandish name — was in the best of health, and well cared for — which I, in the circumstances, found hard to credit.'

Melicent frowned. 'I had, however, no legal right to insist upon entry, and — though I spoke as forcefully as I could — neither of the girls seemed swayed by my arguments. The simple one, indeed, ran away, while the other was — was decidedly *hostile* in her manner. I therefore returned home, and wrote a strongly worded letter, which I posted this morning, to the Social Services. It has always been my habit,' she added, seeing the question on Trewley's lips, 'to read over any correspondence of a — an unpleasant nature after the passage of one night. A fresh morning frequently brings a fresh perspective on the problem — which in this instance, however, was not the case. I posted my letter earlier today — but I did not,' she added, recalling the exact purpose of this constabulary visitation, 'go anywhere near the lodge at any time — I had no need. There is a pillar-box within five minutes of my house . . . '

'And I must therefore enquire,' said the cousin of Sir Joyce Jervaulx, 'what exactly has this — recent incident of which you speak to do with me?'

17

In normal circumstances, Trewley would have established in a matter of minutes who — if, indeed, anyone — could bear witness to Melicent's movements that Saturday morning. But her uncanny resemblance to his old teacher had so unsettled him that it was left to Stone, loyally divining his discomfort, to pose the appropriate question.

Miss Jervaulx bristled. 'Before I accede to your — your impertinent request, I must again ask why the police should concern themselves with my *private affairs*. What can be the nature of this . . . incident for it to result in so intrusive and — and *excessive* and enquiry?'

Stone glanced at Trewley, and received his nod. 'One of the young women, er, living in the North Lodge,' she said, 'has been found dead — in highly suspicious circumstances,' she added, as Melicent

276

gave a little gasp, and turned discreetly pale. From shock? Or from dismay at so soon having the avenging forces of law and order arriving on her doorstep? Impossible to tell . . .

'Dear me,' she said, blinking, and breathing hard. 'Oh — how dreadful. Disgraceful . . . I had no idea . . . I think you had better come in . . .'

And she led the way in silence round the house to the kitchen door, where she kicked off her galoshes and slipped laced oxfords on her feet without another word.

She marched, still silent, to the parlour, where she motioned to her visitors to seat themselves, herself taking a high-backed chair and clasping her hands before her on the table. She looked from Trewley to Stone, and back, with a question in her eyes.

Stone duly obliged. 'The young woman was smothered,' she said, feeling it unnecessary to go into detail. 'After having been hit on the head, that is — and, naturally, we are interested in anyone who's had dealings with the

277

hippies during the past few days . . . '

Melicent's look ceased to be questioning, and began to be restive, the instant Stone spoke the word *hippies*. With a hiss of indrawn breath, a narrowing of prim lips, and one dismissive gesture of her aristocratic hands, Miss Jervaulx indicated her strong disapproval of the squatters in the North Lodge, and hinted that, whatever might have happened to one of them, the fate was undoubtedly deserved . . . She then repeated (aloud) her views on the impertinence of police suggestions — no matter how oblique — that she, of all people, or her actions could possibly be suspect in this case, and folded her hands again on the table, tilting her head so that she could gaze haughtily down her nose at the two detectives opposite.

Stone — Trewley did his best, but his sergeant did better — gazed back.

'I trust,' Miss Jervaulx finally said, in icy tones, 'that I know my duty, Mr. Trewley, Miss Stone. Anyone such as myself, in a position of — of *moral* responsibility (if no longer, alas, *literal*) among the community understands that

278

the forces of law and order should be supported in their struggle against evil doing and crime. However . . . '

A flush darkened the pale patrician cheeks. 'However, if *clearly innocent* persons, Mr. Trewley, are to be *persecuted* with questions as to their whereabouts and actions when the — the courtesy of prompt attention from *certain members* of the constabulary might well have served to stave off this — this lamentable occurrence — '

'Yes, well — I'm sorry, Miss Jarvis!' Trewley ran an unhappy finger round the inside of his collar, and couldn't help letting out a groan. 'I'll be, er, speaking to Sergeant Pleate just as soon as I'm back at the station, Miss Jarvis, believe me.' No need to tell her what the real topic of conversation would be, if only the promise kept her quiet now. 'I'm sorry your complaint maybe wasn't taken as seriously as you'd have liked, but — well, now it's up to me and my sergeant here to try to put things right. We might not be in time to save that poor girl's life, but we can do our damnedest, begging your pardon, to find out who killed her . . . ' Sudden inspiration glowed in the dogged brown eyes. 'And I'd've thought you'd want the same thing, under the circumstance.' He coughed, and shot Stone a warning look. 'There's been some talk,' he said, as Melicent once more primmed her lips, and frowned, 'that you might have been seen in the neighbourhood of the North Lodge earlier today. Now, if you say it wasn't you — '

'Most certainly it was not!'

' — Then stands to reason it was somebody who looked a bit like you — more than a bit, in fact. Enough like to muddle the two of you, being in a raincoat and everything, and only catching a quick glimpse of her . . . ' And might he be forgiven the perjury, he told himself, his collar feeling tighter than ever.

There followed a long, thoughtful pause. Melicent found herself frowning again. She said nothing.

'So you see, Miss Jarvis,' Trewley said, 'if there was anyone who would confirm you'd only left your cottage to post that letter and come straight back, then it'd give us an idea of who else to be looking for . . . '

The flush faded from Melicent's cheeks. She sighed, and lowered her gaze. 'I regret, Mr. Trewley, that I am quite unable to assist you in your enquiries. It is not' — the mental struggle was obvious — 'not that I am *unwilling*, but I very much doubt whether anyone will have noticed my short excursion to the pillar-box — and I have remained within the immediate vicinity of my *house*,' with waspish emphasis on the final word, 'throughout the remainder of the relevant period — and why,' she went on, gaining confidence now that she'd tried her story and it appeared to have succeeded, 'anyone should feel it necessary to spread such rumours about me — or why, should these rumours be in fact true, anyone should wish to impersonate — '

She stopped. 'Oh!' Once more, she paled. 'Oh, how dreadful — that anyone should want to — to frame me . . . '

Her eyes flicked to the pile of library books beside the comfortable easy chair in which she had scorned to sit during the police interrogation. Trewley's gaze followed hers. He blinked. With advancing years had come increasing distance vision — and the titles of Miss Melicent's chosen reading matter contained an unusually high number of references to bodies, blood, and assault-and-battery . . .

'Well,' he said briskly, 'if nobody saw you, nobody saw you, and that's all there is to it — for the moment. Thank you, Miss Jarvis. And unless you can think of anyone around who could pass for you, at a quick glance — you can't? Then never mind.' He rose to his feet, than paused. 'Are you on the telephone out here?'

'No,' said Melicent, blushing again. Her murmurs about *unnecessary electrical intrusion* sounded less convincing than she would have liked when the detectives couldn't help but notice the worn state of her carpets, the faded curtains, and the pulled threads on the upholstery . . .

'But at least,' said Trewley, as the

police car drew away from the West Lodge and headed south, 'we know she's not going to phone ahead and warn her pal Kempshott to come out with one of those oh-my-goodness-how-silly-of-me-to-forget alibis about bumping into her buying stamps or soap powder.' He frowned, rubbing his chin as he brooded.

'Now according to Pleate,' he said at last, 'Kempshott's another queer customer. Probably doesn't have too many friends about the place, so he won't be too keen on blotting his copybook with what's left of the squire's family if she asks him to oblige and he says 'no.' '

Stone giggled. 'Pleate said he thought he *had* said no, sir — remember? When she dragged him into the station, and Pleate wondered if it was a breach-of-promise matter?'

'Umph. Pity he didn't — but there, *I'd* have thought it was a fuss about nothing,' admitted Trewley, 'at the time.'

'Hindsight,' Stone agreed, 'is a wonderful thing, sir.'

They drove on in silence.

The South Lodge, home of Squadron Leader Kempshott, local historian and naturalist, was as neat and well-tended as that inhabited by Miss Melicent Jervaulx — from the outside, anyway. The autumn leaves had been swept from the lawn into piles, set at regular intervals beside the path, as if waiting for Robbie to appear at any minute with two scooping boards and a barrow.

'Good,' said Trewley, opening the gate. 'He's in. You don't leave a job like that half done, in case the wind gets up and you have to start all over again.'

They did not bother to ring the bell at the front, but went at once round to the back of the squadron leader's cottage, both expecting to find him in the region of the garden shed, collecting tools, but — an instance, if they had only stopped to ponder the irony, of Attitudes Analysis in action — Robbie Kempshott was nowhere to be seen.

'He'll have slipped indoors for something.' Trewley was moved to rub the lower portion of his back in silent sympathy. He trod up the two low steps to the kitchen door, and rapped firmly on the sun-faded oak. The reverberations died away with a dull, empty echo.

He knocked again, with more urgency. 'Could've skipped the country by now,' he muttered, scowling at his watch and wondering how much time had been wasted.

'Have a heart, sir. He might just have popped down to the village shop for someth — oh.'

'Oh indeed, detective Sergeant Stone.' Trewley, while always publicly mindful of his sidekick's rank, never used her full title in private unless he thought he'd scored a point. 'Didn't Pleate tell us this Kempshott cadges a lift into Allingham with Miss Jarvis twice a week? They were there yesterday, for heaven's sake. And why would anyone leave their sweeping-up half finished, unless they'd very good reason? I reckon Kempshott's had the gypsy's warning, and hopped it before we had any real reason to think we wanted to talk to him . . . '

'He might,' suggested Stone, warily, 'have heard about the murder and, er, gone along to goggle, sir. Some people do seem to like that sort of thing — and remember, sir, what an odd sort of chap he's supposed to be.'

Trewley scowled. 'He'd go cross-country, so we wouldn't see him — and neither would anyone else girl, if he's one of these woodland types used to hiding in bushes to goggle at birds . . . '

'Or he might,' said Stone, inspired by Trewley's words, 'have seen something this morning while he was bird-watching — something that would give the killer away if he said anything, so he had to be silenced, and he's in the house now, lying on the floor — dead!'

For a long moment, neither said anything more. Trewley groaned. 'You *were* joking, weren't you, Stone? At least — oh, hell. Now you've put the blasted notion in my head, maybe you're right . . . '

'Maybe I am, sir.' Stone gazed around the garden. She knew the superintendent was as keen to look inside the South Lodge as she was. 'Hey — look, sir! Down at the bottom!'

'What? Where?'

Trewley scowled into the distance, where autumn shadows darkened the damp earth at the base of a thick, tall hedge. 'I can't see anything . . .'

'I,' said Stone, with mischief in her voice, 'can see they're awfully lax about security in these parts, sir. Why, I just put my hand on the lock, and the back door opened!' Innocent eyes met his, diverting suspicion from the penknife she was slipping back in her pocket as she thanked her lucky stars she'd lost her propelling pencil some time ago and had changed to the sort which needed sharpening. 'Anyone would say it was positively our duty to investigate this, sir. After all, you said yourself that people don't wander off leaving gardening jobs half done without a very good reason. If the chief constable himself could see the place now, he'd agree we had every right to go in and check things out.'

'If the chief constable could see this place now,' Trewley corrected his sergeant, following her across the threshold of Squadron Leader Kempshott's kitchen, 'he'd run us in for aggravated burglary, my girl. Still,' as she laughed and headed for the hall, 'it's in a good cause, I daresay. The general public's always moaning on at us to improve our crime prevention techniques . . . '

'Quite right, sir. Which is what we're doing, I'd have said — no question.' Stone peered into what was obviously the dining room, while Trewley, muttering, checked the back parlour. They found nothing, and nobody.

At the foot of the stairs, they glanced at each other. Stone shrugged. 'I will if you will, sir. No bloodstains on the banisters, you notice . . . '

They ascended the stairs in single file, walking to one side of the narrow central drugget, just in case. Footprints — or at least depressions — last longer on carpet than many criminals realise. They came first to the bathroom, where they found no trace of anything untoward. They then checked what was clearly Kempshott's study, with its desk, its typewriter under a trim canvas cover, and its RAF-blue two-drawer filing cabinet with models of

World War II fighter aircraft on top. A large bookcase stood against one wall, its shelves crammed with volumes on British bird-life, wild flowers, field mammals, and similar interests of the semiprofessional naturalist, together with assorted tomes on church architecture, medieval farming practices, and the deciphering of Latin manuscripts.

'I always thought,' remarked Stone, gazing round at the unnaturally neat room, 'that people who wrote for a living — even for a hobby — lived in a permanent state of paperwork run riot. Apart from the fact that he obviously hasn't dusted for a day or two, I don't know when I last saw anybody's workplace look so tidy. Forces training, I suppose.'

'Umph.' Trewley, also a member of a national force, shifted irritably as he recalled the state of his — and his sergeant's — in and out trays. 'Perhaps he's just finished a book and is having a holiday,' he suggested. 'Let's get on with it, girl, now we're here — my conscience is starting to bother me.'

They reached the main bedroom. It was exactly what anyone would have expected of an unmarried old-age pensioner of the male sex: once again neat and tidy, though this time — perhaps because in his sleeping quarters he felt better able to relax — not fussily so. A light sprinkling of dust on windowsill and bookshelf (more birds, flowers, mammals, and matters historical) showed that here the squadron leader was no houseproud fanatic. The tallboy in one corner supported a stern, square mahogany mirror, a hairbrush and comb (not matching), and a handful of small change. There were cushions on the easy chair in the opposite corner, arranged so that the sitter could look out into the garden.

'That's an enormous wardrobe, sir.' Stone frowned up at the dark curlicued ornamentation round the top; it reached almost to the ceiling. She stood on tiptoe. 'Saves dusting your suitcases to keep them up there, I suppose, rather than under your bed . . . '

Darting back to peer under the prim

regulation flounce which marched around the bed, she muttered: 'And let's hope he's not weltering in gore on the carpet . . . '

She stood upright again. 'He isn't.' Once more, her eyes drifted to the wardrobe. 'Mind you, I'd say there's more room for — storage — in there than under here, wouldn't you, sir?'

Trewley sighed. He had chosen to ignore her more frivolous gyrations, and was busily examining the top row of books in the case near the window. In the act of turning round to glare at her, he paused. 'He's taken something with him, wherever he's gone.' He peered down at the window sill. 'What d'you make of this?'

Stone abandoned the notion of corpses in the closet, and hurried across to stare down at a dust-free mark about seven inches by three, slightly curved along its length. 'Binoculars?' she hazarded, nodding towards the books. 'I bet he spends hours up here looking for lesser spotted green warblers, or whatever. Probably that's why he's hopped it now, sir — he'll have heard the mating call of the crested artichoke, and gone chasing after it to add it to his diary.'

'Umph.' Trewley scowled, but had to admit she could be right. 'We'll soon find out — if he's gone bird-watching, he'll have taken an anorak with him, at least — and you know you can't wait to see what's in there, can you? Well, since I'm stuck with you for the duration, it seems, I may as well try to keep you happy . . .'

He strode across the room, and opened the wardrobe door. 'Good God!'

Stone rushed to stand beside him. 'My goodness,' she breathed at last. 'Oh, my goodness . . .'

After a further awestruck silence: 'And what a place to keep it — in with all his suits,' marvelled Trewley.

'What *do* you suppose he does with it, sir?' Stone did her best to turn an innocent, enquiring eye upon her superior, who spluttered and turned purple, then muttered that, for himself, he couldn't imagine; and as for her, she shouldn't even try.

'I don't know,' said Stone, 'that I've ever seen one of those before, sir. Have you?'

'Certainly not!' Trewley, recovering himself, glared at his grinning sergeant. Then he chuckled. 'Come to think of it, though, there were a few pictures in those arty mags we did that chap for last year — the perverting public morals one, remember?'

'The nudity-is-natural man from the massage parlour.' Stone nodded cheerfully. 'Oh, yes!'

'*That's* not natural, for heaven's sake.' Trewley jerked an indignant head towards the wardrobe. 'Talk about perverted — Pleate *said* he was an odd sort of bod, didn't he?'

Stone was studying the cardboard box in which the item in question had obviously been packed. 'Bet anything you like this came in a plain brown wrapper, sir — imagine what the postman would have said if he'd seen the small print!' She began to read aloud. '*Love Ewe — the joys and pleasures of your woollicst fantasies in the peace and quiet of your own home. No noise, no mess, no risk of —* '

'Stone, for goodness' sake!' Trewley had turned purple again. 'You ought to be ashamed of yourself!'

He looked really upset by her lack of embarrassment, and she hastened to console him with the reminder that, as a former medical student, there wasn't much she hadn't heard, and what hadn't been heard at college had certainly been brought quickly to her notice once she'd joined the police. The superintendent wiped his forehead with a large handkerchief, and mumbled that he didn't know what the younger generation was coming to, and if any of his daughters —

'Sorry, sir.' Stone, remembering his blood pressure, stopped laughing, and snapped the wardrobe door shut. Without another word, she led the babbling Trewley out of Squadron Leader Kempshott's bedroom, down the stairs, through the kitchen, and out of the back door to safety.

18

'How about that talk we promised ourselves with John Smith, sir?' she suggested, when they were once more sitting in the police car, and Trewley's breathing had returned to normal. 'His cottage — that is, with apologies to Miss Jervaulx, his house — can't be more than a few minutes' drive from here. Even if we decide in the end that the person who killed Alpha *is* one of the Analysis lot, oughtn't we to make sure we can eliminate the — the local suspects, sir? After all, they're the ones likely to have been most . . . disturbed by the appearance of the Phoenixes on their doorsteps. Just look at — Miss Jervaulx,' she hastily amended, as Trewley began to turn purple again. A lifetime's experience of Allshire, even before discovering the private fantasies of Squadron Leader Kempshott, had taught him that *disturbance* could manifest itself in many unorthodox ways . . .

Without waiting for his answer, Stone started the car, and headed eastwards. There was a pregnant pause.

'Now Smith's *another* funny customer,' said Trewley at last. 'The queer way he was talking when we saw him earlier — they're altogether an odd lot around here, for my money. Trying to bamboozle us with fancy speeches — sometimes,' he burst out, 'I'd like to work in the city, with enough men and to spare for keeping an eye on likely lunatics — sorry, girl,' as Stone cleared her throat, very loudly. 'I mean with enough *officers*, dammit. All right?'

'Right, sir.' She hid a smile; now he was almost back to his old self. 'But I do see your point — we simply haven't the resources to carry out investigations the way the big boys do, with incident rooms and dozens of telephone lines and experts by the score hovering in the background. In fact, given the usual size of our — your — operation, sir, I should say the clear-up rate in this corner of Allshire's amazingly high — but then,' with a smile, 'you've picked an amazing team, sir.'

'Umph. Don't get cocky with me, girl — we haven't sorted this one yet, not by a long chalk we haven't. I'm still not ruling out Sir Lionel Tobias, remember . . .'

He fiddled with the car radio. 'We'll just put in that request for a check on his family background,' he muttered. 'Should never have let myself get carried away with all the talk of a grey Morris — blast!'

'Press the switch to the *left*, sir,' Stone told him, as she told him almost every time. 'You could ask them if the result of the postmortem's through yet, as well.'

'Teach your grandmother,' he growled, and Stone kept her eyes firmly on the road ahead as her superior hurled himself for the umpteenth time into single combat with the intricacies of electronic communication.

For the second time that day, the car pulled up outside the East — the current Main — Lodge of Campions Crest. The low hedge, which had been half-clipped, half-ragged on the previous occasion, was now squared-off and regular along its entire length. Of the leather-waistcoated man who had been clipping it, and of the clippings, there was no sign.

'A cup of tea,' suggested Stone, 'after finishing a job well done — that's probably where he is, sir.'

'Don't talk to me about food,' snarled Trewley. Stone thought this a little unjust, as she hadn't mentioned it. She was, however, prepared to excuse her superior on the grounds that the voice at the other end of the car radio (once Trewley had eventually succeeded in establishing contact) had been in one of its temperamental moods. Didn't anyone realise how busy the Voice was? Hadn't anyone noticed it was Saturday afternoon? Just how many people, apart from the Voice, did the superintendent think could be whistled up with one press of a button to produce information at the drop of a helmet? Much though the Voice wished to help Mr. Trewley (which didn't, to Mr. Trewley's irritable ears, sound like very much at all), it wasn't — he ought to know by now — a computer. It could only tell him what the real computer had found out, and the finding out took time. He'd have to wait. The same way he'd have to wait for Dr. Watson to report the results of his postmortem . . .

'One day,' threatened Trewley, banging down the handset in a way which explained why the radio was always in for repair, 'one day, I'll — '

'Let's go and find Smith, shall we, sir?' Stone hopped out of the car before his blood pressure became a problem, and, after a grumbling few moments, Trewley followed suit. Together, the two made their way up the path of the East Lodge, and arrived at the brown front door.

Trewley rapped twice with the knocker, then spotted the bell and, for good measure, rang it before Stone could hint that he hadn't given Mr. Smith much time to respond. There was a long pause.

Trewley yanked on the bellpull. 'Either the blighter's deaf — which I can't say I noticed when we talked to him before — or *he's* gone off somewhere, too.

He's an intelligent bloke — tutors to the gentry aren't idiots — you think he'd have guessed we'd want to talk to him again. Why couldn't he have the sense to stay put for five minutes?' Habeas corpus and the Civil Liberties movement might preclude the wholesale rounding-up of suspects for questioning at the convenience of the constabulary, but sometimes Trewley considered this a great disadvantage.

He scowled, and sighed gustily. Beside him, Stone sniffed. He glared at her. 'What's wrong with you, girl?' The Voice had been bad enough. If Stone, too, was going to go temperamental on him . . .

'Smoke, sir.' She sniffed again. 'Woodsmoke — coming from somewhere round the back, I'd say. What's the betting Mr. Smith's burning the leftovers from his hedge?'

Once more forgetting formality, the two detectives made for the rear of the house, where, as Stone had guessed, they found John Smith, shirt-sleeved and sweating, tending a giant metal-mesh incinerator, humming as he worked.

He looked up at the unexpected reappearance of Trewley and Stone, and nodded a greeting, though he did not stop his stoking until the pair were almost upon him. 'Good day to you both again,' he said, and leaned on his shovel in a manner relaxed and welcoming.

Trewley's bulldog jaw jutted forward. Was the man acting too innocent to be true? 'Mr. Smith, we'd be glad of a chat with you. As soon as possible,' he added, as Mr. Smith glanced at his bonfire, and at the mound of autumnal litter still waiting to be added.

'This sounds,' said Mr. Smith, 'regrettably official, Mr. Trewley. Do I take it that there was indeed a body in the other lodge?'

'Yes, you do.' Trewley scowled. 'There was.'

Mr. Smith, exercising the privilege of the free man in a democracy, scooped up another shovelful of twigs and scattered them in a careful layer on top of the incinerator. He then jabbed his shovel, blade down, into the earth, brushed his hands free of cinders and dirt, and began walking back to the house.

'One of the Phoenixes, I assume,' he remarked over his shoulder to the constabulary caravan behind him.

'A girl calling herself — Alpha,' Trewley managed to inform him, with only minimal hesitation. He supposed you could get used to anything, given enough time.

'Alpha? Dear me.' Mr. Smith's intonation was less one of a shocked man than of a man perhaps not unsurprised by what he had just heard. 'This is a bad business, Superintendent. I knew her, you know — but of course you do. Did I not tell you this myself, a mere matter of hours ago?'

'Yes, sir, you did.' Trewley watched as Mr. Smith applied thoughtful boots to the wicked-looking scraper beside his back door. An artful, wordsy, tricky sort of a blighter . . . and one who knew — or Trewley was very much mistaken — more than he'd so far let on about this whole affair. But he wasn't the sort you could bully or nag . . .

It did not seem to take Mr. Smith long

to resolve whatever dilemma had been troubling him. 'Come in,' he invited, and the detectives followed him into the kitchen.

'A cup of tea, perhaps? Or perhaps not,' as Trewley's bulldog glare spoke volumes. 'Let us . . . chat, Superintendent, since such was your purpose in coming here. You will excuse me, however, if I pour myself a warming glass?'

As Stone settled herself and her notebook at the table, and Trewley dragged out a chair for himself, Mr. Smith went to a cupboard and brought out a bottle half filled with a clear, dark, plum-coloured liquid. The label about its middle was handwritten, and as Mr. Smith fetched himself a glass, Trewley was able to read it.

'Sloe gin? Haven't had any of that for years. Made it yourself, did you?'

'You must allow me,' said Mr. Smith, pouring deep purple into imitation crystal, 'to present you with a small bottle of last year's vintage before you leave — I would not, naturally, offer you alcoholic refreshment when you are on duty, proud though I may be of my accomplishments — for I did, indeed, make it myself from the pick of the crop. I know where the finest blackthorn bushes grow, and I use nothing but the highest quality molasses sugar, with a few drops of almond essence dissolved in the gin in which the fruit is steeped.' He corked up the bottle, collected his glass, and joined the other two at the table. He held up his trophy.

'What could be better than this?'

'Knowing who killed Alpha,' said Trewley, without hesitation. Mr. Smith sighed, and sipped his sloe gin.

He stared into the depths of the glass as he cradled it in his hands, resting them on the table, watching the light play on the smooth ripples from his breath. Finally he said: 'My first encounter with the Phoenixes came as I walked the hedgerows, estimating the likely size of this year's crop. The terms of my tenancy give me the freedom to wander at will over the estate, no matter under whose ownership the manor is held: the same, of course, cannot be said of our young squatters. But they seem on the whole an amiable, harmless crowd — the one called Ocean, who was the first to speak to me, is an interesting character — perhaps the most genuine, in my opinion.'

'Think they're a lot of phonies, do you?' asked Trewley, as Mr. Smith paused, and sipped again.

He permitted himself a world-weary smile. 'I think them innocent and idealistic juveniles indulging in some absurd charade to revenge themselves on an adult world which, by their own account, has treated them none too kindly — and which, on their own evidence, they are not yet ready to join. But it is to be supposed they will manage well enough when they do eventually grow up, when they will be only too thankful they adopted those foolish names to fit in with their fantastic, and impossible, philosophy — only too impossible, poor things. As they have found out . . . '

There were shadows now in his eyes. 'Alpha's death, no doubt, will have set them wondering whether their touching, albeit illogical, beliefs in Fate and

Destiny and Doing Harm to None have perhaps been disagreeably misplaced, now that their noble attempts at mutually rehabilitating one another from the errors of their past lives have been revealed as little more than a waste of time . . . '

Trewley shot him a look from beneath a brow corrugated with much thought. He was more than ever convinced that Mr. Smith was working his way round to spilling the beans — and that those beans would be well worth catching as they fell. 'Time's never wasted,' he said, 'if it helps people to grow up while it's passing. Alpha's might be the first death these youngsters have ever been close to — a rite of passage, isn't that the fancy name for it? Granted, murder's a bit of a drastic measure, but it might just shake some sense into the rest of 'em.'

'Those,' returned Mr. Smith, 'who have sense enough to be used as a foundation, perhaps. Have you heard about Star, for example? They told me her . . . silliness, using the word with its original meaning, results from a drug overdose, and a brain starved, one assumes, of oxygen.' He shook his head, as if pondering the recent overdose and death of young Joscelin Jervaulx, lately under his own care; then he looked up with a faint smile.

'One has to say, however, that it is very much to their credit that they care for her as they do, though little more than children themselves. We must suppose that part, at least, of their muddled ideology has a sound basis, in their concept of the sanctity of all life — at whatever level. A concept,' he added in a dry tone, 'to which not all children are capable of subscribing. Only consider those in *A High Wind in Jamaica* or *Lord of the Flies* — salutary warnings indeed for adults not to trust to appearances where the younger generation is concerned.'

Trewley, father of three, frowned. He hadn't read either of the books in question, but he was beginning to get the picture. 'You're saying — saying Star may not be quite the innocent she seems? She's devoted to the baby, of course, and to the leader chap, Apollo. And he was — Alpha's friend in the first place, if he told us the truth . . .'

'Apollo,' said Mr. Smith serenely, 'now prefers sleeping with Star to sleeping with Alpha — or with Breeze — while Flower has a distinct preference for Ocean, who has — had — less than absolutely comfortable feelings towards Alpha — '

'Good God!' Trewley couldn't help it. 'That lot just upped and told you all this? It's — it's indecent! It's — it's shameless!' And the bloodhound eyes bulged with horror in a slowly purpling face.

Stone looked anxious, but Mr. Smith, carried away by his narration, simply clicked his tongue. 'I told you before, Mr. Trewley, that they enjoy trying to shock me. By the manner of their trying, of course, they reveal rather more about their true selves than perhaps they would like, given that they are, after all, running away from any acceptance of reality . . . Sirius, now.' He favoured Trewley with a look too blank not to have a world of knowledge concealed behind it. 'Sirius is a newcomer to the commune.

308

He sleeps with none of the girls, making excuses into which the others are too respectful of his right to privacy to pry: the sanctity of life, of the soul, of the self, you understand. But when the young women are as physically attractive as are these three — and when the attractions are so freely offered — one wonders, Mr. Trewley, at his *real* reasons for refusing — and for joining the commune in the first place.'

'He's a twitchy sort of blighter,' said Trewley, as Mr. Smith appeared, for the moment, to have come to a halt. 'We couldn't help noticing he didn't look particularly healthy, compared to the others.' He sighed, reluctant to admit that any aspect of the unorthodox Phoenix lifestyle might be of benefit, but he was an honest man. 'All the fresh air, I suppose — not to mention living on grass, or whatever they do,' he added viciously. That impending diet was always in the back of his mind.

Mr. Smith nodded slowly. 'One cannot help but wonder at the possibility that it is not so much he who shuns the young women as they who shun him. Subconsciously, no doubt, but perhaps — living by their instincts as they claim to do — they have sensed something a little . . . '

He paused. Trewley said; 'You mean drugs? We've wondered about that, too.' He did not mention that a computer check — as yet unanswered by the infuriating headquarters Voice — had been run on Stephen Greece aka Sirius. 'You think he might have been rumbled by Alpha, and he had to keep her quiet?'

'If you are thinking,' said Mr. Smith, 'of moral indignation of Alpha's part, I have to tell you that you may be . . . mistaken in her character, Mr. Trewley. I would suggest that his reason for silencing her — if, indeed, he did — would be more in the nature of dispensing with a . . . a blackmailer.' He brought out the final word with some difficulty, paused, and took a large gulp of his remaining sloe gin.

Stone's ears pricked, and Trewley's eyes gleamed: now it was coming! 'You've got some special reason for thinking she could have been blackmailing him?'

Mr. Smith, after a still longer pause, sighed, and seemed to come to some conclusion. 'I have debated with myself the wisdom of telling you — the idea of power being exercised by one over another for some petty purpose is repugnant to me, and I have always supposed that my sympathies, in a manner of speaking, would lie more with the blackmailed than with the blackmailer . . . but in this particular case . . .

'Yesterday evening, Mr. Trewley, I went walking in the woods — a constitutional, nothing more. I often walk in the woods; I move quietly. I heard someone else coming in my direction . . . It was not Alpha, Mr. Trewley. It was a young man, a stranger. I was, I regret to say, curious. On a whim, I followed him — it amused me to see how close I could come to him without his noticing me.

'He did not notice me — and neither did Alpha, when they met. She had obviously been waiting for him . . . She called him Andrew. He called her Angela — ah,' as Trewley nodded, 'I see that you know something of this. In which case —'

'We'd still like to hear your side of it, Mr. Smith.'

John Smith hesitated again. 'Of course. Alpha was very — harsh towards the young man. She blamed him for some incident in their mutual past — there was wild talk of a baby, an abortion, and demands that he should somehow atone by permitting her to stay, with her friends, in the lodge. She was almost gloating in the ease of her ascendancy over the unfortunate Andrew — who, I may add, fled the scene before she appeared to have finished with him. I heard him crashing through the undergrowth near me as I was walking away. She was calling after him, Mr. Trewley. She was alive and well when he left her . . .'

'She wasn't killed until today, Mr. Smith, remember?'

'I remember. And I am not surprised — and I would not wish you to think that, in telling you this, I pointed the finger of suspicion at the wretched Andrew, Mr. Trewley. The exercise was merely to show you that Alpha was perhaps more deserving of . . . that others might have wished to . . .

'Andrew and Alpha and I,' he said, 'were not alone in the woods last night. I could hear leaves rustling, and twigs breaking. Somebody else was there as well — and, whoever it was, he stood and listened to every word that Alpha said.'

19

'Of course, sir,' said Stone, 'it may have nothing at all to do with the murder.' Having realised there was little, if anything, else that Mr. Smith felt they should know, she and Trewley were walking from the East Lodge back to their car. 'Coincidence,' she went on. 'A red herring — you know what this business can be like. Or perhaps it was our Peeping Tom friend — or,' choking slightly, 'the Squadron Leader looking for one of his lost sheep — sorry, sir.'

Trewley managed to stop spluttering, and snapped: 'Coincidence be damned! I had my doubts about Smith all along — I should've got back to him sooner. I thought he was acting a bit strange when we got here — didn't I tell you? Clipping hedges! Bonfires! Covering something up's more the way of it.'

Stone was unlocking the driver's door. 'But covering up what, exactly? That

Alpha had — an opportunist streak in her? I should say that's true of most people, to be realistic about it. I wouldn't have thought — '

'Blackmail, girl, that's what it was. Don't try to put a fancy name on it and make it sound less unpleasant than it was. All those people wandering about in the dark — everyone on that crazy Course saying they were up at the manor being bamboozled together, when half of 'em didn't know the other half and nobody would have noticed one missing — how long,' he demanded, 'did it take for 'em to spot Ryan wasn't there? When he's meant to have been in charge of the whole caboodle, and goes off into the woods to be blackmailed by his sister . . . So just how many people does that leave who could have overheard 'em if they'd wanted?'

'Assuming,' Stone said, 'that Smith was telling the — ' There came an electronic pop, accompanied by a lasting hiss. The radio had crackled into life, and was calling for Superintendent Trewley to reply, if he was able.

315

Trewley grabbed the handset, hesitated, and thrust it in Stone's direction. 'Go on, girl. Show me how the younger generation copes with today's technology.'

She grinned, pushed the button, and assured the Voice that she and the superintendent were all ears. The Voice replied, rather huffily, that this was all very well, but did she wish to take notes of what it was about to impart?

The Allingham force was accustomed to the Voice and its moods. 'I'll borrow your notes,' said Stone cheerfully, 'if I ever decide to write my memoirs in detail. I'm sure the condensed version will do fine, for now.'

'If you say so.' The Voice cleared its throat, and began to speak slowly, giving the simple sergeant time to do joined-up writing if she chose.

'Results of Dr. Watson's postmortem: definitely not a sexual assault. Subject rendered unconscious from a blow to the head before application of the — the gagging medium.' The Voice sounded greatly disapproving of this euphemism.

'Evidence,' it continued grimly, 'of

316

past drug abuse, but indications that subject had kicked the habit — no fresh needle marks, no traces in the system, no blisters or burns on the skin. No signs of terminal illness — subject appears to have been in generally good condition.'

Trewley muttered something about people practising what they preached, for once, but Stone didn't catch every word as the Voice continued its recital.

'Evidence of internal surgery, possibly a botched abortion, as well as clear signs that she had given birth to at least one child — '

Sensation in the car, ignored — perhaps not even heard — by the prim Voice at Allingham's control centre. 'Subject ate her last meal about four hours before she died — a wholefood, macrobiotic diet: bread, vegetables, fruit.' This, the Voice implied, was more like it. 'No signs of artificial preservatives, no alcohol — '

'So I should ruddy well hope,' cried the superintendent, 'at breakfast!'

'Quite so, sir,' said the Voice, for once almost approving. 'That's all,' it added, and was about to sign off when

Stone slipped in a question about the progress of the Tobias enquiries. The Voice, nettled, said that it had already advised the sergeant of *all* information it had been asked to pass on. If she hadn't listened properly, that was hardly something for which the Voice should be blamed . . .

Stone apologised profusely, told the Voice she and the superintendent looked forward to its next bulletin with considerable interest, and signed off half a second after the Voice had pulled the plug at the Allingham end.

There was a brooding silence in the car before Stone, with a sigh, broke it. 'Not a sex crime, then — and maybe not drugs, either. Could there be something in the blackmail theory, after all? In which case, sir, Andrew Ryan *is* our likeliest suspect so far — at least he has a motive, of sorts, although . . . ' She shuddered. 'It's all very well thinking it could be symbolic, but that doesn't make it any the less revolting . . . '

'Whoever it is, he's mad,' said Trewley. 'To have killed her that way, he's got to be — or else he's heard there's a Peeping Tom in the area, and hoped we'd think it was him gone over the top at last — with these loonies, you're never sure which way they're going to jump. The only thing you can be sure of is that being barmy makes them cunning . . . '

Another brooding silence. Trewley coughed. 'An abortion *and* a live birth. How the devil can he tell that?'

'Scar tissue,' explained Stone airily, 'from the abortion — which means that probably came after the baby — and the baby's easy to recognise, sir, from alterations in the mother's body. Her pelvis widens and tilts; the skin of her stomach shows stretch marks; her breasts — sorry, sir,' as Trewley spluttered at her side. 'But you *did* ask.'

He snarled briefly about blasted college show-offs, then was forced to admit that he had. A sergeant can hardly deny information when her superintendent requests it, but he can think twice about asking her again . . .

'Let's get back to the commune,' he said. 'Those conference lunatics at the hall won't get far with Benson and Hedges keeping an eye on 'em, and I'd like to talk to Sirius. Andrew Ryan could well be one of a whole list of folk his sister played her little blackmail games with — that whole blasted gaggle of hippies, from what they say, were wandering about in the moonlight last night. Suppose we take it the conference lot, being from the town, wouldn't be so keen on communing with nature — '

'Excepting Sir Lionel,' Stone reminded him. 'All that Boy Scout camping, remember?'

'I grant you Tobias — I hadn't forgotten him — but . . . ' He scowled at the radio receiver, which remained stubbornly silent. 'But for now I'm more bothered with the hippies, blast 'em. Any one of the blighters could've overheard their pal sounding off at Ryan in the wood last night, and worked out where he came from, and decided he'd make a lovely suspect for us once they'd killed her the way they'd been wanting to do for — well, for whatever reason. They could probably tell just from listening to him with her that he'd never last five minutes under questioning.'

'You know, sir, thinking of Andrew Ryan, I rather fancy Simeon Gotobed,' announced Stone. This considerably startled the superintendent, until her real meaning dawned on him. He sighed with relief as she went on: 'It was Gotobed who found the body, after all — and he wears a suit, of sorts. Remember what Flower said about the man in the suit who turned up at the lodge a few days ago, saying he was lost? Suppose it was Gotobed, being an advance party, spying out the land. If he's as much of an opportunist as he seems, he could have guessed there'd be an unprotected female or two around the place every day . . . '

She sighed. 'Except, if he's that much of an opportunist, we can bet he'll have set up a dozen witnesses to the time he left London. Time . . . It'll give me nightmares, sir, I know, but I simply have to make some bread this evening and time how long the yeast takes to rise enough to — well, to do what it has to — though somehow I don't think I'll be baking it after I've found out, sir.'

'Don't blame you.' Trewley rubbed his chin, and stared at the North Lodge, outside which the car had just arrived. 'Shouldn't think *they'll* eat another slice in their lives, once they find out just what happened to their friend. She may turn out to've been a nasty piece of work in some respects, but nobody deserves to die like that.'

Stone said nothing as she locked the car door. There was no longer any sign of the vehicles belonging to the small forensic team, who must have finished their work and left. Together, she and Trewley walked towards the lodge gate.

'Thinking of Gotobed, though,' said the superintendent, 'you could have a point — maybe. If we could find out what Alpha's reason was for asking Breeze to swap duty days with her, it might get us somewhere — or it might make everything a hundred times more confused,' he added, knocking glumly on the front door, and trying the handle without waiting for an answer.

The door opened. 'Security!' Trewley

rolled his eyes. 'First they bolt it all the time in case of bailiffs, then — oh, what's the use?'

They stepped inside. At the end of the hall, they could see the closed kitchen door. They were about to head in that direction when Apollo emerged from the sitting room, where most of the interviews had taken place.

'Greetings,' he said, in a soft voice. 'We guessed you would return. Is there — is there any news? Your colleagues left some while ago, but they told us nothing.'

'We're getting on,' Trewley said, noncommittal. 'We've some more questions for you, though — starting with — with — S-s-siri-achoo! Achoo!'

A thin wail came from upstairs as the second sneeze made the banisters thrum. Apollo's face briefly showed irritation, before this was banished in favour of his usual kindly smile, and he put a finger to his lips.

'Baldur, I fear, is restless — Flower and Ocean are caring for him, while Breeze looks after Star. The . . . loss of Alpha has finally . . . she had to be told, and the shock was great. The free fresh air will do its healing work — '

'Fresh air? They're outside?'

Apollo seemed surprised, and a little anxious, at Trewley's outburst, which produced another, louder wail from the invisible Baldur. 'They went for a walk,' he hissed hurriedly, beckoning the two detectives along the hall. 'Come in here, where Sirius and I have made a fire — for comfort,' he added, in his normal rich tones, 'and for companionship, which you are welcome to share with us.'

'I'd've thought,' Trewley told him, 'you'd have done better to share 'em with those two girls you've let go wandering off by themselves. How long ago, for the Lord's sake? And do you know where they went? Hasn't it occurred to you young idiots,' as Apollo and Sirius — who had risen from a cushion before the fireplace to nod a silent greeting — 'you may have let them walk right into the arms of a killer?

'Or maybe not,' he added, before either of the young men could say anything. He glared at Sirius. 'Suppose our killer's you, my lad. They'd be safe enough then, wouldn't they, out of this house?'

'If I were — ' began Sirius, but was interrupted by an indignant Apollo, asking how the superintendent could dream of saying such a thing, even as a joke.

'No joke,' Trewley said. He glared at Sirius again. 'They don't know much about you, do they, these youngsters you've taken up within?'

'We don't need — ' protested Apollo, but Trewley glared him down.

'Let him speak for himself, for a change — always assuming he's got anything to say. He's a pretty poor specimen, isn't he? Compared to the rest of you fresh-air fiends — he fidgets all the time, can't string two words together — ah,' as something like a grin flashed across the pale face of Sirius, and his eyes momentarily gleamed. 'Said something to amuse you, have I? Well now, let's see what you can say to make *me* happy, shall we? How about the truth of who you are and where you came from — and what you're doing here?'

'He has joined us to start a new life,' cried Apollo, forgetting, in his excitement, to speak quietly. Above his head, the sound of Baldur's crying could again be heard.

'What better reason — ?'

'No!' Though Apollo had lowered his voice again, Trewley saw no reason to bother: his triple experience of fatherhood had proved to him that babies, once they were in a wide awake mood as Baldur seemed to be, were more than willing to carry on crying for hours, no matter how many attempts were made to placate them. 'We don't need the sermon from you, thanks all the same. It's your friend here I want to listen to. Now. Right?'

Something in his eyes, and the set of his bulldog chin, spoke to Sirius in a way which Stone's previous questioning had not achieved. The young man looked at the superintendent for a long moment, then shrugged.

His mouth twisted in a rueful grin. 'I'll come clean,' he said, 'if you insist. But' — with a sideways look at Apollo, and a grimace — 'this is one of the times I really need my personal space, man. Would you mind splitting, to leave me with the fuzz for a few minutes?'

'Yes,' Trewley growled, 'just — just *split*, will you? But stay in the house, for heaven's sake. He,' jerking his head in the direction of Sirius, 'might need saving from police brutality, if my sergeant here happens to beat him up. You'll need to be on the spot to come rushing to the rescue, won't you?'

Apollo forced a smile, murmured of another joke, and gazed long and hard at Sirius. He then nodded slowly, turned, and without another word walked out of the room, taking care to close the door as he went.

'Right,' said Trewley. 'Your full name, first.'

'I have already informed the sergeant.'

'So now you can inform me. Just check what he says now against what he said before, will you, Sergeant? I'll throw that book at the blighter harder than he could ever imagine if he doesn't come up with the same story twice running.'

Stone had already found the page in her notebook, and, as Sirius announced that his given name was Stephen Harold Greene, she confirmed to Trewley that this was what she'd been told before.

'Right, Mr. Greene. I want the truth. So talk.' It was a command, not an invitation.

Sirius grinned, and nodded in Stone's direction, holding out his hand. 'I'd rather write,' he said. 'And if you'd only waited a couple of weeks, you could have read as much of the,er, whole *truth* as you wanted, at your leisure, over your breakfast . . . '

Trewley's gloomy bloodhound face grew still more gloomy as realisation dawned. 'A journalist,' he groaned, while Sirius, smirking, watched Stone's pencil shorthand its way swiftly down the page, then stumble as the point snapped. 'A blasted bloody journalist!' lamented Trewley, as the sergeant fished out her penknife and set to work.

Stephen Greene looked hurt. 'I've my living to earn the same as you, Superintendent — except that it's not quite the same, because I'm freelance. One of my contacts suggested a feature on the Sixties Revival. New-Age Hippies, Ring Out Again Wild Bells, the Flowers Bloom Once More — you know the sort of thing, I've no doubt. I'm not one to turn down an assignment, believe me — or the chance of my byline on a good story.'

Trewley shuddered. He believed the young journalist, only too well. He could see banner headlines in Stephens's eyes as he gloated over the good fortune which had landed him in the middle of a murder case before it had happened, and he shuddered again.

'We did some research,' continued Stephen, 'and came up with your local equinox jamboree — '

'Don't even mention that word!' cried Trewley, his blood curdling at the very thought of the traffic problems and irritated citizens that were Alingham's annual cross.

'Equinox be damned — '

'I couldn't agree more, Mr. Trewley. Having gone to all the trouble of infiltrating the Phoenixes to acquire what I thought would be the perfect background, you can imagine how I felt when they told me they didn't attend festivals of any kind. They don't even,' he added mischievously, 'go in for orgies — not that my editor would've approved of my joining in if they had, but the temptation didn't arise — and if it had, I would have done my best to resist it.'

A lesser man than the superintendent would have snarled something along the lines of 'Tell that to the Marines' or 'Oh, yeah?' Trewley simply looked, and waited.

Stephen Greene coughed. 'Yes, well. Anyway, I thought I'd better try to salvage something from the wreckage of my plans by staying on just in case the Phoenixes changed their minds, or in case anyone who's gone to the festival joined them afterwards, and I could pick their brains. Someone with a good story about wanting to dry out among the peaceful people — these kids mean it, you know, when they say they don't hold with drugs. They're clean, Superintendent. It wasn't one of them killed the girl under the influence — and I can assure you it wasn't me.'

20

Trewley watched the white fingers twisting together, and uttered a sudden bark of laughter. 'Yes, I think I believe you, Greene — about this lot being clean as whistles — because I've been saying to my sergeant all along you looked like a bloke suffering from withdrawal symptoms — and that's just what you are!'

He laughed again, a bulldog roar which drew another wail from Baldur. 'Oh, you must've had a rough time of it, these past weeks. No booze, no fags — you reporters don't exactly live a healthy life, do you?'

Stephen grinned, then adopted a lofty expression. 'One has to suffer for one's art,' he said, then became quickly serious. 'I was forgetting. Sorry. This isn't art, is it? This is real life — or, rather, real death. And though I'd be the first to write an Inefficient Police exposé if you simply took my word for it without checking, well, you know you *will* be able to check my story, once I give you the editor's name. To be honest, I'm surprised you didn't rumble me earlier, after I'd been interviewed by the good sergeant over there.'

Trewley winced. He recalled, only too well, the contumacious nature of the headquarters Voice. Stone hid a rueful smile.

'You look like a man who's lost his Suspect Number One, Superintendent,' Stephen said. 'I'm flattered — but I'm not that important, really, although anything I can do to help, I will — as far as I'm able.' He paused. 'Of course, it isn't that easy to make helpful suggestions, no matter how much you'd like to, when you're not in full possession of the facts . . . '

Trewley sat up. The journalist — with his sandalled feet, scruffy hair, straggly beard and jeans — did his best to look professional.

'You've told us all along,' he said, 'that Alpha was dead — suffocated, you said — but I couldn't fail to notice that you didn't go into details. The routine guff about not identifying her formally until the next-of-kin have been informed won't wash with me, Mr. Trewley, even if it's kept the others quiet. There was something . . . peculiar about the way that girl died, wasn't there? Something . . . weird!'

The superintendent looked more like a bulldog than he'd done for years, but the imitation failed to quench Stephen Greene. 'Weird. Wyrd. Fate. Alpha was fated to die when and how and where she did. That's what the Phoenixes think, and that's why they're able to be philosophical about it. But your crowd weren't so . . . philosophical, were they? You learn a lot, in my job. Like how to catch the odd sentence or two people would rather you didn't — people like the fingerprint boys and the forensic team who were clumping round here for a while after you'd gone . . . '

Trewley switched his glare from Stephen Greene to the ceiling. 'The sooner that kid's mother comes back from her blasted walk and feeds him, the happier I'll be,' he muttered. He paid no attention to Stephen, who coughed.

'I don't think,' he said, as Trewley said nothing more, 'that I'm planning to eat very much bread in the immediate future, Superintendent. In fact, I'm not really too sure about any of my future plans, except that it's high time I was back in Fleet Street — or at least phoned in a report to reassure them I haven't been eaten by werewolves. A dangerous place, the country. Give me the town any day, where you can rely on the nice friendly muggers and pickpockets and con men, with just the occasional shotgun robbery to vary the routine — '

'Ouch!' The penknife had slipped. Stone tried to grab it as it fell to the floor. Trewley turned towards her, not sure whether to glare or grin — had the interruption been welcome, or not? — when he stiffened suddenly.

'What,' he demanded, 'was that about varying the routine? Sergeant' — he lumbered to his feet — 'you're female, for heaven's sake — have I got this right? Breeze said Alpha asked her to

335

swap their duty days — there's that baby, yelling the place down — and now Breeze has gone for a walk with Star, who was there with Alpha when Miss Jarvis came to call . . . '

As Baldur wailed above her head, Stone gaped at the superintendent for a space of eight seconds, then leaped from her chair, her eyes bright. 'You're right, sir! We've got to find them — she's already killed once! But — but where do we start looking?'

Stephen Greene was staring from one detective to the other, bewildered by the rapid telepathy of a good police team. 'What do you mean? Who are you talking about? How do you know?'

'Where have they gone?' countered Trewley, hurrying in his sergeant's wake as she rushed to the sitting room door and pulled it open. 'What's the usual walk around these parts? Speak up, man — there's a life at stake!'

His bellow brought further howls from Baldur, and Apollo came clattering down the stairs to find out what was going on. Stephen, meanwhile, was gathering his startled wits and trying to describe the Phoenixes' favourite territory. The leader of the Phoenixes took in the scene: Stone was jigging impatiently by the door as Trewley barked questions at Sirius, almost dragging the young man by the scruff of the neck.

'This is madness!' cried Apollo. 'This is violence! You mustn't destroy your inner peace with — '

Stone snapped something that made his mouth fall open; Trewley capped it by commanding him to accompany them on the hunt for Breeze and Star. 'And don't ask a load of damnfool questions — just take us where those girls're most likely to be. If there's more than one place, we'll have to split up into search parties — those two upstairs with the kid — get the lad to — no,' as Stone danced up and down, 'you're right, we're only wasting time. Where the hell are they?'

'We — we usually go through the woods out the back, then across the fields — towards the West Lodge, but not that far . . . There's a lake — '

'A lake!' Trewley's eyes met those of

Stone. 'Can they swim, either of them?'

'There's a boathouse — a punt
. . . Ocean's tried his hand at fishing,
but — '

'Damn the fishing! How far is this lake
from here? Can we get there by car?'

Apollo blinked at Stephen, who said: 'I
suppose down the other drive — from the
West Lodge, where Miss Jervaulx lives.
It might be quicker than on foot from
here — '

'Right, Stone — the car! You two,
with us — and make it snappy!' roared
Trewley. And, as the four pelted down
the front path of the North Lodge, the
shrill keening of a startled Baldur drifted
after them.

In the heat of the moment, they nearly
forgot to buckle their seatbelts as Stone
sent the car racing to the end of the
drive, then took the turn into the road
on two wheels. Apollo, for all his fine
talk of Destiny and Fate, had his eyes
closed as the sergeant exercised cool
judgement and squeaked into the gap
between two approaching juggernauts;
anyone else would have waited to let

the second lorry pass — but anyone else would not have been in so much of a hurry. She glanced in the mirror, stamped her foot on the accelerator, and swung out round the first lorry, slipping neatly back to her own side of the road with just a whisker to spare as a ramshackle saloon, towing a caravan, trundled its way towards them.

'Couldn't you use the siren?' begged Stephen, as the car swooped past a pedalling cyclist who shook his fist at the slipstream. 'Or a flashing blue light — or something?'

'Unmarked,' snapped Trewley, while Stone said, through gritted teeth:

'Nearly there — hang on!' The indicator clattered, she made another two-wheeled turning, and the police car pelted down the road which led to the West Lodge, home of Miss Melicent Jervaulx.

Stone sounded her horn as the car turned again and shot through the gateway, but she did not stop. 'How far along should we go?' she demanded. Apollo, who seemed to be praying, did not reply.

'Near the next big tree,' Stephen said. 'If you pull in by that oak, you'll have room for another car to pass, and we can cut across the fields — look — '

'You mean that walnut?' Exasperated, Stone slowed the car. 'We stop just here?'

'Oh, sorry — yes . . . '

The car crunched to a gravelly halt. 'Everybody out!' Trewley was unbuckling himself as he gave the order. 'Right. Where now? Which way?'

'Stop dawdling,' snapped Stone, as Apollo's shaking hands fumbled with his belt. 'Get out. I want to lock the car — and there's a girl's life at stake!'

'Over there, I think,' said Stephen, pointing. 'But I'm not exactly sure, from this side — there should be a hollow, just beyond the rise — '

'We'll soon find out if there is.' Bloodhound Trewley, setting a good pace for a bulky man on muddy clay, charged off along the trail indicated by Stephen, while Stone sprinted ahead of Apollo, who by now looked as sickly and slow as Sirius had previously done.

The incognito reporter, however, had found a new lease of life. Perhaps the running had boosted his circulation; perhaps it was thc knowledge that he could be on the verge of a scoop. He pounded along behind the two police officers, breathing hard, and — despite his withdrawal symptoms — doing no worse than Trewley, thirty years his senior and overweight.

Stone had put on a spurt and was in front. She stopped, and held up a hand. 'Listen!'

'Don't gasp like that, dammit!' growled Trewley, himself guilty of a bulldog wheezing which threatened to overpower every other sound. 'Stone, are you sure — '

'Listen . . . a cry — somebody shouting — over there, sir!'

She turned, and plunged on. Trewley, trusting her as he always did, thundered after her, leaving Stephen and — a long way behind — Apollo to come as they could. He might be old enough to have fathered the pair of 'em, but it was his job to get wherever they were all going first — his job to be in at the —

Death? Kill? Murder?

Not an accident — though it would be made to look like one — he was sure, and Stone seemed to agree. She'd worked it out just the same way he had, once he'd set her thinking along the right lines . . .

Gasping, he breasted the low rise, to see his sergeant hurtling down the slope to the lake. He saw the boathouse, on the opposite shore; he saw, far out from the shore, a large, rackety punt, drifting . . .

And, threshing about in the water near the punt, people. Two? Three? Impossible to tell, among the foam and splashing and wallowing limbs, the bobbing heads briefly surfacing to scream or shout, then sinking again in a flurry of frantic spray —

'Oh, hell!' He'd caught his foot on a stone — too busy goggling at the lake to notice where he was going. He felt himself go down — twisted sideways — then righted himself with an effort — and swore, as something stabbed at him under his ribs. 'No — don't stop,' he gasped, as

Stephen came up behind him and seemed glad of an excuse to rest. 'Go and help the sergeant — she can't swim!'

Stone was at the lakeside now, running, looking for the miracle of another punt, a floating branch — wondering if she had time to reach the boathouse before the worst could happen in the middle of the waters she, for all her fitness, speed, and strength, was unable to cross unaided . . .

With heavy feet, Stephen Greene panted up to her, and pointed to the tumult in the lake. 'Let me get my breath,' he gasped, 'and I'll — I'll — '

'Is there another punt?'

Saving his breath, he simply shook his head.

'How deep is it?'

'Too deep,' came the answer she'd dreaded. 'And muddy . . . dangerous.' He doubled up suddenly, rubbing his side, with a tortured groan. 'Stitch . . . '

Stone, kicking herself for her helplessness in matters aquatic, knew there was little she could do except hope. Trewley was still making his slow way down the slope, his hand on his side. *Heart attack!* That was all she needed, on top of —

There came a rush and a splash. Apollo — she'd been so worried about Trewley, she just hadn't noticed him — ran the last few yards from the field, kicked off his sandals, and plunged, hardly checking his stride for an instant, into the water. With a confident stroke, he headed straight for the struggle around the punt . . .

And Stephen, galvanised by the sight, overcame the lingering effects of his stitch to go wallowing after him.

Stone risked looking away from the drama on the lake to find out how her superior fared, and was relieved to see him almost upon her, his hand rubbing his side and a tortured look on his face. 'Stitch,' he groaned as he panted his way along, then groaned again as he tripped, stumbled, and for a second time went down, twisting as he fell. 'Bugger!'

There was nothing she could do for the swimmers. Stone left them to their fate, and ran to Trewley's side. 'Don't move, sir . . . let me look at you — '

'Don't fuss, damn you!' The words were jerked out between gasps. 'I'll live, girl. Ricked my blasted ankle — a stitch — tripped . . . Tripped,' he added, in a more thoughtful tone, as, satisfied that he wasn't at death's door, his sergeant stood up to peer, once more, across the lake.

Trewley was still too winded to pick himself up just yet, but he was so busy staring at what had tripped and tumbled him that, even if he'd been raring to go, he would have held back, too busy thinking to bother. Had the inspiration that had struck him — and Stone — been wrong? Was the one they'd both suspected in reality now the victim, not the murderer? If rescue did not arrive in time, would they ever manage to work out the truth?

'Help me up, girl — ugh!' The weak ankle jarred nerves along his entire spine as he set it to the ground. 'What's going on out there? Were we — were we in time?'

Absently, Stone offered her arm and tugged, twisting her head to stare out towards the bobbing, bouncing punt. 'One of the girls is in the punt — Apollo fished her out, but now he's helping Sirius with the other — it's Star, I think. She's being a bit hysterical . . . '

Together, Sirius and Apollo struggled to subdue the panic which had gripped poor Star, assuring her that she wouldn't drown, that they would take care of her. In the end Apollo, begging her pardon, managed to box her ears, and she uttered a little gurgling, bubbling cry before slumping in his arms.

'Into the punt,' wheezed Sirius. 'Then back — to the shore — '

'Not . . . yet. Someone . . . else,' Apollo told him, turning Star's limp form on her back so that he might tow her over to the punt. 'I — think so, anyway — you look, while I . . . hold Star . . . '

With one arm clinging to the side of the punt, Apollo clutched Star with the other, while Sirius paddled in a weary circle around them, peering through the muddy depths into the swirling weeds below.

'I — can't see — anyone,' he called, feeling the air rasp hot and dry in his lungs. 'I'm not . . . sure how much longer . . . I can . . . '

He was on the point of turning back when there was a cry from the shore. 'Don't stop! Keep looking! He can't have got away . . . '

Sirius was now too spent to focus so far, but Apollo, shaking his soaking locks out of eyes into which strands of weed kept slithering, saw Detective Sergeant Stone running round the lake towards the boathouse.

But it was not Stone who shouted. Superintendent Trewley, hobbling, had made his way to the water's lapping edge, and was waving desperately towards those in the centre — waving something which, even from that distance, to the keen-eyed Apollo looked like a small leather case with a shoulder strap . . .

Binoculars . . .

Squadron Leader Robbie Kempshott.

21

Breeze was stirring at the bottom of the punt, shivering, uttering little moans and whimpers. Apollo said, 'Breeze — can you hear me? Help — help me — lift Star — into the punt, then I can . . . help Sirius . . .'

'Star?' Breeze dragged herself up on one elbow, peering over the side of the punt, shaking her head. 'Star — isn't she — is she all right? Will she — did he hurt her?'

'She'll be all right if . . . we can keep her out of the water.' Apollo's voice cracked on the final word; though he was so much fitter than Sirius, even he was failing now. 'Take . . . care of her, Breeze — her arms . . . pull — pull!'

To heave an almost lifeless, waterlogged form over the side of a punt takes an effort — an effort Breeze eventually made. Star, pushed from below and

348

dragged from above, slipped at last from the chilly dangers of the weed-filled lake into the splintery embrace which had already welcomed her friend. Apollo saw her start at the bumping discomfort of her arrival, knew she was regaining consciousness, and knew also that he could allow himself to watch no longer. The Phoenix philosophy was to respect life — all life; even that of a suspected murderer. He must go in search of Squadron Leader Kempshott . . .

Sirius had found a piece of wood, and was clinging to it, exhausted. 'I — I'm not sure,' he gasped, 'but . . .'

Apollo looked down. The water was thick with floating particles of mud stirred by the turmoil, microscopic pondlife, fallen autumn leaves drifting in slow decay to the bottom — the bottom near which, caught in weeds, something which might have been a man's foot could just be seen.

Apollo took a deep breath, held his nose, and forced himself to plunge beneath the surface. He came up again, blinking, gasping, shaking his head.

'I — I can't . . . '

'Hang on!' There came the sound of regular, rhythmic splashes, drawing closer. 'I'm coming!' Detective Sergeant Stone had found a small rowing boat, and was making a hurried, though inelegant, progress to the middle of the lake. 'All right — no,' as Sirius released his plank and tried to seize the side of the boat, 'you'll tip me over — grab my oar — I'll help you round to the stern — it's more stable — '

As Stone steered him, wheezing and spluttering, on his way to safety, she managed to find time to call to Apollo, 'Are they all right? Is everyone out of the water?'

Her arrival had given him new heart. 'I think — I must dive again,' he said, and did so, vanishing into the murky depths . . . to reappear, pushing his hair back from his eyes, shuddering.

'I fear that he . . . has drowned,' said Apollo.

* * *

Help came from the manor, but it came too late. Squadron Leader Kempshott's body was disentangled from the weeds, lifted into the punt, and taken away in the ambulance for which butler Banter had telephoned.

The Phoenixes tried to insist that they must return to the North Lodge to recover from the shock of recent events, but Trewley, after conferring with Stone, refused them his permission. The shock, he said, had almost certainly been greater than any of them realised; he wasn't prepared to accept the responsibility for letting them wander off to a half-heated house without proper medical attention.

'We are all,' Apollo informed him, through chattering teeth, 'responsible for our own actions, my f-friend — and if we ch-choose to go home to b-be with our f-family — '

'Rubbish!' Trewley would have said something even more forceful if he hadn't still been slightly shaken himself. He limped over to the blanket-wrapped Apollo and glared down at him. 'Look, *you* can let yourself die of pneumonia if

351

you like, but you've no right to encourage those girls to do the same, when anyone can see they're in no fit state to argue with you. That'd hardly be a *responsible* action, now would it?'

Apollo glanced at his shivering companions, and sighed. He said nothing more as Benson and Hedges, who had accompanied the manorial rescue party, helped Star gently to her feet and escorted her to their car, while Trewley nodded at Stone to start coaxing Breeze, sitting next to Sirius, into the other.

The commune leader sighed again, rose to his feet, and went to sit beside Star. He spent the whole journey chafing the girl's cold hands, and murmuring words of comfort as she continued to shiver, and then began to sob.

'The man . . . the man . . . in the water . . . the water . . . '

Banter was waiting on the steps as the bedraggled party arrived, and announced that he had instructed soup to be heated, tea to be sugared, and blankets to be warmed before the kitchen fire. 'Equal treatment for all,' he added, with a deplorable wink for Trewley, whose bloodhound face wore so lugubrious an expression that, if his clothes hadn't been so obviously dry, anyone would have supposed that he, too, had been involved in the aquatic adventure.

The disciples of Simeon Gotobed, organised — after some argument from the Brazier contingent — by Sir Lionel Tobias, had provided dry clothes for the dripping survivors of the drama at the lake, and were now clamouring to know what had happened. Nobody was going into details, but it was hardly a secret that a man's body had been dragged from the water — a man who, as one of the shivering young women had blurted out before being hustled away, had tried to attack them . . .

Trewley directed a small party into the side parlour, and set PC Benson to keep everyone else in the sitting room. PC Hedges stood guard outside Trewley's lair, ready to repel invaders as necessary while his superiors finally got to the bottom of the Campions Crest Case.

Apollo said, in a low voice: 'I feel

353

ashamed — terribly ashamed.' Star, sitting as close to him as she could press, stared in dismay as he buried his face in his hands. With a nervous little murmur, she laid tentative fingers on his arm; her touch seemed to hearten him. He lifted his head, and faced the room bravely.

'That I,' he said, 'who claim to hold all life sacred, should fail to make the — the supreme effort to save a drowning man . . . No matter if he had killed once, or a dozen times: even then, what right would I have to judge him? I told myself — I believed I was exhausted, that there was nothing I could do . . . but I can't be sure that was the truth.' He shuddered. 'The awful guilt of it — I'll wonder to the end of my days whether it was — was just that there was nothing more I *wanted* to do to save him . . . '

Star, whimpering, clung to him, and Breeze roused herself from her trance to utter a weak protest; but Trewley, who disapproved of adolescent histrionics, favoured him with a sour look. Anyone other than a father of three might have supposed the young man to be sincere in the sudden development of a conscience and a sense of responsibility, but the superintendent merely rubbed his chin, and frowned round at his assembled audience.

The action was enough to draw the attention of everyone in the room away from Apollo towards the superintendent. He coughed.

'All life is sacred? Couldn't agree with you more, lad. You're not the only one who's sorry the squadron leader's dead, because the man was a hero, as far as I can make out — and there's precious few of them around, these days.'

'A hero,' Breeze said, bitterly. 'You — your whole generation . . . full of hate and violence . . . glorifying war — '

'No!' barked Trewley. 'I'll thank you not to put words in my mouth, miss. I said the man was a hero, and I'll say it again — and I don't expect you, of all people, to start arguing with me.' He stood up, then remembered his wrenched ankle, and remained where he was instead of striding across the room to glare down at her.

'A hero,' he said again. 'Gave his life to save you and your friend Star, didn't he?' Breeze, suddenly still, opened her mouth to deny it. 'Or rather,' Trewley went on, 'he gave his life to save Star . . . because you were trying to kill her, weren't you? To kill her, the way you killed Alpha — and he chucked his binoculars on the ground and went galloping to the rescue, and you hit him on the head for his pains — and he must've drowned,' turning to Apollo, 'before you or Sirius or anyone else got there. He didn't stand a chance after your precious Breeze had knocked him out.'

Nobody spoke. Apollo stared. Star, still upset by her idol's emotion, was oblivious to everything Trewley had just said. Sirius, in his Stephen Greene persona, was obviously making mental notes for his front-page story. Breeze, frowning, was as obviously making up her mind how to reply to the superintendent's charge. Her eyes darted about the room; she saw Stone shift on her chair near the door, and frowned again.

'It's not true,' she said at last. 'Why would I do such a — a terrible thing? We of the Phoenix Family hold life to be sacred — all life, as Apollo has said. To — to do what you accuse me of would be . . . sinful. The Fates do not permit anyone else to take the life of another . . . '

'Especially,' Trewley said, sitting down to produce his trump card, 'when it's by means of an abortion.'

Apollo gasped. 'Breeze had an abortion? But — but if she did, that was in the past, before — before . . . '

'Before she came to see the error of her ways?' Trewley finished for him, above Breeze's cries of startled outrage. 'Well, she could have done, I suppose — just at the moment, I don't particularly care, and I certainly don't know. The person I *do* know about is Alpha, and there's no question but that she had an abortion. And,' with a nod in Stone's direction, 'according to the medical evidence, she probably had it after she'd given birth to a live baby — a baby,' louder, above more startled cries, 'she told lies about when talking to its father in the woods on Friday night.'

Apollo said, 'We all went for a walk on Friday night, and the woods are a favourite place. Do you mean' — his eye turned to Sirius — 'that Alpha's baby was — was — '

'Oh, no.' Trewley didn't usually have much time for the press, but he wouldn't torment them, or see them tormented, without good cause. 'No, young, er, Sirius there's nothing to do with any of this. One of the folk attending the conference centre's the bloke who got mixed up with Alpha ten years ago — and that,' he added grimly, 'is how you lot come to be in the lodge in the first place, because for all your fancy notions about Fate, and fish and chips, it was a spot of blackmail that straightened things out for you — leastways, that's what Alpha meant to happen. She'd have had everything arranged for you nice and cosy, if someone hadn't stopped her mouth — '

'Someone? The — her baby's father!' cried Apollo, while Breeze huddled deep in her blanket and shook her head to and fro in silent denial. 'This poor man — a stranger to our way of life — he can't have understood she would never — he must have panicked, and been afraid Alpha would — would . . . But he didn't have to kill her,' he added, in a whisper. 'He could have spared her that.'

'Now, you listen to me.' Trewley was stern; he would make this idealistic young idiot see sense before this case was done, if he had to dunk him in the lake again to do it. 'I don't think Alpha was as committed to being a — to your way of life,' he amended, quite unable to speak the words he thought so ridiculous, 'as the rest of you — as some of the rest of you,' glancing at Sirius, glaring at Breeze. 'Oh, she'd had a rough time of it, I don't doubt, one way and another — and it had taught her to play rough, too. She was hoping to blackmail the baby's father into letting you stay in the lodge by saying she'd spread the word she'd had an abortion, and it'd been his fault — and the poor sap's the type who's got no idea of telling her to publish and be damned, because he's just landed a new job here, and . . . well,' bringing himself up sharply, 'well, it wouldn't suit him to have everyone know about it.' Whatever relationship there might be between Andrew Ryan and Simeon Gotobed was their own private business.

'Which is what your Alpha relied on, when she told him the tale. He'd turned up yesterday, all eager to start his new job, and heard about the squatters in the lodge from the butler chap. He's young, and keen. Thought he ought to do something about you, or at least find out what sort of folk you were — so he went down to the lodge, and guess who opened the door?'

'Alpha,' said Apollo, in a dead voice. 'It was her duty day yesterday — she and Star were taking care of Baldur . . . '

'Baldur!' Star's vacant eyes gleamed as she woke up to what was being said. 'Dear Baldur — my baby — he's not been feeling very well, poor darling.'

'Teething, probably,' Trewley nodded to Apollo. 'The baby wasn't fit to be carted round the fields with the rest of

360

you, so he stayed at home while the girls took it in turns to stay with him and, er, dust, or whatever. And yesterday it was the turn of Star, with Alpha — Angela, as the chap from the conference centre had known her. It was one hell of a shock for him to see her again — not so much of a shock for her, of course. She must've been expecting to bump into him sooner or later, after that write-up in the newspaper, but she hadn't expected to have him appear on the doorstep — and she certainly didn't want to start pushing him to do what she'd planned when there was the risk someone could overhear the way she was carrying on.'

'Star,' said Apollo at once, with a fond look for the girl at his side; thoughts of Baldur seemed to have taken her back into another daydream. He lowered his voice, and said, 'But I don't know how much of what . . . Alpha said to this man poor Star would remember — I don't see how anyone could have seen her as a threat. She's too . . . gentle,' he said, daring Trewley to find a harsher adjective.

'So she is,' agreed the superintendent at once. 'Never said she wasn't — and it's thanks to her, in a roundabout way, we got to the bottom of this case. You see, it was Star who told us there'd been a visitor to the lodge yesterday afternoon. No,' as Apollo started to say something, 'I don't think she ever noticed Alpha's ex — too busy with the baby, most likely. If she did see him, she's never said, has she? But what she *has* said, if you remember, is that *a cross old lady* called — and she said it in front of Breeze. And Breeze was smart enough to realise she'd been handed a lovely scapegoat — and made a great palaver of telling us about an elderly woman driving a grey Morris, who quarrelled with Alpha on the doorstep . . . '

Breeze muttered something, but, muffled in the blanket, her words were indistinct. Apollo looked at her, then away.

Trewley went on. 'What Breeze didn't let on, of course, was that she'd overheard at least part of Alpha's conversation with her baby's father — enough to make her curious about what they were going to say to each other later on. They couldn't talk then — the lad would've been in too much of a state, I daresay, to make much sense, and Alpha would be worried one or other of your lot would turn up and, well, not go overmuch for the way she was blackmailing the poor blighter. So Breeze made up her mind to follow Alpha when she slipped out that evening — and she did. And she heard what the two of them had to say — and she made up her mind that Alpha had to die.'

22

Sirius, wearing his invisible reporter's hat, spoke for the first time. 'Can it really have been Breeze, of all people, who killed Alpha? Wouldn't the father of her baby be a more likely bet — or the old girl with the Morris — or that man always on the prowl with his binoculars — or almost anyone else, for heaven's sake!'

Apollo, his arm round Star's shoulders — whether to give or to receive comfort, Trewley couldn't tell — said sadly, 'The — the abortion, I suppose.' He could not bring himself to look at Breeze to see if she confirmed his theory. 'She was — is — devoted to Baldur — our baby, our hope for the future. The idea that anyone could voluntarily deprive anyone — an unborn baby — of life — '

He broke off. His eyes widened. 'But that's what she did herself! It's no worse than . . . killing Alpha, or — or anyone else . . . that man in the lake — the man I thought had tried to harm the girls . . . '

'He was trying to save them — save Star, anyway. Breeze got her out in that punt to drown her — she'd've told you it was an accident, I daresay, or even suicide — upset about Alpha, she'd've said.' Trewley shot a cautious look at Star, who seemed mercifully unaware of the discussion going on about her, smothering a yawn and snuggling close to Apollo. He said quietly, 'She might even have had the nerve to try putting the blame for Alpha's death on the poor creature — and if it hadn't been for Miss Jarvis, we might have swall — er, fallen for it.' He hadn't intended to use that particular phrase: he supposed the memory of how Alpha had met her death was never far away.

He said, 'Miss Jarvis told us that when she came to have her talk with Alpha, she was worried about drugs, she wanted to know just what sort of people you were — she could hear the baby crying. She accused Alpha of neglecting him, and Alpha told her it was none of her business, but he was hungry, and his mother'd be back any minute to, er, take care of him.' A deep red flush crept up the superintendent's cheeks. 'The rest of you can shove bottles in his mouth as often as you like, but you're always going on about being natural, and — yes, well.' He coughed. 'So that's what Breeze was doing when she must have overheard all the commotion at the front door, and sneaked along the hall to listen . . .

'And it's what she tried to make out she was doing yesterday, after Alpha's body had been found — and found a bit earlier than she'd expected, which must have surprised her. She'd thought she'd make the discovery herself, which would give her time to check she hadn't left any clues that she was the one who'd done it. Then I suppose she planned a nice fit of hysterics about the wicked stranger who'd come along and killed her friend . . .

'She was wrong about not leaving any clues. Oh,' as for the first time Breeze looked Trewley straight in the face, and seemed to shake her head, 'there were no fingerprints, nothing of that sort — nothing so small. What gave her away was bigger than a fingerprint, and must weigh ten or twelve pounds' — a brief vision of the bowl of rising dough flashed across his inward eye, but he banished it — 'the baby.'

'Baldur?' Apollo blinked. A smile curved Star's drowsy mouth, and she sighed, and nodded sleepily. 'Baldur?'

'She came back,' said Trewley, turning purple again, 'to — to take care of him. Only he wasn't hungry — he didn't wake up until she made a deliberate racket outside so he'd hear her. Then she scooped him up and went off' — he gritted his teeth — 'to feed him, she said — but *he must already have been given that feed*. That supposedly hungry baby stayed fast asleep with a crowd of strangers crashing round the place taking photographs and fingerprints — and a baby just won't sleep if it's hungry. It was his regular time — the evidence of Miss Jarvis told us that — so if the baby's mother had been in the house to feed him, it suggests very strongly that she must have been there when Alpha . . . '

He hesitated. 'Died,' supplied Apollo, very quietly.

' . . . Was attacked,' said Trewley. He cleared his throat once, then twice. 'I've never told you how Alpha died,' he said. He looked straight at Breeze. 'My guess is you left it to this precious Fate you all believe in — you quarrelled with her, perhaps. Called her a phony, a liar, a murderer — maybe you threw something at her, maybe she slipped and hit her head. Either way, she was knocked unconscious — and you took a piece of the dough from the bread she'd been making, and stuffed it in her mouth to gag her. Then you went away, and left Fate to decide whether she'd come round in time to spit the stuff out, or whether . . . '

Even Sirius, who'd already guessed what had happened, looked sick as Trewley ended his explanation. Breeze smiled an enigmatic smile, and gave the faintest of nods; Apollo had turned deathly pale. He gulped, and clutched at

Star for comfort; she stirred, sighed, but did not move.

Trewley went on: 'You waited a fair time for Fate to work, didn't you? You made every second count. When you thought your friends would start to wonder — when you knew you couldn't leave it any longer to come back to give your baby the feed only *you* knew he didn't need, you were careful to come in at the front of the house, not the back. None of you normally come in the front way — that's been made very clear.' His tone was grim, though he, like Apollo, could hardly bring himself to look at her. 'You really wanted Alpha to die, didn't you?'

After a moment, Breeze nodded again. 'She was a hypocrite,' she said. 'She had taken a life — she didn't deserve to keep her own. But I left the decision to Fate . . . and Fate decided Alpha should not live.'

Apollo forced himself to address her to her face. 'The shock of learning Alpha's secret may have — have overturned your judgement, Breeze, but' — his arm tightened about his slumbering companion — 'what harm had Star ever done to you, for you to wish her dead? I can't believe . . .'

Breeze smiled a lopsided smile. 'I'm sure the superintendent has an answer,' she said.

Trewley coughed. 'I can guess, all right, though I'm not swearing to the details, but — my guess is that Star heard or saw a little too much for her own good, either this morning, when you came back to have it out with Alpha, or yesterday, which is more likely. She was on duty day with Alpha when young — when Alpha's ex turned up out of the blue. She'd have heard her making plans to meet him later, no doubt. Maybe she spotted you creeping round eavesdropping, and wondered what you were up to — and when you and Alpha swapped duty days, she'd have wondered even more.

'Because,' said Trewley, with his best bulldog glare, 'you've been lying to us right from the start, haven't you? It wasn't Alpha that asked you to change

370

with her, it was you that did the asking. You wanted her alone in the house, so you could talk things over in private — maybe you guessed she'd make bread, I don't know. Maybe you planned to kill her right from the start — I don't know that, either. But if you're going to plead provocation, I'd say you're skating on very thin ice . . .

'And Star,' Trewley said, with a smile for the sleeping girl, her head on Apollo's shoulder, 'knew too much, so you took her out for a breather, and decided to get rid of her, for safety. It was your bad luck, and her good luck, that Squadron Leader Kempshott was in the bushes by the lake with his binoculars, looking for the lesser spotted artichoke, or something of the sort.' He threw a rueful grin in the direction of Stone, who acknowledged, with a discreet bow, her superior's adaptation of her earlier words. 'Only a real emergency's going to make a naturalist as keen as him drop an expensive item like those glasses and risk breaking them — an emergency like spotting some murderous female trying to murder her second victim in the middle of his favourite lake . . . The poor devil,' said Trewley, staring thoughtfully at the feet of Sirius and Apollo, 'didn't even have time to take off his shoes, he was in such a hurry to save Star — and I suppose he *did* save her, even if it was only by getting in Breeze's way and slowing her down in time for us — for Sergeant Stone to reach her. And it's just too bad,' he concluded grimly, 'that we weren't in time to save him . . . '

Stone, over by the door, stirred, but said nothing. She couldn't help recalling the earlier words of Sirius, when he spoke of *that man always on the prowl with his binoculars*; and she was hardly likely to forget the remarkable contents of Kempshott's wardrobe. She knew her logic was as shaky as that of Breeze, but if — now that the squadron leader was dead — there were no more reports of a Peeping Tom, she felt that Alpha would not have been the only person to atone, by their death, for their actions in life.

She shook herself briskly. Superintendent Trewley, if he'd had the remotest idea of what she was thinking, would have uttered a few very forceful words on the subject of *you blasted women and your cockeyed logic* —

'I *said*, Detective Sergeant Stone,' came Trewley's voice in the Repeat mode she, of all his subordinates, seldom had to hear, 'that if this young woman's got nothing to say for herself, she'd better come down to the station and say it in a police cell. Fetch Benson in here, will you? And then give Hedges a shout. They can take her along with 'em back to town, while we tidy up a few things here.'

With a discreet blush, Stone jumped to her feet, and was about to open the door when Trewley said:

'No, hang on. We don't want to make any mistakes with all these trick cyclists wandering around — budding social workers and legal aid types every one of 'em, I shouldn't wonder. Just turn back in your notebook to where you interviewed the lot at the North Lodge, will you? You said you'd got their real names out of them. If we're going to charge her, I want it nice and official.'

While Stone hunted through the pages, Trewley regarded his suspect with a long, thoughtful gaze. Calmly, she returned that gaze. It seemed that, as Fate had decreed her crime should be uncovered, so she was willing to submit to Fate's ruling — a ruling she'd never given Alpha the chance to refuse . . .

As his sergeant's nod told him she had found the relevant passage, Trewley said, 'Look, you do the necessary, will you? I'll fetch the others. I don't know why, but I fancy a breath of fresh air.'

And Stone, watched in silence by Sirius, in disbelief by Apollo, cleared her throat. 'Barbara Rebecca Evesham' — a strange little smile quirked Breeze's lips, but otherwise she did not move — 'do you wish to say anything?' Breeze, still smiling, shook her head.

'You are not,' continued Stone, 'obliged to say anything unless you wish to, but . . . '

★ ★ ★

374

Apollo and Star (who had been coaxed awake, and was starting to worry about Baldur) insisted on walking back to the North Lodge rather than wait for a lift from Trewley and Stone. Sirius, gleefully abandoning the hippie life for the chance of a nationwide scoop, had found a conveniently private telephone, and was dictating into it, with Stone (on the lookout for breaches of confidence) hovering nearby.

Trewley took it upon himself to review the case before a sitting room audience which had drunk numerous cups of coffee, and now considered itself sufficiently alert to cope with any amount of reviewing. He was only slightly surprised to observe Banter among the listening crowd; from the man's behaviour when the dripping lake party had appeared, the superintendent had more than half expected to find the butler, with his socialist tendencies and his lively curiosity, eventually mingling, with no trace of embarrassment, among the Attitudes Analysts and their victims, Braziers and Allshires together . . .

Together. Even as he was laying before his audience as many of the facts as he thought wise, Trewley's subconscious had set to work on yet another little problem. As he came to the end of his impromptu report, he coughed.

'I think you'll understand, ladies and gentlemen, why I'm not at liberty to give you any more information than I have already. You couldn't reasonably *expect* me to, now could you?'

As he spoke the final words, his glance moved swiftly from Brash Archie Brazier to Sir Lionel Tobias, and he nodded slowly. 'You'll be reading all about it in the papers soon enough, I don't doubt,' he said, and spoke a general farewell in his most decided tones. Banter, still in many ways the perfect major domo, moved towards the door to escort the superintendent to his car.

'I'd just like a private word with a couple of the folk in there,' Trewley said, as the butler was quietly closing the sitting room door. 'Could you fetch Sir Lionel and the Brazier chap along for a few minutes? Thanks.'

'This is all most . . . unexpected, Superintendent,' said Sir Lionel Tobias as, with Archie Brazier lounging along in the rear, he entered the little morning room. At the look on Trewley's face, he closed the door before advancing to the most comfortable armchair. 'Should one sit down? Or is that the clanking of handcuffs I hear in the distance?'

'Umph.' Trewley waved him to the chair, then nodded to Archie. 'Yes, sit down, if you want — this isn't the third degree. And it shouldn't take more than a minute or so, if you two're willing to give me a — a straight answer to a straight question, that is.'

'The, ah, same question?' enquired Tobias, as Archie Brazier's saturnine eyebrows lifted. 'Surely not, in the, ah, circumstances.' He lowered his voice in a conspiratorial fashion, man to man. 'The Wardrobe War, you know. One could hardly expect a member of the Allshire company to have anything whatsoever in common with a member of the family which runs Brazier's Boots . . .'

'With,' corrected Trewley, his eyes on

the grinning Archie, 'the member of the family who *owns* Brazier's Boots. The *new* owner — who's always said he's having too much fun going round nightclubs and casinos to waste his time on business ... and yet here he is, wasting a whole weekend, if you want my honest opinion — and that's the straight question I wanted to ask the pair of you. Do you believe in this Attitudes Analysis or not?'

Sir Lionel looked at Brash Archie Brazier. The playboy, shrugging, looked back. Then he winked, and nodded.

Sir Lionel chuckled. 'You've rumbled us, Superintendent, but we must ask you, please, to keep your deductions to yourself for a little longer. There is to be a — a closer than heretofore relationship, as you have inferred, between the Allshire and Farther Clothing Company and Brazier's Boots. For a start, Archie here is to sell me his personal holding of stock — but the matter hasn't yet been finalised. We have no wish to bring our respective Boards into the affair until absolutely necessary, you see.'

'Or,' supplied Archie, 'our lawyers, especially after what happened last time. You know what the blighters can be like — niggling over the fine print, finding snags in every little clause, bumping up the costs and making more money out of the deal than anyone, including me. Good grief, if I want to lose a fortune, I can have a damn sight more fun doing it at the tables!'

'We are, in fact,' Sir Lionel interposed, 'very nearly ready for the legal departments to be called in, but there were one or two points which had to be cleared up before the deadline — and we were looking for genuinely neutral ground on which we could meet without arousing suspicion. Modern electronics are sadly insecure modes of communication, Mr. Trewley — telephones can be tapped, faxes intercepted, radio calls eavesdropped, offices bugged — as I'm sure you don't need me to tell you. We've managed up until now by snatching the odd few hours at the homes of various very discreet acquaintances, but when the need arose for a longer period of time, for more detailed discussion . . . '

'You decided to get Analysed,' said Trewley, with a grin. 'Fair enough, I suppose, if it was privacy you wanted.' He became confidential. 'D'you reckon he's bonkers — the Gotobed bloke?'

'Have a heart,' begged Archie, as Sir Lionel appeared to give it some serious thought. 'You said *one* straight question — and an officer of the law like you ought to know better than us the laws of libel!'

'Slander,' Trewley said; the correction was automatic. 'Slander, when it's spoken — and I promise you it won't go beyond these four walls, whatever you say. You've seen more of him than I have — you must've done, fixing this course and everything. Wouldn't you say it's all been a waste of time — apart from your business dealings, I mean?'

Sir Lionel coughed delicately, and smiled. 'A waste of time? Good heavens, no, Superintendent. To judge by the events of the weekend so far, I should say that the Campions Crest Conference Centre may become the training success of the decade.' He smiled again. 'With a slight, ah, modification in personnel, perhaps — what do you say, Archie?'

What Archie said was unprintable. Trewley was thankful that Stone, for all her liberated notions, wasn't there to hear him; but he had to agree the man had a point. He tried his best to look disapproving . . .

And all three men burst out laughing.

* * *

Stone was waiting in the car as Trewley, still laughing, emerged from the house with Banter, forgetting his butler pose, shaking him by the hand and thanking him. The superintendent thought it better not to ask the reason for this gratitude. He'd watched Sir Lionel close the door of the morning room after he and Archie Brazier had been summoned — he'd heard the click as the catch snicked to . . .

And he hadn't missed the silent way the same door had opened when the tycoon and the playboy had gone out

381

again. Banter had been hovering in the hall, looking as lofty as any butler has a right to be — he'd admitted earlier that he'd eavesdropped on the Attitudes session in the attic . . .

'What? Sorry, girl.' It was Stone's turn to have to repeat herself. 'Yes, back to the station — there's some interviewing needs to be done. Maybe you'd better tackle her — all girls together — you're bright enough to make quite a good job of it, I daresay . . . '

'Thank you very much, sir,' said Stone, primly.

'Oh, I've never said your fancy education was a waste of time.' And then Trewley made up his mind. It would only be — a chuckle rose in his throat as the aptness of the phrase struck him — an academic question . . .

'You college types are supposed to know most things, girl. Any idea how someone like me'd go about finding a stockbroker?'

A LANCE FOR THE DEVIL
Robert Charles

The funeral service of Pope Paul VI was to be held in the great plaza before St. Peter's Cathedral in Rome, and was to be the scene of the most monstrous mass assassination of political leaders the world had ever known. Only Counter-Terror could prevent it.

IN THAT RICH EARTH
Alan Sewart

How long does it take for a human body to decay until only the bones remain? When Detective Sergeant Harry Chamberlane received news of a body, he raised exactly that question. But whose was the body? Who was to blame for the death and in what circumstances?

MURDER AS USUAL
Hugh Pentecost

A psychotic girl shot and killed Mac Crenshaw, who had come to the New England town with the advance party for Senator Farraday. Private detective David Cotter agreed that the girl was probably just a pawn in a complex game — but who had sent her on the assignment?

THE MARGIN
Ian Stuart

It is rumoured that Walkers Brewery has been selling arms to the South African army, and Graham Lorimer is asked to investigate. He meets the beautiful Shelley van Rynveld, who is dedicated to ending apartheid. When a Walkers employee is killed in a hit-and-run accident, his wife tells Graham that he's been seeing Shelly van Rynveld . . .

TOO LATE FOR THE FUNERAL
Roger Ormerod

Carol Turner, seventeen, and a mystery, is very close to a murder, and she has in her possession a weapon that could prove a number of things. But it is Elsa Mallin who suffers most before the truth of Carol Turner releases her.

NIGHT OF THE FAIR
Jay Baker

The gun was the last of the things for which Harry Judd had fought and now it was in the hands of his worst enemy, aimed at the boy he had tried to help. This was the night in which the past had to be faced again and finally understood.

PAY-OFF IN SWITZERLAND
Bill Knox

'Hot' British currency was being smuggled to Switzerland to be laundered, hidden in a safari-style convoy heading across Europe. Jonathan Gaunt, external auditor for the Queen's and Lord Treasurer's Remembrancer, went along with the safari, posing as a tourist, to get any lead he could. But sudden death trailed the convoy every kilometer to Lake Geneva.

SALVAGE JOB
Bill Knox

A storm has left the oil tanker S. S. *Craig Michael* stranded and almost blocking the only channel to the bay at Cabo Esco. Sent to investigate, marine insurance inspector Laird discovers that the Portuguese bay is hiding a powder keg of international proportions.